THE
LONELY
WITNESS

D0062042

THE
LONELY
WITNESS

A Novel

WILLIAM BOYLE

PEGASUS CRIME
NEW YORK LONDON

The Lonely Witness

Pegasus Books, Ltd.
148 West 37th Street, 13th Floor
New York, NY 10018

First Pegasus Books hardcover edition May 2018

ISBN: 978-1-68177-795-5

10 9 8 7 6 5 4 3 2 1

Printed in the United States of America
Distributed by W. W. Norton & Company, Inc.

for Katie Farrell Boyle
It's a wonderful life that you bring

Life is a series of obsessions one must do away with. Aren't love, death, God, or saintliness interchangeable and circumstantial obsessions?
—E. M. Cioran, *Tears and Saints* (translated by Ilinca Zarifopol-Johnston)

I don't know what the chords are. They keep changing all the time.

—Nick Cave in *One More Time with Feeling*

Around here it is not a matter of finding the truth but of deciding which lie you live with better.

—Flannery O'Connor, *The Habit of Being: Letters*

1

When Mrs. Epifanio opens the door, Amy can tell right away that something's wrong. Monsignor Ricciardi had told her a few months ago, when she started doing this, that Mrs. Epifanio was prone to fits of dementia, that some days she'd probably seem very confused about where she was and what year it was and who was dead or alive. But Amy's only seen that side of Mrs. Epifanio once or twice. She's usually cheery and bright-eyed in the morning, so lively for a ninety-year-old, standing with her shoulders hunched, her bobby-pinned, rose-colored hair wild, her taped-on-the-bridge-of-the-nose glasses hanging recklessly around her neck.

She's wearing a housedress now, which isn't normal. Amy knows she likes to get dressed up for communion. Usually, she's in a floral-print blouse and slacks. Her eyes are almost quivering, as if she's on the verge of tears, though it's sometimes difficult to tell with an old woman. She looks over Amy's shoulder, out at the street, glancing up and down the block.

"You okay, Mrs. E?" Amy asks.

"I'm sick over here," Mrs. Epifanio says.

"What's wrong?"

"You know Diane, the woman from church who sits with me four days a week?"

"A little bit."

"Last two days, her son comes in her place. Vincent. Real creep. I sit at my kitchen table, playing solitaire, picking at my Meals on Wheels; he goes into my bedroom and starts digging around. I call into him, I says, 'I'm gonna call the police!' He says, 'Don't worry, Mrs. E,' like we're pals. 'I'm just cleaning up a little.'"

"You sure?" Amy asks.

"Of course I'm sure."

"Maybe you imagined it."

"I don't think so."

"What's Diane say?"

"He says she's sick with the flu. I can't get through to her."

"What time's she usually get here?"

"Ten."

"And you're worried he's going to come again?"

"Yes."

"How about I hang around and we straighten this out?"

"Oh, that'd be wonderful. Thank you, dear." Mrs. Epifanio looks relieved.

Amy motions to her bag. "I've got communion for you."

"Come in, come in," Mrs. Epifanio says. She points down the narrow hallway, where a door opens on her small kitchen.

Amy crosses the threshold.

"You know, I was just telling my grandson Rob all about you on the phone," Mrs. Epifanio says.

"Rob is Elaine's son?"

"Yep. They live over in Metuchen. Supposed to come visit again on Sunday, but we'll see. 'Amy Falconetti,' I says to him. 'Originally from Flushing. Brings me communion. Such a nice girl. Pretty. Dark hair. Tattoos, just like you,' I says to him."

"That's really nice to hear."

Amy's not sure how Mrs. Epifanio knows about her tattoos. They're all on her back and thighs, traces of her old life. Word gets around, she guesses. Someone found out, saw her in the summer with a tank top and shorts on and spread the word. She's not embarrassed about her tattoos, and she doesn't regret them. It just feels like they belong to someone else. It's also still weird to her that she has dark hair. It's been a few years since she dyed her blond hair eerie black, and she's never quite adjusted. She sometimes looks in the mirror and can't recognize herself. But it felt like a necessary change.

"Just the truth. Last one who brought me communion, Immacula, you should've seen her." Mrs. Epifanio puts out her arms like a zombie. "Walking dead. Kill you to have a little enthusiasm? I mean, I know it's not the most exciting thing in the world, bringing communion to an old lady who can't leave the house, but I think you've gotta carry yourself with grace. And you do."

"Thanks, Mrs. E," Amy says. "I try. And I always look forward to seeing you."

"I'm better than all the other ones, right?"

"All the other what?"

"All the other old bags you visit."

Amy laughs. "You're great."

They're in the kitchen now: Mrs. Epifanio settling onto her padded chair, Amy sitting across from her. The table is strewn with scratch-offs, church bulletins she's brought over the last few months, word-puzzle books, prescriptions, junk mail, and pillboxes. Amy always takes in the picture on the wall: Mr. Epifanio as a young man, standing in a subway tunnel with a clipboard in his hand. Amy's not sure what exactly he did—it's tough to get straight information from Mrs. Epifanio—but she's pretty sure he worked for the MTA. He died back in 1986, right after the Mets won the Series, which Amy will never forget, because she was in first grade and Queens was rocking. That was more than thirty years ago now. Crazy how time moves.

Amy's always listening to Mrs. Epifanio tell stories about her husband. Mostly they seem to revolve around his clowning around in bars or staying up all night to hunt a little mouse with a BB gun.

"You doing okay with your pills, Mrs. E?" Amy asks.

"My pills," Mrs. Epifanio says, waving her off. "Who knows anymore? Half of me's going this way; half of me's going that way."

"The visiting nurse is still coming?"

Mrs. Epifanio nods into her chest. "She comes. I can't hardly understand her with that Russian accent."

Amy welcomes this opportunity to transition into administering Holy Communion to Mrs. Epifanio. She's supposed to hold off on any conversation until after the parishioner receives, but that's awfully tough to enforce, especially with Mrs. Epifanio, who is starved for company. Amy uses the short-order rite that she uses for all lonely widows. She takes the Bible, the cross, the candle, and the white cloth out of her bag. Then they go through their prayers.

The reverential attire Amy's wearing—blue slacks and a white blouse—is a far cry from how she used to dress. For years, she had pretty strict fashion rules: rockabilly-girl hair, sometimes with a bandanna, paired with pencil skirts, swing skirts, cropped trousers, swing trousers, short-sleeved shirts, vintage sweaters, sarong dresses, and halter-necked tops. Everything was red, white, black, and navy, with polka dots, stripes, checked gingham, or leopard-print patterns. Acceptable motifs included cherries, skulls, anchors, horseshoes, dice, bows, and pin-up girls. She wore flats or pumps on her feet. It was like she was always dressing to go see Social Distortion or serve as an extra in a John Waters movie.

Memories of her past life—past *lives*, really—come only in flashes now, a haze of bars and music and tattoos and drugs and booze and women. Things getting dark with Merrill, her gutter-punk girlfriend with scabies and a mean dog on a frayed rope leash. Meeting Alessandra at Seven Bar, where Amy worked for years, and then moving here, to Gravesend in Brooklyn, to live with her. That was five years ago. Alessandra hated the neighborhood and had spent her life trying to escape it or stay away, but she'd been filled with guilt about leaving for Los Angeles after high school. She'd wanted to make it as an actress and hadn't been around when her mother got sick and died, so she'd decided she should stay for a while and tend to her father. Like almost everything with Alessandra, the decision was more a projection of who she thought she should be rather than who she was.

They were happy for a bit. Amy took the train into the city to pour drinks at Seven Bar, while Alessandra stayed with her father and got a little extra work in movies here and there. When Alessandra's father died suddenly of a pulmonary embolism, she ditched Amy and moved back to Los Angeles without much notice. Amy sank into a big, black depression after that. She thought about chasing after Alessandra but didn't. She sold all her records for cash, quit her job at Seven Bar, ate cheap, lonely meals at Liu's Shanghai on Bath Avenue, her favorite Chinese place. She stayed behind. Staying behind was what she'd always been good at.

She went into St. Mary's one day, when she thought she was being followed by a man after getting off the train at Bay Parkway. Her childhood church in Queens came back to her in an instant. The organist was practicing in St. Mary's. She was beautiful. Her name was Katrya. She was Ukrainian. Amy felt safe. She started going to church weekly again for the first time since middle school, since before her mother died.

She liked Pope Francis. He seemed to reflect everything good about Catholicism. She decided she wanted to do something useful. She wanted to help. She'd spent enough time not helping. She became a Eucharistic Minister, went around and brought communion to old people, mostly old ladies like Mrs. Epifanio. She liked hearing their stories and making them smile. She liked that they thought she was so young, even though she was in her mid-thirties now and was starting to feel old.

After she receives, Mrs. Epifanio closes her eyes and prays quietly. She crosses herself and then uses a toothpick to dislodge some of the wafer from between her teeth.

When they're done with the rite, Mrs. Epifanio says, "Can I get you anything? Coffee? I have some delicious seeded cookies. Some good rolls, too. I've got a hundred of those little cartons of orange juice from Meals on Wheels. You like orange juice? Take a few. Take them all. I don't drink orange juice."

"I'm fine," Amy says, looking up at the clock. Ten to ten. Diane—or her son—is set to show up soon. Amy wonders if Mrs. Epifanio is just dreaming it all up. What she's fully expecting is that Diane will show, Amy will ask about Vincent, and there won't even be a Vincent.

"I'm not imagining this," Mrs. Epifanio says, as if reading her mind.

"I believe you," Amy says.

"It's too bad this Vincent's such a creep. He's about your age."

So many of these old ladies feel the need to try to hook her up with their grandsons, nephews, guys from the block, anyone they can think of. Amy always shakes it off. Most of them she doesn't even consider telling the truth. You can only explain so much to a ninety-year-old who has spent her whole life thinking one way.

"Yeah, doesn't sound like my type," she says to Mrs. Epifanio.

"He's got these nasty eyes."

"I don't know, Mrs. E. Maybe it was just a nightmare."

"You'll see."

The door opens a few minutes later. She *does* see. The man she assumes is Vincent walks in. He's got the key. He's at least five years younger than she is, maybe not even thirty. He does have dark, unsettling eyes, with dark hair to match. He's wearing a black trench coat, looking like one of those Columbine shooters from back in the nineties. He's skinny. He's got a dirty smile.

"And who are you?" he says, coming into the kitchen and sitting across from her at the table.

"See?" Mrs. Epifanio says. "What'd I tell you?"

"Why do you have a key?" Amy asks Vincent.

"It's my mom's. She's sick with the flu. Asked me to come over and sit with Mrs. E in her place." Vincent waves at Mrs. Epifanio like she's blind or an infant, raises his voice to talk to her. "How you doing today, Mrs. E? You remember me from the last couple of days? Vincent."

"Go shit in your hat," Mrs. Epifanio says.

"She doesn't like me much," he says to Amy.

"She says she called your mother and can't get through," Amy says.

"My mother can't even get out of bed. Who are you, you mind me asking?"

"I'm from church. I bring Mrs. E communion."

"Okay, well, we're all good here. 'Less you got one of those little wafers you want to throw my way. I'm the only one I know loved the taste of them as a kid. Like licking a nun's armpit. Hey, you're not a nun, are you?"

"I'm not a nun."

"All I'd have to do is lick your armpit to find out if you're lying." That smile. Yellow teeth. Foul breath she can smell from where she's sitting.

"Who talks like this?" Mrs. Epifanio says.

"Mrs. E doesn't need you today," Amy says. "I'll be sitting with her until your mother gets better."

He rubs his hands together and doesn't respond.

"Have you been back into her bedroom?" Amy asks.

He exhales, as if he's exhausted with this line of questioning. "My mother told me to dust in there."

"Mrs. E isn't comfortable with that."

Vincent stands. "Look, lady. I've got better things to do. I'm trying to do my mother a favor here, that's it. You don't want me around, I'm out."

"Leave the key, okay?"

"I'm not gonna leave the key. It's my mother's."

"It's Mrs. E's house."

"I am most definitely not leaving the key." Vincent starts to walk down the hallway, then pauses to turn back and address them. "I don't know what the fuck this is about. Try to do something nice and you get treated like a thief. Diane's not gonna be happy." He goes out through the front door, leaving it unlatched and slightly open.

Amy gets up and goes over to close the door behind him. "Jeez," she says, as she comes back to the table and sits down again. She's been trying for a while not to curse so much.

"I told you I wasn't imagining it," Mrs. Epifanio says.

"Maybe we should call the cops."

"They won't do anything."

"I don't like that he has the key."

"Me neither."

"I'll sit with you awhile longer. We'll figure out a plan. Do you have Diane's number handy? Let's try her."

Mrs. Epifanio leans on the arms of her chair and rises to her feet slowly. She makes her way over to a pantry on the far side of the refrigerator. She comes out with an ancient green address book. "Her number's in here some-where," she says. On the way back, she stops to open the refrigerator and grabs a few small cartons of orange juice, cradling them against her chest. When she gets back to the table, she pushes the address book and the orange juice in front of Amy. "Have an orange juice," Mrs. Epifanio says.

"Oh, I'm okay," Amy says. "Really. Thanks."

"Have one."

"Maybe in a bit." Amy flips through the address book, all yellowed pages and Mrs. Epifanio's nearly illegible script. Lots of names and addresses and numbers are scratched out. A stack of Mass cards is stuck in the middle of the book.

"Probably ninety percent of the people in there are dead," Mrs. Epifanio says.

"That's sad," Amy replies.

"It's sad to think that I'm in someone else's address book and they'll just scratch me out when I croak like I scratch them out when they croak." Mrs. Epifanio laughs.

"What's Diane's last name?"

Mrs. Epifanio thumbs her chin. "What is it? I say her last name so rarely. Grasso? No. That's her neighbor Edna. . . . Marchetti. It's Marchetti. Same last name as my cousin Janet."

Amy finds Diane's number in the last column on the *M* page. She goes over to the rotary phone on the wall and dials it. She lets it ring ten times before hanging up. "Nothing," she says. "For a second I thought Vincent might pick up."

"I appreciate the company. I really do, Amy."

Amy walks down the hall and peeps through the curtained window in the door. Vincent is in front of the apartment building across the street, vaping, pacing through his cloud of smoke. He seems to be talking to himself.

She goes back to the phone and dials the rectory. She tells Connie Giacchino, the secretary, that she can't do any more home visits today. She explains that Mrs. Epifanio needs her help. Connie says Monsignor Ricciardi will certainly understand and maybe Immacula will be willing to step in. Amy thanks her and returns to the table.

"I'll get out the cards," Mrs. Epifanio says. "We can play Rummy 500."

"Sounds good."

Something about Vincent has Amy extra uneasy now. It occurs to her that he reminds her of someone. When she was a sophomore in high school and living full-time with her grandparents, she watched from her bedroom window as their neighbor Bob Tully strangled a man to death in his driveway and then dragged him into his garage. The man's face was red, his eyes were popping, he was gasping for breath. Bob Tully's hands were monstrous. He was thick-necked and so strong and seedy-looking. Amy often saw him from her window, because she had just started smoking and she spent a lot of time blowing smoke out over the fire escape. He looked up at her as he was dragging the man to the garage and smiled. Did he really look like Vincent, or is she just conflating their faces in her mind now?

Bob Tully must've seemed old to her then, but he couldn't have been more than twenty-eight or twenty-nine. She didn't call the cops, didn't say anything to her grandparents. She closed her blinds and wondered if she'd actually seen what she thought she'd seen. The next day, Bob Tully came out as she was walking to school. He was peeling an apple with a pocketknife, smiling, saying she didn't see what she thought she saw, and she should just forget anything she thought she saw, and if she didn't, there'd be a lot of trouble, because girls with big mouths sometimes wound up hanging from trees. He showed her the knife. She'll never forget his thumb on the knife. She saw Bob Tully around a lot after that. He'd wave to her from his stoop. The more she stayed quiet, the nicer he was.

One day, she followed him as he bounced from the garage where he worked to the bar where he drank to the house of the woman he was seeing. She searched the newspapers for a sign that someone was missing—a husband, a son. Nothing. She never knew the identity of the man Bob Tully strangled. She started to consider she'd imagined it. And she continued to follow Bob Tully. She got to where she looked forward to following him. She wondered if he knew she was following him. Catholic school was boring. The nuns were boring. Her grandparents were boring. Smoking was boring. She wasn't sure if she watched Bob Tully in the hope that he'd do something else terrible, or that he'd be caught, or that someone would come to avenge the murder of the man he'd killed.

When Amy was nineteen, done with high school and working at a bakery in the neighborhood and thinking about how to get out of Queens, Bob Tully got drunk and drove his car head-on into a fruit truck. She wasn't there to see it, but she heard the story. Bananas and apples everywhere in the street, and Bob Tully ejected through the windshield, splattered on the sidewalk outside a barbershop.

He couldn't have looked as much like Vincent as Amy thought he did.

2

Vincent's still standing across the street when she goes back to check forty-five minutes later. Amy can only figure that he's waiting to confront her about something, or maybe he's just dumb enough to think that she won't see him when she leaves. She sees less of Bob Tully in him now that she's studying his awkward posture.

She wishes she had someone she could call as backup. Her life in the neighborhood is pretty small. It says a lot that the only people she can even think of to call are Monsignor Ricciardi, Connie Giacchino, and her landlord, Mr. Pezzolanti.

Back at the table, Amy reports that Vincent is still out there.

"Real creep, I told you," Mrs. Epifanio says.

"Who can I call? Maybe Elaine?"

"Don't bother Elaine."

"Mrs. E, I'm a little worried here. I leave, he's got the key, and he can waltz right in. I have to leave at some point."

"I know."

"I'm going to go out and talk to him."

"Be careful."

Amy leaves her bag behind and walks outside. It's hard to go from the bottled-up feeling of the house to the bright world outside. It feels a little warmer than when she headed over. Unusually warm. Very little winter weather this winter. She's surprised to find that Vincent is gone. She looks all around and doesn't see him.

Mrs. Epifanio's block, Bay Thirty-Seventh, is like many of the blocks in the neighborhood: newish condos next to her old, green frame house on both sides, the apartment building across the street, lots of other three-family houses. New trees have been planted by the city, with their sad little white tags and mounds of mulch. On a February morning like this, the kids in school, Amy can hear buses on Bath Avenue and the traffic lights clicking. She walks to the front gate. Vincent has left it open, pointed out to the sidewalk. She pulls it closed and latches it and takes another good look around for Vincent.

She goes back in and tells Mrs. Epifanio he's gone.

"That's good," she says.

"But I'm still not sure he's gone-gone. I'll probably leave in a little while, but I'm going to write down my number." She takes out her old Samsung flip phone. She's about the only person she knows of who doesn't have a smartphone. It's hard to even get these anymore, but they keep them on the market for senior citizens and technology-averse people like Amy. "You can call me whenever, day or night. If he comes back, let me know. I only live a few blocks away."

"That's so kind."

Amy finds a scratch pad and a black Sharpie and writes her name and number in big, blocky letters. "Do you want me to leave it here on the table, or should I post it on the fridge?"

"Table's fine."

"Okay. Do you feel a little better?"

"Sure."

"Did Vincent touch anything in your bedroom?"

"Nothing I noticed."

"You checked the drawers?"

"I didn't see anything missing." ·

Amy goes back into the bedroom. It's dark. She feels around on the wall just inside the door and finds a knob to twist. Three lights in the brass chandelier overhead flicker on. Everything is out of time. A bed with a chenille spread from the fifties. Swag flowers. Fringes. Penny-flat pillows. She looks up. Popcorn ceiling. A simple gold cross on the wall next to her. Under that, an antique Singer sewing machine with its original desk and bench. She runs her fingers over the scuffs on the desk. A clay-colored French provincial dresser with nine drawers runs along the far wall. Propped on top of it is a framed picture of Mr. and Mrs. Epifanio on their wedding day. She can't imagine what Vincent was doing in here. It doesn't look like anyone has so much as sat on the bed in ages. She knows that Mrs. Epifanio, like many of the old people she visits, sleeps in her recliner in the living room with the television on.

Her instinct is to go through the dresser. She stops herself. She wouldn't even know what might be missing. She hopes that Mrs. Epifanio doesn't have envelopes of cash stuffed in the drawers—another thing these old folks tend to do—that she doesn't remember putting there. One woman, Mrs. DiPaola, once asked Amy to go down to the basement and put her laundry on the line after communion. What Amy saw down there was an open cigar box on the table next to the washing machine, so much money inside. At least ten thousand dollars. She closed the lid of the box, hung the clothes on the line, went upstairs, and told Mrs. DiPaola it was a bad idea to leave so much money sitting out like that.

She sits on the bed. Something reminds her of her father—the ceiling. The apartment her father lived in after he'd left her and her mother had ceilings like this. Amy was only there twice before he stopped coming around to pick her up on weekends. She was twelve. Her mother died the next year. That was when she moved in with her grandparents, next door to Bob Tully. She never heard from her father again. He left Queens and moved to Poughkeepsie, and then her grandmother found out he was on the skids in Kingston and Hudson and all over upstate. But Amy remembered ceilings just like this in his apartment in Pomonok. She remembered staring up at those ceilings while he went out to the bar.

She stands and smooths the wrinkles out of the bedspread.

Back out in the kitchen, Mrs. Epifanio has opened a large-print sudoku book and is struggling with a puzzle.

"Didn't see anything unusual," Amy says, returning to her seat at the table. "Maybe I'll try Diane one more time." Address book in hand, she dials Diane's number on her cell phone, since it's out already and she doesn't feel like dealing with the rotary again. After six rings, she's about to drop the call, but then someone picks up and doesn't say anything. "Diane?"

"Diane's sick," a man says. Vincent.

Amy pushes the END button with her thumb and folds the phone shut. She's immediately sorry that she called from her own number. "It was Vincent," she says to Mrs. Epifanio.

Mrs. Epifanio shakes her head and looks down at the table. "I sure hope he didn't kill his mother. Happens all the time. Guys like him, they come home to rob their mothers. Mother's got nothing to rob and ends up with her throat cut. Poor Diane."

"Jeez, Mrs. E. You don't really think that, do you?"

"Who knows anymore? This day and age."

"Where's Diane live?"

"Second floor of the little brick two-family across from that house with the lions out front."

"I know that house."

"Giorgio Gianfortune. He owns the fish market. Thinks he's a big shot."

"I'm going to walk over there."

"That a good idea?"

"I just want to see if there's anything unusual."

⟐

Amy packs her bag and tells Mrs. Epifanio to close and put the slide lock on the kitchen door. Because there's a vacant apartment upstairs—Mrs. Epifanio stopped renting it after Mr. Epifanio died—the kitchen door has its own lock. Amy is thankful it's there. Mrs. Epifanio says she'll lock it. Amy points to her phone number again and tells Mrs. Epifanio to call for any reason. *Really*. But she also says that if Vincent comes back and starts knocking on the door or anything, Mrs. E should absolutely call the police. It's not okay for anyone to enter her house without asking, no matter his intentions.

Amy walks into the hallway and waits for Mrs. Epifanio to close and lock the kitchen door. Mrs. Epifanio struggles over to the door and shoulders it closed. The sound of the slide lock being engaged on the other side follows.

"Okay?" Mrs. Epifanio says.

"Good. I'll call you after to check in."

The house with the gaudy cement lion statues at the driveway entrance is only a few blocks away, Bay Thirty-Fourth between Bath and Benson. There could be other houses with lion statues, but she knows this is the one Mrs. Epifanio is talking about.

Amy pauses on Mrs. Epifanio's front stoop and then walks slowly to the front gate, keeping an eye out for Vincent. She exits through the gate, closing it carefully behind her, and then crosses the street and turns right onto Bath Avenue. She stops at Augie's Deli to get a coffee. She wonders if Vincent stopped here on his way home.

Bath Avenue is quiet this time of the morning. She passes the recently sold lot where Flash Auto once was. When she and Alessandra briefly had a car, they took it there for repairs. Having a car turned out to be nothing but a pain—parking, winters, maintenance. Alessandra was a terrible driver. Amy wasn't great either. She preferred walking and taking the bus or subway when she needed to go into the city, anyway. She would walk for hours, if she could. She often took long walks to Bay Ridge and Sunset Park, to Coney Island and Brighton Beach, listening to music. She'd sold all her records, but she'd held on to her childhood Walkman and some tapes she'd made in high school. Liz Phair, Tori Amos, Stone Temple Pilots, Alice in Chains, Nirvana, Hole, Sonic Youth, L7, the Breeders. The stuff she listened to as she smoked out her window. She could've gotten an iPod touch or something like that pretty cheap, she guesses, but she likes her old Sony Walkman, which fits so neatly in her palm. The battery cover kept in place with duct tape, the headphones stiff. It's a tank. She likes the act of flipping the tape, too. She likes to measure time by the sides of a tape.

She wishes she had it now. Instead, she's carrying her communion set, wanting so badly to ditch it back at the church, anxious because she's about to do surveillance on Diane's apartment. A hundred what-ifs run through her mind. What if she bumps into Vincent going up the block? What if he walks out of the house and sees her? What if he leans out the window while he's vaping and yells down to her? What if *he* calls the cops on *her*? *Officer, there's this girl outside being awfully suspicious*. What if she sees something that leads her to believe that Diane's been killed?

By the time she turns onto Bay Thirty-Fourth Street, her heart is racing. An old woman pushes a shopping cart along on the cracked sidewalk just ahead of her, its wheels clattering. The woman is out collecting bottles and cans. She stops in each yard and goes through recycling bins. She's wearing rubber gloves. Amy says hi as she passes.

She stops in front of the house with the lion statues, turning to look across at the brick two-family house Mrs. Epifanio identified. Second floor, she said. It's a small, boxy house, with three windows on the second floor facing the street, shades drawn, and a bay window on the first floor. Plants on the sill. A white cat sitting there. Only one door, which must be the entrance for both apartments. A small garden out front with a statue of St. Francis of Assisi and a line of withered tomato plants. The fence is painted red, a BEWARE OF DOG sign hanging crookedly from the gate with a twist of wire.

She's ambivalent about just standing where she is. She walks up and down the block a few times. Nothing changes. She gets tired and leans against the chain-link fence of a house a little farther up the street, putting her communion set down on the sidewalk, keeping one eye on Diane's place.

When Vincent emerges a few minutes later, dragging on his vape pen, he doesn't notice her because she's behind a parked car. He walks past her on the other side of the street, headed for Benson Avenue. She's torn about what to do. Go to the house and ring the second-floor buzzer and see if Diane answers? Or follow Vincent? He could be going back to Mrs. Epifanio's, though he doesn't seem to be headed in that direction.

She makes a snap decision to follow him, that old Bob Tully thrill coming back.

⇒

It becomes clear to her—as Vincent makes a left on Eighty-Sixth Street under the El—that he's not returning to Mrs. Epifanio's house. Amy continues to follow him anyway, staying half a block behind. She followed Bob Tully from this same distance, ducking behind telephone poles and trees.

Vincent rushes across Eighty-Sixth Street at a green light, holding on to whatever's in the pockets of his trench coat so it doesn't fall out. He's still got the vape pen in his hand. He stops in front of the HSBC on the corner of Twenty-Third Avenue and takes a drag. Amy crosses over once he starts moving again. She looks over at the liquor store where she used to go with Alessandra to buy wine and gin. Nothing special as far as liquor stores go. She hasn't been back in since Alessandra split town. She's mostly given up drinking.

Vincent passes in front of St. Peter Catholic Academy, once called St. Mary's. The church—still St. Mary, Mother of Jesus, as it has been for more than 125 years—is right up the block. Amy's apartment is a few doors down from the church. She's tempted to give up and just go home. She could drop the communion set back at the church and have the rest of the day to herself. Go get lunch at Liu's Shanghai. Talk to Xiùlán. Read. Listen to her Walkman. Whatever.

Amy feels like she's doing something she can't come back from. Maybe it's a bad decision to resume this behavior. A stupid decision. Say she follows Vincent into a scary situation. But that old thrill pushes her on. After Bob Tully died and she got her own apartment in Queens and started working in the city, she'd chased the feeling of purpose she'd had following him. She dated a dominatrix who liked Amy to watch her sessions with doughy businessmen. She dated a trapeze artist who felt alive only in the air and once got drunk and scaled the Brooklyn Bridge for kicks while Amy shook nervously on the walkway below. Vincent's a creep, wearing that trench coat on this nice warm day, rummaging around in Mrs. Epifanio's bedroom. Those eyes. She wants to understand him. She wants to see what his life is like.

Twenty-Third Avenue to Stillwell to Kings Highway. Vincent never once looks over his shoulder. The routine comes back. It's easy to keep him in sight, to linger just far enough behind that nothing looks unusual. Bob Tully lumbered along with his head down, but Vincent is a dramatic walker. He throws his arms back and forth a lot. He dances over cracks in the sidewalks. He takes out an iPhone and almost trips looking down at it. He stops to take a picture of some graffiti on a telephone pole.

On Kings Highway, between West Ninth and West Tenth but closer to the corner of West Tenth, Vincent ducks into a bar called Homestretch. Amy's been there twice, both times with Alessandra. From what she remembers, it's a divey little sports pub with Quick Draw and darts and a horse-racing mural. There was a ravioli buffet one Saturday night they were in there. Lots of old, grizzled regulars. From outside, it's the kind of place tourists to the neighborhood take pictures of. Hand-painted sign: HOMESTRETCH in meticulous white script over a background of red, BAR

& GRILL in neat black lettering over white. A black awning runs overhead, with HOMESTRETCH BAR printed in white paint, off-center, and a series of harness-racer reliefs on a white strip under that. There's a Budweiser sign in the window and blue-and-orange flags advertising Quick Draw hang from the awning. A lonely bench sits out front. Delis on both sides, shabby-looking apartments upstairs with battered window air conditioner units.

Amy crosses Kings Highway and Quentin Road and stands on the corner of West Tenth, outside 3 Stars Laundromat.

There aren't many bars left in the neighborhood. She doesn't go to bars anymore, though she and Alessandra spent many nights looking for something to do that wasn't just pizza or Chinese food. Alessandra talked about the Wrong Number, but it was closed by the time Amy moved here. There were a couple of others that had come and gone, but she can't remember the names. On Eighty-Sixth Street and Bay Thirty-Second, there's a new Georgian bakery she really likes; she's pretty sure there used to be a bar in that spot. Once she stopped working at and going to bars, she mostly stopped thinking about them.

She's not going in after Vincent, that's for sure. She checks her phone for the time and can't believe it's only just noon. She wonders if Vincent will spend all day in Homestretch. When she worked at Seven Bar, there were regulars who would come in around noon and stay until they closed at four in the morning. Some would stay past close, if she let them. A few nights, Amy was drunk enough that she locked the door and whoever was in there kept the party going with shots and pool and everyone just wound up sleeping in the booths. She'd actually met Merrill on a night like that.

She feels silly standing there. Every car that passes, she thinks the passengers are looking at her, accusing her of something. The family that comes out of the Laundromat, hauling bags of clean clothes, they give her a once-over. A bearded guy with untied shoelaces and a steaming deli coffee passes and winks at her and says, "How much?" She looks away. He laughs. In the old days, she would've gotten in his face, said something like, "Who the fuck you think you're talking to?" In the old days. There's no peace in that. The guy's inconsequential.

How long to stand there? That's the question. With Bob Tully, there had been a sense that something might happen at any moment, but Vincent seems more and more like a neighborhood weirdo with nothing better to do than make an old lady uncomfortable. And she's so different now. Too old to be guided by mere curiosity.

Vincent comes out. He sits on the bench, vaping. Another guy follows fast on his heels and sits down next to him. This other guy is pasty, wearing red, low-hanging basketball shorts, flip-flops, and a plain softball T-shirt with black sleeves. He and Vincent are talking. Vincent looks mad. Amy can't hear anything. She moves around to the side of 3 Stars, afraid she's right in Vincent's sight line. She leans against the glass window. Her feet are getting sore. She should leave. She wants to leave. But she's glued there.

Vincent is motioning wildly with his hands. He stands up suddenly. Amy thinks he might throw a punch. He doesn't. Instead, he storms back into Homestretch. The other guy follows him.

Amy stands there for another forty-five minutes. A little girl in the Laundromat makes faces at her. Amy curls her tongue and crosses her eyes. The girl laughs. Amy decides it's time to go. Seeing the little girl has set off something in her. Vincent's a waste. Creepy, sure, but that's it. She leaves, taking a different route back to the church. She turns around a few times to make sure Vincent's not following her now. She thinks she sees him once and then realizes it's someone who doesn't look anything like him.

3

Amy drops the communion set back at St. Mary's and stops to light a candle on the way out.

She lights a candle at least once a week, always under the stained glass St. Thérèse. Therese was the name she chose for her confirmation. When you grow up and move away from the church, you forget about things like confirmation names.

Her full name is Amy Lynn Therese Falconetti. She loved St. Thérèse as a girl. The Little Flower. She read whatever books she could find about her in the library. Thérèse's childhood, how young she was when she became a nun. Her years at the Carmel of Lisieux. Her tragic death at twenty-four from tuberculosis. Amy had even read *The Story of a Soul,* Thérèse's autobiography. Her confirmation gift from her mother was a St. Thérèse medal. She lost that medal when she was in college, drunk one night. Showering in the dorms with a bottle of gin, she took it off and left it coiled on the ledge by her shampoo bottle and forgot all about it. When she remembered the next morning, she went back to check and it was gone. She has always wondered if the medal is still out there somewhere, worn around someone's neck, kept in someone's bedside table drawer.

When Amy regained her faith post-Alessandra, she started thinking about St. Thérèse again. Her words on charity, especially. Amy realized how much of her life had been devoted to selfish, empty things, and she wanted to help a little. She knew she was no saint, but she thought she might be able to bring a little light into people's lives: a visit to the nursing home, a trip to the grocery store for someone who is homebound, praying with and talking to people who are alone.

The stained glass St. Thérèse—like all the representations of saints in the windows at St. Mary's—is made of jagged shapes. The original church in this spot, built in 1889, burned down in 1967. The church that's there now was built soon after that and opened in 1971. It's very much marked by architectural decisions specific to the period. The layout is bell-like. The altar is spare, the windows trippy. Candles flutter with a sad radiance. The church is quiet now and smells of myrrh. It's mostly quiet these days, the congregation having shrunk significantly. Many old Italians remain, but the young in the parish are Chinese, Russian, Mexican.

Praying is hard. Amy's never sure what to pray for. She finds herself thinking about Vincent and Bob Tully as she kneels in front of St. Thérèse and the candles. She prays for Mrs. Epifanio and for Diane and for Vincent and for Bob Tully and for the man he killed, too. Prayer is strange.

Back outside, she clicks RECENT CALLS on her phone and tries Diane again. No answer. She doesn't have Mrs. Epifanio's number saved, but she somehow remembers it and calls her to check in. Mrs. Epifanio says everything is great, she took a nap like a baby, and she feels less worried. Amy says she's glad and reminds her to call if she needs anything.

It's a short walk to the house where her apartment is. Mr. Pezzolanti, her landlord, is standing outside by the open front gate, flipping through a Rite Aid circular, when she arrives. Amy is thankful every day for him. He lets her rent out the basement apartment in his three-family house for almost nothing. Four hundred dollars a month. He's a regular at St. Mary's. She used to know bar regulars; now she knows church regulars. He's a nice guy. Genuine. He takes the collections at Mass on Saturday evening. Wears a tweed blazer and clips his nose hairs and slicks his hair back for church. Now, he wears a blue cotton work shirt she can see through, a plaid Italian cap, dark pants, sandals. He has moles on his shoulders and arms.

Mr. Pezzolanti's only son died of a heart defect at seventeen. His wife died of cancer in 2001. He has money saved up; he doesn't have to rent her the apartment. He doesn't rent the upstairs anymore. He treats Amy like a daughter. He tells her often that he doesn't want her to pay. She insists. Four hundred is what she can afford. Most of what she does is volunteer: Eucharistic Minister, running clothing donation drives, working at soup kitchens in other parts of Brooklyn. For money, she babysits and cleans houses when she needs to. She does a little bookkeeping for the church and a doctor's office on Bay Parkway, but that's only now and then. Occasionally, someone asks her to help out with their elderly mother or father at Sea Crest in Coney Island or Haym Salomon on Cropsey. A couple of months back, Kathy D'Ambrosio paid her twelve bucks an hour to sit with her mother at Sea Crest Mondays through Thursdays while she was at work. That was nice. Mrs. D'Ambrosio told her stories about Coney Island, and they watched the Game Show Network. If Amy's really desperate for money, she gets a register job at one of the Russian markets on Eighty-Sixth Street for a few weeks. She's only had to do that three times, and they're always happy to have her in reserve, the way they go through girls over there.

"Guy came around looking for you a little while ago," Mr. Pezzolanti says.

"What guy?" Amy says. Her mind goes first to Vincent. It wouldn't be hard to find out who she is and where she lives.

"Older guy. Never seen him before."

So, not Vincent. "He say what he wanted?"

"He was a little shaky. Had a little bit of—you don't mind me saying—a bum quality. Didn't say much, just he was looking for you."

"Thanks, Mr. P."

"You need anything? You good down there? How's the hot water?"

"Good. Everything is good. Thank you."

She's waiting for what she knows is coming: Mr. Pezzolanti asking why she doesn't have a boyfriend. A lot of eligible bachelors around, guys with good jobs. Sanitation workers, electricians, lawyers. They should be lining up. Amy again chooses not to deal with it, never taking the time to explain. If he ever saw her around with Alessandra before she moved in, he must've thought nothing of it. And no one comes home with her these days, so there's not much she needs to account for in the way you need to account for things with nosy old-timers.

"I see this bum-looking guy," Mr. Pezzolanti says, "I think, *When's Amy gonna get herself a nice boyfriend?* You know Nicky DiMarzio's son? Little younger than you, but he works at the gym on Twenty-Fourth Avenue. Nice kid. Respectful. Doesn't drink."

"I'm good, Mr. P. Thanks."

"You do a lot for a lot of people. Let someone take care of you for a change."

Amy smiles and walks past him. The entrance to her apartment is down a small flight of cement steps. Mr. Pezzolanti has wrapped the railing in tinfoil and glued red felt flowers in rows on the sides. She's never asked why. The front door has a little brass knocker. She takes out her key and sees scratches around the keyhole she's never noticed before. They're probably normal marks from inserting and removing the key several times a day. She turns the knob and pushes in the door.

The studio apartment is pretty bare. She likes it that way. A box TV with a digital antenna that someone up the block had put out for trash; twin mattress on the floor; foldout table with folding chairs. She misses her records and the artwork she had up on the walls in her old place in Queens, but she feels so far removed from that version of herself. She's kept a few things—a small stack of records, sketches of her tattoos, three of her favorite outfits—and they're in an egg crate on the top shelf of the apartment's only closet.

She doesn't have a dresser or a couch. She keeps her new clothes—blouses, slacks, underwear, socks, jeans, a hoodie, a few T-shirts—in a plastic bin. She has a mini fridge stocked with yogurt and juice and ice pops. The apartment doesn't have a stove. She makes do with a hot pot and an electric kettle, mostly for rice and tea. In the corner is a stack of books she has out from the library, Dorothy Day's diaries, her book about Thérèse of Lisieux, and a book about the Catholic Worker Movement. Amy's Walkman is next to the books, the headphones coiled over a small stack of cassette tapes. What looks like another closet in the back is actually her bathroom, a tiny space just big enough to fit a toilet, a sink, and a shower stall. She's never been in a mobile home, but it's the kind of bathroom she imagines she'd find in one.

Who is this man who came to see her? She can't stop wondering about him. She's grateful at least that he's pushed Vincent from her thoughts for the time being.

She thinks about going to get lunch at Liu's Shanghai. It's her one vice. The food is excellent. And she loves to see Xiùlán, who works the counter seven days a week. Xiùlán was born in Bath Beach. Her parents own the restaurant. She and Amy don't seem to have much in common, so they talk about the weather. Sometimes they talk about the news or the neighborhood or something strange one of them has witnessed. Xiùlán is beautiful, and Amy most definitely has a little crush on her, but nothing will ever come of it outside of a loose, casual friendship. She knows the mechanics of such encounters. Plenty of bar patrons developed crushes on her simply because she was their bartender and they liked the routine of knowing her, or the easy way she struck up conversations, or how she poured drinks. That didn't mean fire. That didn't mean connection.

Amy has seen Xiùlán with the man who must be her boyfriend. She never asks about him. She doesn't want to know. She doesn't think she'll go to Liu's Shanghai today after all. It's too much to go four times in four days. Yesterday had been so busy that Xiùlán only had time to look up from the phone and say hello.

What Mr. Pezzolanti said about her doing a lot for a lot of people, she guesses that's true. Lately, at least. But she doesn't feel like doing anything else for anyone today. She sits down on the bed and kicks off her shoes. Plain, boring shoes with plain, boring laces. She crosses her left leg over her right knee and rubs the bottom of her foot. Maybe she should take a nap, like Mrs. Epifanio. Just read a little and see if she can't close her eyes. Try to shed some of the anxiety she's managed to pick up.

Amy rubs her other foot and then curls up on the bed. She doesn't even reach for a book. Times like this, she feels intensely alone. There were plenty of other women before, but she mostly misses Alessandra. Gravesend is, after all, Alessandra's neighborhood. Bensonhurst, too. Bath Beach and the blocks around it. She goes to church in one of the two churches Alessandra went to as a child. She attends meetings with the monsignor who presided over Alessandra's father's funeral. The streets are haunted by Alessandra's stories. Where those new condos are, that's where the D'Innocenzios lived. And here's the Calabrese house. And that's the Rite Aid where Stephanie Dirello worked. Amy is glad that Stephanie and her mother decided to move to Jersey last year. She'd still see Steph around every once in a while before that, and it was always uncomfortable. She can't think too hard about how much she misses sleeping with Alessandra. She's not sure what to do with the pain that accompanies such yearning.

A knock on the door.

"Hold on," she says. She wonders if it's the stranger who came around looking for her before. Her curiosity carries her to the door. She wishes for a peephole. "Who is it?"

"It's Mr. P. The guy who stopped by looking for you before, he's right here with me."

Amy is glad that Mr. Pezzolanti had the forethought to stay with the man, not to just let him knock and find Amy on his own. She opens the door.

The man standing beside Mr. Pezzolanti is her father.

4

Fred Falconetti is nervous and shaky. He's wearing a red sweatshirt with holes around the neck and battered chinos and dirty black Nike sneakers. He's got a gray beard that's so unkempt, it's almost dreaded, arrow tips of tangled hair crawling up his cheekbones. His neck is sugared with tufts of hair that look like balls of dust. His hair is wavy, mostly gray, and he seems to have tried to comb it for the occasion. He has a surprised look on his face, one she recognizes from her days at Seven Bar: an alcoholic who's sober and risking his dignity to ask for something. In this case, what? Forgiveness? A few years ago, she might've told him to fuck off. Now, the way she is, the way her life is, what can she do but allow him in and give him a chance? He has tears in his eyes.

"You know this guy?" Mr. Pezzolanti says.

"Amy Lynn," Fred says.

"Who is this guy?" Mr. Pezzolanti says.

Amy is speechless.

"I'm her old man," Fred says.

Mr. Pezzolanti looks at him, shocked. "Her old man? I didn't think she had an old man." To Amy: "You've got an old man? *He's* your old man?"

Amy nods. "I didn't know I had an old man anymore, either, but I guess I do."

"Missing in action, huh?" Mr. Pezzolanti says.

"Something like that," Fred replies.

"Last time I saw him, I was twelve," Amy says.

"Good Lord," Mr. Pezzolanti says. "You two have a lot of catching up to do, I take it."

"Can I hug you?" Fred asks Amy.

Amy nods again, and he moves in. He smells of cigarettes and bad cologne. His beard sandpapers her cheek. She's the one with tears in her eyes now. She's thinking about her mother. Fred's laughing a little, awkwardly, nervously, probably thinking how he expected things to go south, fast, that she'd turn him away. That's what she suspects. She feels it in his body language, the tender hug and quaking arms.

"I'll leave you to it," Mr. Pezzolanti says. "You need me, Amy, I'll be right upstairs."

"Thanks, Mr. P," Amy says, pulling away from Fred and wiping her eyes with the heels of her hands.

"Can I come in?" Fred says.

"Sure," Amy says. "It's not very comfortable. I only have a couple of folding chairs."

"I don't care about comfortable."

They sit across from each other at her little poker table, the folding chairs stiff and hard. Fred puts his elbows up on the table and smiles.

"I don't believe this," Amy says.

"Me neither," Fred says.

"All these years."

"How are you?"

"How can I answer that?"

Fred leans back in his chair. "I know, I know. Do you want me to start?"

Amy gets up and paces. "Why now?"

"It can take your whole life to wake up to certain things, when you're like me. I had my priorities all out of whack. I'm sorry for that. I wish I could go back."

"I don't want to just start going through each other's histories. How we got here. Who we are." Amy catches herself. This is her old voice. This is the way she would've responded a few years ago. She should try compassion. But she can't make her lips say anything that might be perceived as a willingness to start over.

She sits back down. "What do you want? Are you in trouble?" Such doubt and anger in her tone. The man must be here for selfish reasons. He's broke and needs to mooch from her. He's homeless. He's on the run from a crime. He's dying and can't pay for treatment.

He hesitates.

"I don't have much money," she says. "Mostly I just volunteer through the church."

"You go to church? That's good."

"I pretty much stopped after Mom died, except when they made me go at school. I just started again a couple of years ago."

"I've been going to church again, too. Not here, obviously. Over where I live in Queens. It's nice to feel welcome somewhere. I wore out a lot of my welcomes over the years."

"How did you find me?"

"I put out feelers."

"You're in Queens?"

"I moved around a bit. Wound up back there about three years ago."

"You put out feelers how?"

"Most people, seems like, you can find them on the Internet if you really need to. But you don't have social media or anything, huh? That's healthy. Shit's poison. All these zombies on their phones. Now you've got this bat-shit reality TV show president Twittering and whatnot."

"Who'd you talk to?"

"I went back to the old neighborhood. Found someone you went to high school with at St. Agnes. That led me to the bar you worked at in the city. This was more than a year ago. They told me Brooklyn, but Brooklyn's big as hell. From there, I had to do some serious investigative work. I was pretty impressed with myself, actually. It was the hardest I ever worked at any-thing." More laughter. "I'm not here for money or anything, I swear."

"Okay," Amy says.

"I'm sorry I left. I'm sorry about your mother. I'm sorry about everything."

"Okay."

Fred stands up and crosses his arms. "Listen, I'm in your hair. I don't want to crowd you. I know it's not great, showing up unannounced like this. You need time to process this. Maybe I can come back another time and we can get lunch or coffee or something?"

She nods. "Sure," she says. It's the best she can do.

"Tomorrow? Same time?"

"That's fine."

"How about one more hug for the road?" Fred says.

They embrace. Fred walks out, gazing back at her once before he closes the door behind him.

That really happened, she thinks. Her father was in her little apartment, and now he's gone. Her *father*. She had just been thinking about him at Mrs. Epifanio's because of the popcorn ceiling in the bedroom. She'd long ago figured him for dead.

She latches the dead bolt and goes back to the bed, curling up again and trying to empty her mind, wanting to hide.

As she lies there, Amy finds it impossible not to think about her mother, Barbara. How she did everything for her growing up. Fred off at the bars, off with other women—just *off.* Barbara deserved better. After Fred finally disappeared for good, Barbara fought like hell to have the marriage annulled, and Amy prayed that her mother would find someone better. Someone with a job. Someone who would come home after work and stay home. Play cards with them. Share meals. Know how to be kind.

Barbara had one date that Amy remembers. Guy's name was Terry De Santis. Worked over at a cabstand in Ozone Park. He showed up in a nice, new-looking suit with a short, stubby red tie. He opened the door of his Lincoln Continental for Barbara and took her to Don Peppe's. Amy stayed with her grandparents and couldn't relax until Barbara got home and told her what a wonderful time she'd had, what a gentleman Terry had been. Amy was happy and hopeful. The next week, Barbara was diagnosed with pancreatic cancer. Terry never came around again.

The visit to her doctor had merely been a routine checkup. Barbara seemed totally fine one day, then deteriorated quickly. She lost a lot of weight, and her skin turned yellow. She was gone in fewer than eight months. Amy's grandparents hunted for her father, to no avail. They didn't have to do that. They knew they would take responsibility for her. But they thought Fred deserved the right to have some stake in her life. Amy got mad. She turned her back on God. She tried not to think about her father. She tried not to give her grandparents too much trouble. They only knew that she went to school and got good grades. She lied to them about going to church. They believed her, for some reason. They never caught on about the smoking. They didn't know Bob Tully except to say hi to him. He'd only moved in next door a couple of years before her mother died. Her grandparents never knew what she'd seen. They never could've guessed that Amy was following him every chance she got.

Now, having returned to God, Amy's being asked to give her father a shot? She's not sure she can. She's not sure she has that kind of strength.

Her father didn't beat her. He didn't beat Barbara. He was a drunk, no more and no less. His absence from her life didn't make her who she is. Her mother and grandparents made her who she is. She wishes Fred had the guts to stay away. This isn't for her—it's for him. She knows the story.

She gets up and takes off her clothes. In the little bathroom, she runs a shower. The water pressure is great. She turns the hot water all the way up—Mr. Pezzolanti has just adjusted the knob on the water heater, and she has more hot water than ever. The bathroom is a pocket of steam. Staying under the water soothes her. The noise of the shower drowns out everything else. She closes her eyes. She's being wasteful, and she knows it. She stays in the shower until the water starts to turn cold; then she twists the knobs off and reaches for a towel. She dries herself. She walks naked to her plastic bin, her arms crossed over her chest, and picks out fresh clothes. A purple T-shirt, jeans, a black hoodie, and her black Converse. She's decided she *will* go to Liu's Shanghai. She makes sure she has her phone, in case Mrs. Epifanio calls. It's in her pocket, the ringer on vibrate.

Outside, Mr. Pezzolanti is standing by the gate. He seems to have been waiting for her. He notices her hair is wet. "That hot water's really blasting now, isn't it?" he says.

She touches her hair. "I'm sorry I took such a long shower."

"Oh, no sweat. That was really your old man, huh?"

"It was."

"Doesn't look much like you."

"I take after my mom."

"How'd it go?"

"I don't know."

Mr. Pezzolanti nods. "Say no more. I don't mean to pry." He leans against the gate, looks up at the telephone wires. "I wasn't always the best as an old man. I've got regrets."

"You were around."

"Chris was only a kid. We had a few falling-outs. I'm in no position to give you advice. But your father's your father. Blood's tough."

"It is."

Part of Amy wants to invite Mr. Pezzolanti along to Liu's Shanghai or at least ask him if he wants anything for takeout. But she beats back that desire to be kind. She wants to be alone. She wants to sit with her fried wontons and scallop soup dumplings and steal glances at Xiùlán. She says good-bye to Mr. Pezzolanti, telling him she'll see him later. He gives her a salute.

⟞⟐⟞

Eighty-Sixth Street is full of late-afternoon action. She must've stayed in her apartment even longer than she thought after Fred left; she hasn't looked at a clock. The fruit markets are bustling, and trains come and go overhead. Commuters pour out at the Bay Parkway station. Double-parked cars are lined up at the curb. Garbage is ribboned around telephone poles. Dirty puddles have collected in the crosswalks. Squashed cigarette boxes, newspapers, and food wrappers dot the ground. Kids pass with bubble tea. The Chinese markets have laid out wild displays of dried mushrooms, dried shrimp, dried everything. Chicken and duck carcasses hang in the windows of Chinese restaurants; crowded fish tanks fill other windows. An old lady sits on an overturned orange crate outside one of the Russian grocery stores with a folded shopping cart at her feet and a wilted yellow tulip in her hand. Amy remembers Alessandra's story of a guy with a guitar who used to stand on the corner of Bay Parkway and serenade everyone as they passed by. She remembers Alessandra pointing out where Sam Goody once was, how she bought her first Pixies tape there.

Liu's is fairly far away, on the corner of Nineteenth Avenue and Bath Avenue, technically in Bath Beach, thirteen blocks past where she turned off earlier for Diane's apartment. Amy continues along Eighty-Sixth Street now. She prefers walking under the El. The avenue is crowded and alive, but it seems to be dying at the same time. Closed riot gates full of rust and graffiti. Battered El columns in the street spidering along endlessly. People tossing away their garbage as they walk—abandoned scratch-offs, beer cans in brown paper bags, pages from a child's coloring book. Half-hearted new construction projects all around, paired with a roof caving in here, a broken window there. Graffiti over a beautiful half-hidden old shoe store sign. Everything feeling partly poisonous. Or poisoned. Here are men with decaying teeth, with decaying smiles, and women trudging along with their shoulders hunched. A bike without wheels is chained to a lamppost.

Most days, Amy isn't sure if she likes one single thing about the neighborhood. She's never liked anything about it, really. Alessandra hated it, so she'd seen it first through that lens, and that impression stuck. But not liking it had led her to want to stay. She felt like she could disappear, at first. Then she felt like she could live among the forgotten and bring some light to them. *Maybe I'm being overdramatic*, she thinks. Sometimes the dreariness hits her full force.

At Nineteenth Avenue, she makes a left and then continues straight, crossing Benson. Liu's appears, an unassuming white awning wrapping around the corner, the name of the restaurant and some Chinese characters in green and red, along with two Shanghai shadow skylines. From the outside, it could be like any of the other Chinese dive joints in the neighborhood, serving up musty egg drop soup and bad fried rice. What had drawn her in first was a review she read somewhere. She can't quite remember where. Maybe *New York* magazine. The review sang of the soup dumplings, of the vegetarian duck, of the fish-head casserole, and of the braised lion's-head meatballs. She'd started simple with Shanghai-style lo mein and worked her way up to more adventurous stuff.

People have been catching on over the last year, coming from other neighborhoods to eat there—even coming from the city. It's a small restaurant, and it's usually crowded from dinner until close. She's hoping that it's early enough now that she'll get there before the rush.

When she enters, she's surprised that the place is almost completely empty. She sits at a table by the window. Xiùlán comes out of the kitchen and waves, then goes over to the phone on the counter, picks it up, and says something in Chinese. She's short, probably about five two, and her hair is black. She wears a pink cap with little fox ears sewn onto it, a black blouse, and jeans ripped at the knees. She finishes the call and comes over.

"How are you?" she asks, her voice soft.

"Same," Amy says. "You?"

Xiùlán shrugs. "Annoying phone call."

"I hope you're not getting sick of me. I come in every day now."

A smile. "Never. What can I get you?"

Amy doesn't need to look at the menu. She orders her two favorite things: A1 and A3. Scallop soup dumplings and fried wontons. The fried wontons come in a peanut and hot sauce. She's not even that hungry. Her stomach is unsettled because of Vincent and Fred. She thinks how strange it is that days can just go to these unexpected places. Her routine unaltered for the last couple of years, and then this.

Xiùlán brings the order into the kitchen. She comes out and goes back behind the counter to fetch Amy's ginger ale, which is free with the meal. She doesn't even need to ask what Amy wants to drink, and that makes Amy happy. "Here you go," she says, setting down the can in front of Amy.

Amy says thanks as Xiùlán joins her at the table. They talk about how nice it is out for this time of year, how they can't believe it's February already, and about the state of things in the world. How scary it is. This guy as president—an absolute idiot. The immigration ban. Xiùlán telling stories of what some of her family members have been going through, their fears and worries, how hard they've worked to get here and how it all seems to be collapsing. Amy shakes her head and says how sad that is. She can't wait for it to be over. Xiùlán expresses doubt that it'll be over any time soon.

They switch gears. Xiùlán asks if Amy heard about the double murder on Bay Twenty-Third, the woman who killed her husband and son. Terrible. Amy asks how the woman did it. Xiùlán makes a gun with her hand. "Shot them both," she says. "Bullet went through the floor and almost killed the old man in the apartment downstairs, too."

Amy wonders if she should tell Xiùlán about Vincent and Fred. It seems stupid and selfish. She decides not to. The food comes, and Xiùlán leaves her to eat.

Amy gets hungry as she smells the food in front of her. The first scallop soup dumpling bursts in her mouth, perfect. She picks up a wonton with her chopsticks. Spicy. Also perfect. She plows through the food, thinking about how good it tastes, trying not to think about having to get lunch or coffee or whatever with Fred. She won't bring him here. She'll bring him somewhere dumb and unimportant, like Starbucks, somewhere that could be anywhere. She washes down the food with her ginger ale. Xiùlán comes to check on her. Amy lets her know how good everything is, as usual.

Amy walks up to the counter and pays. The food isn't expensive. Her total comes to just over seventeen dollars. She gives Xiùlán the exact amount and leaves five bucks as a tip. Xiùlán says it was nice seeing her again. Amy says, "It's always nice seeing you," and then she worries that she's being too forward. Nothing registers in Xiùlán's face.

As Amy leaves Liu's Shanghai, her phone rumbles in her pocket. She takes it out and flips it open. "Vincent's back," Mrs. Epifanio says. "He's pounding on my kitchen door right now."

5

Now it's getting dark out. Amy runs the first half of the way and fast-walks the second, once she's short of breath. She's not sure what she'll find at Mrs. Epifanio's. Vincent, having given up, slumped at the door? But maybe he's not just some neighborhood weirdo after all. Maybe he'll have broken down the door and gotten inside and strangled Mrs. Epifanio to death. Or maybe Mrs. Epifanio will have called the cops, and Amy will merely be an ornament on the edges of disorder.

It takes her fifteen minutes to get there, maybe a little longer. The front door is open when she arrives. She goes inside. There's no sign of Vincent. The kitchen door is closed. She tries the knob. Locked. She knocks.

"Who is it?" Mrs. Epifanio says from the other side.

"It's Amy, Mrs. E. Is he gone?"

"I guess so." Mrs. Epifanio sighs and opens the door. She looks tired and uneasy. "He just stood out there and pounded on the door. He called me an old bitch, said he was gonna break the door in. I'm so glad you told me to put the slide lock on."

"Did he say what he wanted?"

"No. Just he needed to get in."

"Why didn't you call the police?"

"I called you."

"I'm not the police. What could I have done?"

"I know. Come in. Have some coffee."

"I can't, Mrs. E. I'm sorry." She's not sure why her impulse is to say no. She technically has nowhere to be. Wouldn't this be part of what she considers her work? To help calm down Mrs. Epifanio, to tell her everything's going to be okay, to call the police for her and file a report? But instead, it's a clipped *no*. Her old self is coming through again.

"I understand," Mrs. Epifanio says.

"Just keep that slide lock on," Amy says.

Mrs. Epifanio nods and closes the door, still distressed and now disappointed. She was probably taking for granted that Amy would stay for a little while, nice girl like her.

Amy locks the front door from the inside and then pulls it shut behind her. She looks for some sign of Vincent. She's thinking he was so harried that maybe he dropped something. He had the key out and maybe he dropped his vape pen or his phone, left some trace of himself. But there's nothing that she can see.

She's down the stoop and out the gate. She wants to follow him again. That same impulse from before. She's got only two leads. He either went to Diane's or to Homestretch. If he's not at one of those places, there's no following him. This time, she thinks, she wants to confront him. She wants to ask him a couple of questions. She never had the guts to confront Bob Tully. She guesses Homestretch and heads in that direction.

So much walking. Her feet still sore. When she gets to Homestretch, she stands outside and peers in through the window. The Budweiser sign casts a red glow over the small crowd inside. She doesn't see Vincent. She goes in and takes the only empty stool at the bar, down by the end. The bartender looks like a plumber. He wears a gold chain over a T-shirt with the Italian flag on it. He's got a mustache, and he's eating a folded slice of pizza.

"What can I get you?" he asks.

"Just a club soda, thanks," Amy says.

Bar like this, he doesn't laugh. He probably suspects she's an alcoholic who just wants to be around it all. Maybe she looks like that in her plain clothes. Unassuming. Like someone running from her past.

He brings her back a club soda on the rocks in a pint glass with a lime wedge on the rim and puts it on a coaster in front of her. She leaves three singles for him. He takes one. She pushes the other two forward to indicate that it's a tip. He nods and says, "Thanks, sweetie."

Homestretch on the inside is pretty much just as she remembers it. The TVs are on, playing MSG. Football's over. Baseball hasn't started yet. The hockey fans are waiting for the Rangers to come on. She grabs a straw from a dispenser on the bar, rips off the paper, and pushes it into her glass. She takes a long sip.

She isn't surprised when Vincent comes out of the bathroom and sits at the other end of the bar. He doesn't see her. He's got a Bud Light there waiting for him. He seems to be alone. She puts one elbow up on the bar, shifts her bottom on the stool, and covers her face with her hand as best she can.

Out of the corner of her eye, she sees Vincent drawing on his vape pen. A bluish cloud of smoke rises around him. Some of the old-timers lined up at the bar look at him like he's dissecting a frog right on his cocktail napkin.

"I told you to knock that shit off," the bartender says to him.

"Bernie, come on," Vincent says. "It's okay to do it inside."

"That's not the point. You're making yourself look like an idiot. You're making us all look like idiots. You're gonna do it, go outside."

Vincent sighs. "I've seen people in here racing cockroaches on the bar top and you're gonna give me shit for vaping?"

"Even the name," Bernie the bartender says. "*Vaping*. What is that? Just go get a pack of cigarettes."

Vincent swigs what's left of his beer and goes outside. He sits heavily on the bench. Amy puts down her hand and readjusts on her stool. She can see only the top of Vincent's head in the corner of the window. She can go out there and talk to him, if that's what she wants. Now is ideal. She imagines what she might say to him. She'd want it to be good. Something like, "Mrs. Epifanio sends her best." He'd look up and smile.

And what if he's truly dangerous, like Bob Tully? What if he lashes out at her? That can't be what she's after. But maybe the mystery of whether he could be capable of what Bob Tully was capable of is what's driving her. She's embraced another kind of mystery, but it's been so dull.

She knows she should've just stayed with Mrs. Epifanio and called the police and given them Vincent's description and told the officers she was worried about Diane.

Through the window, there's only the dark patch of his hair and the smoke rising over it and lights from passing cars. Someone walks up to him. A man wearing a hooded sweatshirt. Not a light hoodie like hers but puffier, fuller, with the hood cinched tight around his face. It could be the same man from earlier, just dressed differently. The man sits next to Vincent on the bench. More smoke.

Bernie comes over to check on her. She says she's good. She stands up, leaving her club soda, and walks over to the wall and studies a poster for the Mayweather-Pacquiao fight from a couple of years back. A cocktail table arcade machine is shoved up against the wall nearby, a scatter of empty bottles on top of it. Next to that, propped on a stool, is a big bouquet of fake roses. She touches the papery petals.

If she walks out the front door right now, there'll be no choice but to face Vincent. She'll pull open the door and practically be on top of him, sitting there with the other man on the bench. If he's looking down at the sidewalk, she guesses, it's possible she could pass without his noticing her.

"Have a good night, sweetheart," Bernie says, as she makes a move to leave.

"Thanks," she says. "You, too."

As she opens the door, she tilts her head to the left, expecting to make immediate eye contact with Vincent. But she's surprised to see that both he and the other man are gone from the bench. She takes a few steps out toward the street and turns around in a circle, scanning everywhere for them. She notices them then, ducking onto West Tenth Street, headed toward Highlawn Avenue. Her gut tells her to let this go, but she feels committed. She follows them.

West Tenth between Kings Highway and Highlawn is quiet and residential, mostly row houses with half-blocked driveways, notes left on windshields, garbage cans and recycling bins out at the curb. The street is crowded with parked cars in a battle for position. Newspapers curl in the gutter under the murky glow of streetlamps. The dark seems so much darker here than out on busy Kings Highway.

Amy keeps a safe distance and stays on the opposite side of the street. She pulls her hood up to obscure her face. The other man—now she can see him in full—wears drooping jeans with a hole in the back pocket and Timberland boots. His hood is still up. The fact that she's seen only the back of him so far makes it difficult to tell if it's the same guy from earlier.

Vincent seems overanxious. He's talking to the man, gesticulating wildly, trying to explain something.

The man is talking back. He seems pretty relaxed.

Amy can't hear anything either of them is saying. She wishes she could.

She wonders where they're heading. Her mind wanders in a million bad directions: drug deal, shakedown, secret whorehouse, to beat the hell out of some poor working stiff who owes on a debt.

They stop in their tracks. So does Amy, crouching down behind a Nissan

Maxima with a birdshit-splattered windshield. Vincent's getting louder. She hears the word *mother*. The two of them are facing each other now. Toe to toe. She can sort of see the other man's profile behind the curved edge of his hood. He has a long nose and a square chin. The guy Vincent was with earlier, she only saw straight on. She didn't really take note of his features, more what he was wearing. Those basketball shorts and flip-flops. His easy slouch on the bench.

Vincent throws out his arms and pushes the man.

The man folds back, hitting the side of a parked car with a thud. He comes up with a knife in his hand. Amy only sees it at first because of a glint on the knife from the streetlamp over them. It's a short, stubby blade. She can't make out much else from her position.

Amy ducks lower, covering her mouth, not wanting to make a noise. If something happens, she doesn't want the man to know she's here. She makes a noise, and he'll come after her. She wonders if other people are witnessing this from their windows. It's probably just a show of force, of dominance. Alpha male bullshit. Nothing will happen.

But the man lunges at Vincent and stabs him in the throat. Vincent is too slow to get his arms up to block the attack. Amy hears a wet sound, Vincent coughing. He puts his hands over his neck as if he's trying to hold something in, and then he crumples to the sidewalk behind a car and out of her view. The man, without hesitation, bolts away up the block, charging into the middle of the street, looking back once, and then making a quick right onto Highlawn Avenue. The sound of his boots on the pavement is terrible.

Amy rises to her feet and peers over the hood of the Maxima. She still can't see Vincent. She crosses the street, twisting her head around to see if anyone else has witnessed this. She should take out her phone and call 911. She doesn't. It's as if she's looking out the window at Bob Tully again. She had thought Vincent looked like Bob Tully, but now she's realizing that Vincent looks like the unknown man Bob Tully strangled. She's got to stay quiet.

She walks up to Vincent. He's on his side, close to the curb, knife still in his neck. Blood spreading out neatly under him. His eyes bulging. His mouth open in the shape of desperate silence. Blood fountaining from his lips, between his fingers. He manages to yank the knife from his throat—the worst move. A thick cord of blood gushes from his neck, his hands finding few things to do now.

Amy stands near him, by the front gate of an unassuming little row house with a cardboard Valentine's Day heart hanging from the door. She's fascinated by the blood. Revolted by it. She was just sitting with Vincent at Mrs. Epifanio's table that very morning. She doesn't know if he deserves this. She tells herself that he doesn't. She thinks of St. Maria Goretti, eleven years old, stabbed in the throat by her would-be rapist. She can't remember where she read that. Some book of saints she got out of the library. St. Maria Goretti forgave her attacker with her dying breath, said she wanted him in heaven with her. Amy guesses that's why she was a saint.

She squats down and says, "It's going to be okay, Vincent."

Vincent notices her then. He chokes out two words: "Call . . . someone."

His blood is trickling into the street, into the dark crevice between the curb and the front tire of the parked car. Amy smells the rubber of the tire. She smells Vincent's distress. He's looking at her with his sad, dying eyes. She pulls back her hood so he can see her face. Black hair. Pale skin. Caring eyes. She wonders if he thinks she's a saint.

He doesn't say anything else, the life going out of him. The place he's stabbed, there's no helping him anyway. Amy's playing a role now, that's it. She's realized it's her duty, to be with this stranger in his agony.

She reaches out and puts her hand on his chest. He's a harmony of stillness.

Next to him is the knife. She picks it up. A stiletto switchblade, about eight inches open, burnt bone handle, sharp steel blade. Vincent's blood feathered on it. She stands and folds the blade, locks it, Vincent's blood marking her palm. She puts the knife in the pocket of her hoodie and walks off in the opposite direction of Vincent's killer, back toward Kings Highway.

6

When the reality of what's happened kicks in, Amy begins to shake with fear. She feels like a killer with the knife in her pocket. She's not sure she should go home. And how can she ever go back to church? She's sure she'll see Vincent there on the altar, his hands at his neck, his blood pouring down the marble steps. She's sure that Katrya's organ will mimic his choking. She's sure she'll smell that rubber and distress when she takes the communion wafer on her tongue. She's sure she'll see his blood in the chalice and taste it on her lips. And in the stained glass windows, as she kneels to light a candle, Vincent will appear. Murdered like a saint, after all. And she, in that moment, his last, mistaking *herself* for a saint.

She's walking wherever. Hand in her pocket over the knife. Blood on her hand. Spots of blood on the tips of her sneakers, where she must've edged against the puddle of blood when she reached out to put her hand on Vincent's chest or when she picked up the knife.

She'd wandered left on Kings Highway, away from Homestretch, to Seventy-Eighth Street, past Bay Parkway, all the numbered avenues running down. Seventy-Eighth Street looks more or less like the street where Vincent was stabbed, like all the side streets in the neighborhood. Trees. Fire hydrants. Iron front gates. Mary statues in the yard. Garbage cans at the curb. Tight parking. Dull bloom of streetlamps. Cars rattling up the block every so often, their lights a disaster of possibilities. As she passes through Bensonhurst, headed for Dyker Heights, row houses give way to larger two- and three-family houses with private driveways. When Amy looks up and realizes she's about to cross Sixteenth Avenue, she remembers the Roulette Diner.

The Roulette's on Sixteenth and Eighty-Sixth. It's an old dive of a diner that Alessandra took her to a handful of times, open twenty-four hours. She makes a left and hustles the eight short blocks.

When she gets there, she walks up the crumbling stoop. A laminated sign on the door reads THE ROULETTE WILL BE CLOSING ON APRIL 15, 2017. THANK YOU PATRONS FOR 44 GREAT YEARS! Amy opens the door. A bell clangs. It very much looks like a place at the end of its run: Naugahyde booths patched with duct tape, mirrored walls dirty and cracked. What once must've felt casino-flashy now feels casino-sad. Waiters and waitresses in black vests and button-up shirts look like they've been working at a low-stakes blackjack table all night. An old man is huddled at the front register with a *Daily News*, glasses low on his nose.

Amy settles into a booth overlooking the parking lot, taking her hood off. Half the parking lot is torn up by some purposeless construction. A few other people sit scattered around at tables and booths. It must be late, but not that late. She's afraid to look at her phone. A couple of giggly girls across from her are taking selfies of themselves with two big plates of disco fries. Amy remembers Alessandra ordering the disco fries.

A waiter comes over, long nails and tired eyes with a crusty green stain on his vest. He hands her a sticky menu and fills her water glass. The glass has a white film of dishwasher residue on it. She thanks him and orders a coffee.

She gets up and walks to the bathroom. It's nasty in there. Pink foam from the broken soap dispenser has left a trail around the sink. Another broken mirror. Broken tiles on the floor. There are two stalls, each with graffiti on the outside of the door—tags, phone numbers, half-peeled stickers. She washes the blood off her hand before doing anything else.

In one of the stalls, she spreads toilet paper on the seat and sits down to pee. She looks at the tattoos on her thighs. Used to be her favorite pieces. Mexican sugar skulls, bright and cheerful fraternal twins. One good, one evil. Done in Flushing by Joey Assassin. It seems fitting to focus on them now, thinking about the joy and purpose she felt watching Vincent die.

She unspools some toilet paper and wipes the blood from her sneakers. She drops the crumpled paper between her legs into the water. She takes the knife out of her pocket and unfolds it. She pictures it lodged in Vincent's throat, hears him gurgle around it. She sees the killer's profile. The blood is there. It's real. The knife is real. Her legs are falling asleep. She wipes the blood from the knife with a ribbony heap of toilet paper and stands up. She deposits the bloody paper into the toilet and flushes hard, as if it will be rejected if she hits the handle too softly. Red swirls in the water.

She sets the knife on the toilet tank and pulls up her pants. She wants to clean the blood from the knife, but she's afraid to do it at the sink. What if someone walks in? She dips the blade in the fresh toilet water and pushes it around, like she's doing dishes in a basin. More red in the water. She turns it over in her hand and holds it by the blade and washes the handle that way. When she's done, she dries the knife with more toilet paper and then gives the toilet another forceful flush. She closes the knife and puts it back in her pocket.

She's not going to have a mirror moment. She rinses her hands in the sink and avoids looking at herself in the broken glass, as she did on the way in. She's not sure what or who she'll see reflected in the grime.

Back at the table, her coffee's waiting for her. It's still steaming. She wraps her hands around the mug and puts her chin over the steam, her elbows up on the table. The coffee smells bad. She looks out the window again. It occurs to her then that she could've been followed. Who by? Someone who witnessed her witnessing the crime? Or what if the killer doubled back, wanting to recover the knife, and saw her perched over Vincent? Every dark shape outside is the killer. Every El column provides him cover. Around every corner, he peers with greasy eyes, hood drawn tighter so his face is a beam of meanness.

"Amy?" a voice says.

She looks up. It's Mr. Castricone from church. He takes the collections at eight fifteen Mass on Sundays. She almost doesn't recognize him out of his bulky tweed jacket. He's wearing a windbreaker and gray sweatpants and a battered Mets cap. He's probably in his late fifties, but he looks even older dressed down, like a guy you'd find sitting on a bench outside the OTB with a short dog of wine. She realizes she hasn't responded to him.

"You okay?" Mr. Castricone says. "You look troubled."

"I'm just a little out of it," Amy says.

"Anything I can do?"

"That's nice of you. I'm good."

"How about some company?"

"Really, I'm good."

Mr. Castricone sits down across from her anyway. "You ordering anything to eat? I had the chicken souvlaki." He kisses his fingers. "Delicious. 'My compliments to the chef,' I says to Carmine. Carmine over there's my regular waiter. He's been around forever. Gonna be sad to see this place go. Forty-four years they been open; forty-four years I been coming here. I came here after my confirmation, you believe that? I had my bachelor party here. Me and the boys. 'Don't take me to no strip club,' I says. 'Take me to the Roulette.' I came here every Sunday after church with my wife and daughter. After my wife died in '06, my daughter would still drive in from Jersey to meet me here on Sundays, and Carmine would set a place for my wife. When my daughter had the kids, she stopped coming every Sunday, but I'd still be here and Carmine would set the two other places. Where am I gonna go? Nowhere's left in the neighborhood for me."

"I'm sorry," Amy says.

"I'm intruding," he says.

"I'm just . . ."

"You need someone to talk to, I'm here. I got a lot of wisdom to pass on. Been through some shit." He pauses. "Excuse my language. Been through my wife dying. Been through union battles. Got my ass handed to me by this pyramid scheme out of Bay Ridge. You heard that story? Sucked up my savings. I was one of the guys got taken. I trusted the guy who did it. Took him in like family. I'm talking too much. My wife always said I talked too much. My daughter, too. I remember correctly, you're from Queens, right?"

"Right." Amy drinks some coffee. It tastes worse than it smells. Sour and weak. She pours in two packets of sugar and tries to make it palatable. She wonders if it's just what she's witnessed that's making it taste so off. After Bob Tully threatened her with the knife, she remembers, her sense of taste faded. Her grandma took her to the doctor because she was losing so much weight.

She drinks again. The coffee's awfulness is merely masked by sweetness now.

"Flushing? That's right, right? See, I still got some of my memory left."

"Mr. Castricone, I hate to be rude," Amy says, leaning back in the booth. "I appreciate you looking out for me. You don't mind, I just need to be alone."

"I got you," Mr. Castricone says. "A little heartbreak, perhaps? Fella done you wrong. I see. He's got rocks in his head, that's what I say. You're a beautiful girl." He stands. "I heard you've got tattoos. I have one, too. From when I was in the navy. My wife hated it. We've all got secrets."

Amy ignores this. When Mr. Castricone finally gets up and leaves the diner, she feels some relief. The waiter comes back and asks if she wants to order any food. She says she's going to just stick with the coffee. The waiter says she should try the rainbow cake if she's in the mood for cake. It's just like a rainbow cookie; the best thing on the dessert menu. She says she's not feeling very well, but she'll get it next time she's in. He reminds her there won't be many more next times. She gives in, and he brings her a piece of the rainbow cake, insisting she won't regret it.

She presses the tines of her fork into the cake. It's mushy, and the frosting seems to be sweating, as if it's been sitting out in a hot display case for days. She can't eat it. She won't.

She thinks about Alessandra to get her mind off Vincent and his killer. One time, sitting in this very booth, Alessandra had told her a story from high school. How she'd come here after a school play senior year and downed a pint of peppermint schnapps in the bathroom with a girl named Marilu Pirraglia, and then they'd eaten two slices of chocolate cheesecake each and puked in the parking lot and laughed all the way home.

The waiter shuffles up to the table. "How's the cake?"

"Good," Amy says.

"But you've barely touched it."

"I'm sorry. It's my stomach."

He shrugs. "I shouldn't have pushed it so hard."

"Can I ask you a favor?"

"Sure."

"Do you think someone can call me car service?"

"We can arrange that." He goes over to the old man at the register and says something to him. The old man picks up a red phone and taps the numbers slowly, talks into the receiver. He holds up his hand to Amy to indicate that they'll be here in five minutes.

Amy's only desire is to be home now. She's walked so much, she doesn't have it in her to walk the mile and a half back to her block. And she's not sure what's out there in the dark. She hates taking a car service. She'd rather take the bus or train a couple of stops, but she knows she'll wait a while at this time of night, and that means standing out on the corner or up on the El platform, too exposed.

She leaves ten dollars on the table, more than enough for bad coffee, a slice of cake she didn't even want, and a tip for helping arrange the ride.

A black eighties Town Car pulls up a few minutes later, its lights hazy in the half-destroyed lot. Amy rushes out of the diner. Stenciled on the door of the car in white letters is GRAVESEND & BENSONHURST BEST CAR SERVICE. The driver doesn't open the door for Amy. She hops in, her hand tight on the knife in her pocket, afraid that she'll lose it in the seat gap.

The driver has a massive back. He's wearing a white Kangol and a black leather jacket with a raised collar, plus a heavy dose of what smells like Drakkar Noir. His eyes in the rearview roam from her face down to her chest. "Where you headed, sweetheart?" he says.

The bad-cologne smell is so overwhelming, Amy's got to roll down the window. "You know St. Mary's?"

"Sure."

"I'm going there. The Eighty-Fifth Street side." She's hesitant to say her address, to let him know where exactly she lives.

"A little late-night confession?"

She doesn't say anything in response.

He pulls out of the lot and takes a left onto Eighty-Sixth Street. Amy watches storefronts zip by through the open window, hoping to avoid any other interaction with the driver. Tile and marble store. Tire shop. Tasty Chicken. Tasty Bagels. Paint store. The New Utrecht branch of the library. East Ocean Buffet. Threading salon. Marshall's. New Utrecht Avenue brings the El with it where it intersects Eighty-Sixth Street, Capelli's Funeral Home on the corner. Under the El, red lights flash. Brake lights. Double-parked cars. A woman on a treadmill in the window of a brightly lit 24 Hour Fitness. Duke's Deli. That Polish restaurant. Meats Supreme. Cigar Emporium. A few sushi joints Amy doesn't remember being there before. A Popeyes with Chinese writing on the sign.

"You know a lady named Betty Clay?" the driver says.

"Don't think so," Amy says.

"My aunt. She goes to St. Mary's. I used to go to Most Precious Blood growing up. Is that church even still there?"

"It's still there." She'd gone to Most Precious Blood on Bay Forty-Seventh with Alessandra a few times when they first moved back. Alessandra went to school there, but the school had closed years ago, and her father liked St. Mary's better.

"You should cheer up, you know? Smile more." The driver's looking at her in the rearview mirror.

"You don't know me."

"You're pretty. Smile."

"Go fuck yourself."

The driver laughs. "Whoa, there."

They turn onto Twenty-Third Avenue, passing the bright Russian market on the corner. He drops her in front of the church on Eighty-Fifth Street and says how much the fare is. Amy pays it to the penny and doesn't tip. She gets out of the car, and the driver is pulling away before she can even fully close the door.

She walks up the block to her apartment. As she opens the front gate, she looks up and sees Mr. Pezzolanti watching her from his window. He puts up his hand. Amy stops before descending the steps to her apartment. Mr. Pezzolanti's door opens, and he steps outside. He's wearing slippers and a fluffy robe with a big splotch of ice cream on it.

"I was worried," he says. "I look at the time, I think, *This is unlike her*. Your old man back around, I didn't know what to make of it."

"I'm fine, Mr. P."

"You sure? You look a little rattled."

"I'm good. Just tired. I took a long walk."

"You need anything, you just let me know." His concern is real, but he's also curious. She can see the questions burning in his eyes. Where was she? Who was she with?

She goes into her apartment and doesn't turn on the lights. She sits on her bed and kicks off her sneakers. She sees herself leaning over Vincent, a streetlamp making a halo over her head. She sees Vincent's mouth up close. Blood. Choking. His hushed plea for her to call someone. Then, the killer's profile and his boots on the pavement. She tries to remember everything she can. She thinks about Bob Tully again, about who she was and what she saw and how that had shaped her life and especially how it had shaped everything she'd done from the minute she got to Mrs. Epifanio's. Her inaction had been the inaction of the girl scared to death by Bob Tully. The thrill she'd felt following Vincent was the same thrill she'd felt then, too. She seemed to see herself from outside now. She'd become so *boring*. She'd allowed herself to get carried away.

She takes out the knife. She lets it sit in her hand like something she discovered buried in the woods. The handle is still rimmed with blood. She brings it into the bathroom and washes it with her sandalwood-spice hand soap. What's left of Vincent's blood runs down the drain. When she's done, she dries the knife with a coarse black towel.

She wonders if Vincent's body has been discovered yet. She can imagine the scene: an ambulance with its back doors thrown open; two EMS workers huddled over the body; cops milling about; neighbors out on their stoops, shaking their heads, shocked something like this could happen on their block. She wonders again if any of them saw anything—something like two men fighting and a woman crouching behind a car, then the woman rushing over to the fallen man after the killer fled. The woman not helping, not in any way they could see. The woman picking up and pocketing the knife and rushing away.

If she's going to keep the knife, she has to hide it. She goes to the fridge, where she keeps a package of raspberry-mint ice pops in the freezer. She drops the knife into the box, then goes back to the bed and pulls on her hood. She buries herself in her aloneness. She tries to forgive herself. She asks for God's forgiveness. She prays. She swears she hears the front gate open in the yard. She hears leaves crunching underfoot. She misses her records. She puts on her headphones, but the batteries in her old Walkman are dead. She feels forsaken. She can't sleep. She sees Bob Tully's smiling face. She wonders if she'll ever sleep again.

7

Amy doesn't remember sleeping at all. When she sits up at seven thirty the next morning, her eyes are burning and heavy. She doesn't feel like changing her clothes. She goes into the bathroom and brushes her teeth. She avoids the mirror again and puts on her sneakers and steps outside.

The weather has changed a little, dropped about ten degrees. The day before felt like spring. Today's not that much different, but it's leaning back toward what February should be.

Amy's relieved to see that Mr. Pezzolanti is not out front waiting for her.

She goes to the Russian market on Twenty-Third Avenue and buys the *Daily News* and a coffee. She flips through the newspaper, looking for the story, for a picture of Vincent. She half expected it to be on the cover. She guesses everyone feels that way about a crime they've witnessed or been a victim of, like it's the only story in the city. She remembers feeling this about Bob Tully, too. But that crime didn't show up in the papers; the man was never so much as missed. Vincent's murder is nowhere that she can see, not even buried in the middle in small print. She drops the newspaper in the garbage can on the corner and sips her coffee. It's at least stronger than the diner coffee. The blue paper cup is hot and alive in her hands.

She read once about saints and sleeplessness, how insomnia teamed with fasting could produce visions. Is she in the middle of something like that now? Not that she's a saint. But as a regular person, hit by this trauma. No food, no sleep, her nerves a jangle of fears. Everything seems sharper and brighter and more defined to her. The train overhead is louder. Time feels thinned out, like she's inhabiting an illusion.

Testing the dread, she walks to Eighty-Fourth Street and enters the St. Mary's rectory. She's supposed to do things today. She's supposed to pick something up and walk somewhere and deliver something. She's supposed to be a light soul. She's supposed to be helpful.

Connie Giacchino is sitting at the main desk hoisting a red mug that reads PRAY BIGGER. Prayer cards are fanned out in front of her. Her tinted glasses don't hide the shock in her eyes when she sees Amy.

"You okay?" Connie says, setting down her mug.

"I'm not feeling well," Amy says, her voice sounding strange in the stuffy room. She looks at the walls, as if seeing them for the first time. Sacred Heart calendars, mysterious certificates, framed pictures of Pope Francis. "Can you please tell Monsignor Ricciardi that I'm not going to be able to do anything today?"

"Of course." Connie rises to her feet. "You don't look well. You want to sit down? Can I get you anything? Tea?"

"I'm going back home."

"Did something happen, Amy?"

"What do you mean?"

"I don't know, exactly. You just look like something happened."

"Nothing happened."

"It's no problem, really. Immacula helped yesterday, and she'll help again today. God knows, she's got nothing going on."

"Thank you."

"Do you want to talk to Monsignor Ricciardi? He'll be back in fifteen minutes."

"Do I need to talk to him?"

"I just meant if you'd be more comfortable talking to him than me. You know, if you've got something going on you want to talk to him about."

Amy steps back. "I told you, I'm fine, Connie."

"I believe you." Connie picks up the phone. "I'm just going to call Immacula."

Amy turns and walks out of the rectory. She drinks some coffee and then spits it out because it's cold. She pauses to pour the rest down a sewer drain and ditches the cup in a small garbage can by the fence.

She cuts through the parking lot to the Eighty-Fifth Street side of the church. Her father is sitting on the front steps, the glass doors behind him shivering with reflections of the morning light. If she hadn't just seen him the day before, she would've figured him for a resident from the home down on Cropsey Avenue. Wild hair. Unkempt beard. Rheumy eyes. Too-big clothes from some donation drive. Filthy sneakers. Hands cupped over his knees like a scolded kid. His chest looks scarecrow-stuffed under a ratty flannel. He smiles at her.

"What're you doing here?" Amy says.

"I'm a little early for our lunch date. I thought I'd just sit out here and enjoy the morning."

Amy's taken aback. Fred's voice melts into the noise of everything else. She'd forgotten she said she'd go to lunch with him. And it's not even close to lunchtime. "A little early? It's, what, eight fifteen?"

"Something like that. I was just gonna kick around a little. Try to stay out of trouble. Are you okay?"

"I'm fine."

"You don't look okay."

"I've heard."

"You want, we can just go grab breakfast or coffee now. But I don't mind killing time. I like to walk around. I can just explore the neighborhood a little."

Amy looks up at the rooftop of the apartment building across the street. Pigeons perch on the edge. "That's fine," she says, aware of how much she's using the word *fine*, as if it's a thing to lean on, as if it'll be true if she says it enough.

⇒

She takes him to the Starbucks on Eighty-Sixth Street, just past the corner of Twentieth Avenue. It's right next to Lenny's Pizza. As they enter, Fred says, "They have a computer at the place where I normally stay, and I was reading how that pizza joint right there is famous, because it was in *Saturday Night Fever*. You know, I never saw it. I remember it being a big deal. Travolta. I saw him in that O. J. Simpson miniseries, playing Bob Shapiro, and he was pretty good. I watch TV when I can now. I'm rambling. Sorry."

"I saw it, sure," Amy says. "*Saturday Night Fever*. Not the O.J. thing."

"I ought to see it sometime, too."

At the counter, she orders a grande Americano, and Fred gets a blueberry muffin and a tall coffee. Amy tries to pay, but Fred stops her and shoves a crumpled ten at the barista in the black visor and green apron with a dragon tattooed on her forearm.

They sit at a booth by the window, watching people walk by on Eighty-Sixth Street with shopping carts and baby carriages and plastic bags from markets. The Manhattan-bound D rumbles by on the El overhead. A traffic cop is out giving tickets to cars whose Muni Meter receipts have expired. Trucks are making deliveries at the curb. Amy zeroes in on a woman in blue shoes eating a Sausage McGriddle from McDonald's over her hand. Her hair has streaks that match her shoes.

"Can't believe this is February," Fred says.

"Yeah," Amy says.

Fred takes the lid off his coffee and blows on it. "Is this me doing this to you?" he says. "You look wrecked. I don't want you to be wrecked about me showing back up in your life. That's not the end result I was hoping for."

"What *are* you hoping for?"

Fred looks out the window. "I don't know. I just want you to know you still have a father. I haven't been a father to you in your life, I know that much, but I want to try now."

"Being a father is taking me out for coffee and paying?"

"I'm sorry. I'm trying."

"You've gotta understand how strange this is for me," Amy says. "I figured you for dead. I was a kid when you left, and I hardly spent any time with you then. You're flashes in my memory, that's it. I didn't even remember your voice until you spoke."

Fred tears up. Spit webs the corners of his mouth. "I wish I could take it back. I wish I could be there for you and your mother. I made a lot of bad decisions." He picks at his muffin. "Can I be honest with you? And I'm not saying this because I want you to pity me. I've been on the verge of throwing myself off a bridge many times over the years. I've cut my wrists. Stabbed myself once. Took an overdose of pain pills I stole from a woman I was seeing. A lot of that's from knowing how much I let you down. You were born, I had one job, and I didn't do it. Maybe I should've offed myself. Maybe my gift to you should've been staying out of your life. You've done pretty well without me."

Amy doesn't want to feel pity for Fred right now. She refuses to accept it as one of the conditions of this encounter. She looks away. A line about four or five people deep has built up at the counter. The last man in the line, she thinks she recognizes him. Same boots. Same drooping jeans. His hands are in his pockets. He looks jumpy. She's sure it's Vincent's killer.

His hair is dark. She can't see his face. She thinks, just from the quick look, that it can't be the guy who'd sat with Vincent on the bench outside

Homestretch, but that doesn't mean it can't be the killer. She has no proof that they're one and the same, and her initial read of the guy on the bench hadn't been great. She puts her face against her arm, slumping down in the seat.

"You're distracted," Fred says, wiping tears from his cheeks. "What is it?"

"It's nothing," Amy says in a low voice.

When this man gets to the front of the line and turns to order and she sees his profile, Amy will know for sure if it's Vincent's killer. But if he's following her, if he followed her *here*, why would he be waiting in line for coffee like a schmuck? Maybe he knows she's not a hundred percent on his identity. Maybe he's toying with her.

"You look like you saw a ghost," Fred says.

"Maybe I did," Amy says.

"I'm putting my heart on the table here."

"It bums you out I'm not giving you my full attention, huh? Now you know what my childhood was like."

Fred, defeated, rips off the cardboard sleeve from around his coffee. "I deserve that." He begins to pick it to pieces, piling them on the table next to his cup.

When the man makes it to the front of the line and turns to face the barista, Amy remains silent, fidgeting. She watches him closely. She studies his profile. This man, he's Chinese. She's sure the killer wasn't Chinese. He had that long Italian nose. Looked like one of those guys from the neighborhood whose last name has a lot of zs in it. She lets out a breath. She's just being paranoid. "It's not him," she says aloud.

"What's going on, Amy?" Fred asks.

"I said nothing's going on."

"Who's not who?"

"Forget it."

"You've been staring at the man at the counter. You know him?"

"I don't."

"What I said, you got any response? A big part of my recovery is letting people know how I feel and living resentment-free. I know I've got no right to ask you for help or anything."

"Resentment-free?"

"I just don't want to walk away from this opportunity feeling like you haven't heard me at all."

"And you're gonna resent me if I don't listen to you?"

"I'm trying to be frank."

"You're in AA?"

"Been clean five years. One thousand, eight hundred, and sixty-three days, to be exact."

"That's good. I don't drink much anymore. I never had a problem, but I gave it up after I quit working at the bar when Alessandra left. I saw what it did to people. I'd seen my whole life what it did to people. I didn't want to drown in it, too."

"Alessandra?"

"She was my girlfriend for a while. She's why I moved to this part of Brooklyn."

"I didn't know her name. The people at your old bar mentioned that you moved to Brooklyn with someone."

"We're doing exactly what I didn't want to do. Going through each other's histories."

"It's nice to catch up. I want to hear about your life."

Amy remembers her Americano. It's cooled down enough to drink. She takes a sip. The relief she's feeling has allowed her to let her guard down a little. She likes that Fred didn't act surprised or shocked about Alessandra. She likes that he hasn't asked a follow-up question. Maybe he knows. Maybe someone at Seven Bar told him she's gay. Maybe he knows that asking dumb questions won't get him anywhere. Maybe he's okay with it.

"Alessandra grew up around here," she says. "Gravesend. Bensonhurst. I stuck around after she went back to Los Angeles. I started going to church, and I just felt like I could hide out and maybe help people."

"I get that. Noble as hell, wanting to help folks." He sifts through the pieces of the cardboard sleeve, thumbing a bigger hunk into a folded square. "It's so nice to be talking to you. I waited a long time for this chance. The day I got clean, I made it my number one goal. I wanted to get to a point where I could stand in front of you and not be embarrassed of who I am at that moment. I mean, I'll always be ashamed of who I was."

"Look, I'm glad you're in a good place."

"But."

"But. I can't see how there'd be any future for us."

"I understand." Fred wears his heartbreak on his face.

Amy wonders what he was expecting. She wonders why she's turned so fast from softening up to being cruel. Everything she's been doing these past few years has taught her that she should accept him into her life, forgive him, learn to love him again. That would be the good thing to do. The right thing.

"Maybe, if you have a few days to reflect on this, you'll feel differently," Fred says.

"I don't know. I don't think so."

"You don't even want to be in contact?"

"I'd prefer if we just left things the way they are."

"Can I ask, if I'm not being too far out of line here, are you in some kind of trouble? It's like you're on the run from something. I've been there. A lot of my life, I was looking over my shoulder."

Amy has a moment where she feels like she might open up to him, tell Fred about Vincent and what she witnessed last night.

"You don't want to tell me," Fred says, sensing her hesitation, "but it's something. Is someone threatening to hurt you?"

"Fred, I told you. I'm okay." She figures if she lets anything slip, she's letting him in. And letting him in now means letting him in for good. She's not prepared for that. She pushes away from the table and gets up, grabbing her coffee. "Thanks for reaching out. Thanks for trying to make things right. But it's too late, Fred."

8

Amy stands in front of the lions again. Bay Thirty-Fourth is quiet. The same old woman from yesterday passes by with her shopping cart full of bottles. Jesus, was that just yesterday? She heads across to the house where Diane lives, passing through the red fence and looking at the St. Francis statue. St. Francis's nose is missing. His feet are chipped away.

Amy rings the buzzer for the upstairs apartment. Her guilt has guided her here. It occurs to her that Diane could be dead inside. Dead for days on the kitchen floor. Amy guesses she might smell something, in that case. How long does it take for a body to start to stink?

The door opens, and Diane stands there, dark bags under her eyes, her nose as red as the fence, her lips dry. She's pale. She's swimming in an XXL St. John's Redmen sweatshirt that must be thirty years old. They've been called the Red Storm since at least '94. She's got on flannel pajama pants and purple slipper socks. Her gray hair is plastered down on one side, fluffed up on the other.

"Amy? Please."

She walks out of the Starbucks and rushes across Eighty-Sixth Street, dodging a little wobbly driver's ed car. She cuts a quick right onto Twentieth Avenue. She knows Fred will go back to her apartment. She knows he won't give up so easily. She's not going home now, though. She has something she needs to do first.

"Amy Falconetti?" Diane says.

Amy's at a loss for words. Diane's not dead.

"What are you doing here?" Diane asks.

"You remember me from church, right?" Amy says.

"Of course."

"I brought communion to Mrs. Epifanio yesterday. She was worried about you. We tried to call."

Diane gives Amy an understanding look. "Oh, I'm sorry. I've been laid out with this flu. I'm feeling a bit better today. I couldn't even move the last couple of days. I sent my son, Vincent, over there to take my place. Did he not show up? He told me he did."

"He showed up."

"Oh."

"He just wasn't very clear with her, I guess. She was worried something bad had happened."

"My son's a real piece of work, let me tell you. You want to come in? I have some masks and plenty of sanitizer."

Amy's thinking about Vincent again. How she looked down at him as he died. She can't believe she's standing here with Diane. It's strange to know what she knows. "I shouldn't."

"Please, come in. I've been starved for company."

Amy nods and follows Diane in. They walk up a narrow staircase. The railing is warped. Diane wheezes as she walks. When they pass through her front door, Diane points to a box of surgical masks sitting on top of the cast-iron radiator in the hallway and tells her she should put one on. Amy stops and pulls a blue mask on over her nose and mouth.

Diane's apartment is small. The hallway they're in leads to four rooms: going clockwise, a bedroom, a bathroom, a living room, and a kitchen. All spare. There's a Swiss clock on the wall in the hallway and a TV on in the living room playing some game show. Church bulletins rest on top of a bookcase filled with romance paperbacks. Vincent doesn't live here with

Diane; that much Amy can sense. She wonders where he lives. *Lived.* She can only imagine a cluttered apartment full of video games, clothes strewn on the couch, and a kitchen counter overflowing with pizza boxes.

Diane guides Amy into the kitchen. "I'll make tea," she says.

Amy sits at the two-person kitchen table in front of a window with its shade drawn. A Pellegrino bottle with fake flowers stands on a lace doily in the center of the table. Amy breathes into her mask. She fingers the edges of the doily, not sure what to do with her hands, and looks around the room. There's paint peeling from the ancient cabinets. A humming refrigerator covered in Mass cards and shopping lists, kept in place on the freezer door by silly, fruit-shaped magnets, sits to one side.

Diane puts water on to boil in a ceramic kettle on the stove and then slips on a pair of surgical gloves she yanks out of her pants pocket. "I'm wearing gloves," she says. "I don't want you to get this flu. It's the absolute pits."

"I'm not too worried," Amy says, her voice stifled and deepened by the mask. "I got my flu shot."

"I don't buy into flu shots. Immacula's daughter, she got the flu shot last year, it turned her into a wild person. She was hitting the walls. You sure you're not sick already? You look pretty run-down."

"I haven't been sleeping well."

"Insomnia's a real bitch. Most nights, I can't sleep. I pace around. I watch TV. There's nothing ever on. Getting sick was a blessing in that way. Forced me off my feet, knocked me out for a few days. I had strange dreams, but I slept." Diane sits across from Amy, waiting for the water to boil. "You know Rosie Parascandolo?"

Amy nods.

"She was having trouble sleeping, she went to this Chinese acupuncture place up the block. You've seen this place? Little hole-in-the-wall. She's sleeping like a baby now. You should look into it."

Amy's on the verge of crying, wanting to say, *Your son's dead. I thought he might've killed you, and now he's dead. I'm sorry. I saw it happen.* Instead, she says, "Acupuncture, huh?"

Diane shrugs. "Worth a shot. I don't like needles, but these Chinese know what they're doing. They're very healthy. I see the old ladies doing their stretches in the Cavallaro school yard every morning."

The kettle whistles. Diane gets up and shuts off the gas.

"Can I help?" Amy says. "You should sit."

"I'm good," Diane says. "I only have Lipton. That okay?"

"Fine."

"You take milk or sugar?"

"Plain's good."

Diane pours two mugs of tea. She hands Amy one and then fixes her own with milk and sugar. She sits back down at the table and waves her hand through the steam.

Amy lowers her mask around her neck and blows on the tea.

"It's so nice to have company," Diane says.

"I'm glad you're okay."

"Speaking of Rosie Parascandolo, you know her son? Georgie. He lives in Westchester County. Chiropractor. He just got arrested for embezzling a million dollars from the group he works for. Got into a real hole financially, I guess. Had a mistress, too, this whole double life that was bleeding him dry. His wife was in shock. I heard this from Antoinette Parisi. She's in the know. And Mary Magliozzo confirmed it."

"Huh," Amy says.

"I'm sorry I'm talking a mile a minute. Like I said, I'm starved for company. My son comes and goes these days. It's too much to spend five minutes with your mother?"

"Where'd—?" Amy catches the slip and corrects herself: "Where's your son live?"

"He's got a little apartment over on West Eighth between Highlawn and Avenue S, right near where you get the N train. He's only been there about a year. He stayed here with me before that. Too small for the both of us. We used to have a bigger apartment, just up the block, but the Salernos sold the house for condos. Vincent's friends made fun of him for still living with his mother, so he got his own place. You think he invites me over? Never. I've been there only to clean up. He gives me a key, tells me his landlord's pulling an inspection and he needs the place spick-and-span. You believe that?"

Amy realizes that Vincent was only a couple of blocks from home when he was stabbed. Maybe they were headed back to his apartment before things suddenly turned rotten between them.

"I babied him too much growing up," Diane says. "He can't hold a job. He always wants to borrow money. What're you gonna do?"

"He's your only child?"

"My one and only. His old man ran off when he was one. Moved to Philly with some woman from work he was seeing on the side. I never took up with anyone else. It was always just me and Vincent."

"That must've been hard."

Diane nods. "Especially when Vincent started having trouble in school. He had this one teacher in seventh grade, she was just real nasty. Fat pig, if I can be mean for a second, but that's no crime. She was a grade A bitch, first and foremost. Heavy drinker, too. And she just homed in on him, like he was the only one getting in fights. These kids would start with him and Vincent would fight back, and he'd be the one to get in trouble. That's always been Vincent's luck."

She drinks a little tea. "Enough about Vincent. Tell me about yourself. I see you at church all the time, but I hardly know anything about you."

"Not much to tell," Amy says.

"Nonsense. Pretty girl like you, you must have the guys lining up."

Amy, uncomfortable, doesn't say anything. It feels so wrong to be proceeding with, even encouraging, this small talk. And now she's painted into this familiar corner by Diane, who has all the typical qualities of a lonely, nosy parishioner.

Diane reads her discomfort. "You don't like to talk about yourself. I get it."

The front-door buzzer sounds.

"Who the hell is this?" Diane says, standing up. "Hold on a sec, sweetie." She abandons her tea and trudges downstairs to answer the door.

Amy hears Diane open the door. "Yes?" Diane says, and it sounds like she's right there in the room with Amy, the hallway amplifying her voice.

"Ms. Diane Marchetti?" a man responds. Official. A cop.

"That's me."

"I'm Detective Barrile, this is Detective Vlamis. Is this photograph of your son, Vincent?"

"Yes, that's Vincent."

"We're sorry to have to bring you this terrible news, Ms. Marchetti." Detective Barrile pauses, takes a labored breath. "Your son was stabbed and killed. The investigation is ongoing, but we're actively working to follow any and all leads."

"What do you mean?" Diane asks.

"I'm very sorry, Ms. Marchetti," a woman says. The other cop. She has the voice of a heavy smoker. "Very, very sorry."

"Vincent and his personal effects are at the Kings County morgue on Winthrop Street," Detective Barrile says.

"What do you mean?" Diane asks again.

"This is never easy, Ms. Marchetti," Detective Vlamis says. "We can walk you through the procedures you'll need to follow from here on out. Vincent lived with you, is that correct? His license lists this as his place of residence."

Diane doesn't answer.

Amy peeks out from behind the shade drawn over the window. An unmarked Crown Victoria is double-parked in the street. The two detectives, Barrile and Vlamis, are standing down at the front door, both in suits. Amy can see only the tops of their heads.

"Vincent is dead?" Diane says.

Detective Vlamis again: "Yes, ma'am. We're very sorry."

Diane slams the door. A terrible silence lingers in the hallway. Amy watches the detectives go back to their car and get in. They're somber. She can't imagine how hard it is to do a job like that. She's learned a lot these last few years, spending so much time with old people. Widows. People who have lost children. She wonders why it took the detectives so long to get the news to Diane. She wonders if Vincent wasn't discovered until the morning. Can that be? Did he just lie on the sidewalk all night?

Diane comes back upstairs. She's drained of whatever color she had left. "Is this real?" she says to Amy.

"Diane, I heard them," Amy says. "I'm sorry. I'm so, so sorry."

"What am I supposed to do?"

"I don't know the exact protocol."

"I didn't even ask any fucking questions. Was he robbed? Was it a fight? What was I thinking? I didn't tell them about his apartment. Why did I slam the door? Oh Jesus." She collapses into her seat at the table across from Amy.

"Is there anyone I can call?"

"I've got no one. Vincent was it. I'm all alone now."

"Cousins?"

"There's no one."

"Who lives downstairs?"

"The Russos."

"Can they help with anything?"

"They're worthless." The tears finally start to come. She's blubbering into her hands. "My poor Vincent. My poor, poor Vincent."

Amy pulls her mask back on out of instinct. She considers that this is the last opportunity she'll have to tell Diane the truth. *I was there. I followed Vincent. I was thinking of something from high school. I was scared and fascinated. I saw the other man stab Vincent. I didn't see the man's face, I swear. I was with Vincent when he died. He wasn't alone. I'm sorry.*

What she says instead is, "I should leave. You need time to process this."

"Don't," Diane says, gulping back her tears. "Please, stay."

And so, Amy stays. She agrees to go to the morgue with Diane. She puts on surgical gloves and cleans the teacups while Diane goes into the bedroom to change clothes.

Diane is in panic mode. Amy can hear her talking to herself, asking what to wear for an occasion like this. There's terror in her voice. She comes out in an outfit Amy's seen her wearing at church: black slacks, a floral-print black blouse, and a red cardigan.

"How will we get there?" Amy says.

"Car service, I guess," Diane says. "I've got a couple of numbers in the drawer there."

Amy riffles through the junk drawer next to the stove. The first number she finds is for the same car service she got at the diner. She doesn't want to call them, on the off chance they'll send the same driver. The other car service is called My Way. She takes out her phone and types in the number, taking off the mask and telling the dispatcher the address and where they're going. She's surprised by the fact that she knows Diane's address. She must've absorbed the house number when she was watching from across the street by the lions.

"I'm so fucking angry," Diane says.

"You have every right."

"I'm angry at *Vincent*. Like I said, he was always the one to take the fall. He always put himself in bad positions. He had his whole life ahead of him, and now he's just dead."

The car arrives ten minutes later. They go downstairs, Amy holding Diane's arm as they take the steps one by one. Diane seems more fragile by the moment. The car is almost identical to the one Amy caught at the diner, except I DID IT "MY WAY" is stenciled on the door in yellow letters. Amy helps Diane in.

The driver is cheerful. He has an innocent face and pretty eyelashes and wears a battered Knicks cap. "My name's Vincenzo," he says.

Diane starts bawling again.

"We just got some bad news," Amy says. "Some devastating news."

"I'm sorry," he says. They drive away in silence.

Amy's never been to a morgue. Her grandparents dealt with everything when her mother died, and both her grandparents died in hospice within a year of each other. Her father's parents died before she was born. She's been to plenty of funerals and wakes, some for friends who had died well before their time. Rudy from Seven Bar had been hit by a taxi while riding his bike. Merrill's junkie friend, Addie, had OD'd in Amy's bathroom and the ambulance was too slow getting there. And then there was Ruth from college, who had just started working at Cantor Fitzgerald on the one-hundred-and-first floor of the North Tower at One World Trade Center in September 2001 and was one of the 658 employees of that firm to die in the attack. But Amy has never been to a morgue, and she doesn't particularly want to go now. She certainly won't go in, if she can avoid it. She doesn't want to stare down at Vincent's body. She doesn't want Diane to collapse into her arms.

"Can I borrow your phone?" Diane says. "I forgot mine, and I need to call Andy Capelli at the funeral home."

Amy hands her the flip phone.

Diane stares at it in her palm like it's an artifact from a different era.

"I'm sorry," Amy says. "I haven't caught up with the times."

Diane manages a little laugh. "You're like the senior citizens." She opens the phone and enters a number from memory. Amy can make out Andy Capelli's voice on the other end of the line. He's a regular at church, and he took over running Capelli's, the funeral home on New Utrecht Avenue, when his dad passed away. Andy's a nice enough guy, always wears a wooden cross hanging outside his shirt. Fond of turtlenecks, too. Hard of hearing. Diane has to say almost everything twice. It's difficult enough to say once that your son has died, his body is at the morgue, and you need to set up funeral arrangements.

Amy goes through a list of things she might say to Diane when she gets off the phone. She's running low.

Diane hangs up and gives her back the phone. "Who would do this?"

she says. "Who would hurt my baby? The detective said they're following leads. That means they don't know. That means he's out there, whoever he is, probably not even giving a thought to Vincent."

Amy wonders how it would sound if she explained that she had the murder weapon at home in a box of raspberry-mint ice pops. That she had cleaned it off in a diner toilet and then again in her own sink, impeding an investigation for no good reason. Diane would probably think she'd absolutely lost her mind.

"You can't get caught up thinking about that now," Amy says. "One thing at a time." She's learned from so many of the old people she visits and sits with how to rely on clichés. It's something she hadn't had to do in a long time, not since her grandparents.

"You're right." Diane reaches out and puts her hand on Amy's knee. "I'm so glad you're here. God sent you to me today for a reason."

———◆———

At the morgue, Amy manages to stay out of the way. She sits on a hard blue chair in a waiting room of some kind, while Diane deals with the medical examiner and his assistant. The morgue has the feel of a loading dock. It's cold and eerie. The strange, strong chemical smell in the air is overpowering.

The driver is waiting for them outside. That was Amy's idea. She doesn't know how long anything will take, but she wants to have the car there, ready to go.

Diane wanted her to come along to see Vincent, but Amy refused. She said she didn't think it was appropriate to see him like that, since she didn't know him. Diane said okay.

Amy wasn't even sure what was going on now, to be honest. Was Diane identifying the body, or had she already done that? Was she simply saying good-bye? Was there a grief counselor present to give her some advice? Would the detectives be back?

Diane comes out and collapses into the chair next to Amy. "I can't any-more," she says. "The funeral home takes over now."

"What can I do?"

"Nothing. I'm glad you told the driver to wait. I want to go home. I just want to be home."

They go outside and get back into Vincenzo's car. Vincenzo is respectful enough to remain quiet. They head back to Diane's, passing other cars, people on sidewalks, action everywhere, but nothing seems real.

"It didn't even look like him," Diane says. "He looked so little. He'd been"—she raises her hands to her throat—"butchered."

"I'm so sorry," Amy says again. How many times has she said that already?

"The medical examiner was an arrogant prick. 'That's my Vincent,' I says to him. He just scoffed. He sees people like me all the time. People who can't handle this. I was firm. I didn't let him see my cracks."

"Forget him. People with jobs like that, they become desensitized."

"I can't believe I forgot my phone. What if the detectives are trying to call me? What if they have the guy who did this in custody?"

"I'm sure they'll be in touch again soon."

"What if they're not? What if this is it? My son's dead, and his killer just goes free. There's hardly anyone to even come to his wake. I'll ask Monsignor Ricciardi to do the Mass. He'll do a nice job. What else? What's my life now?"

Amy thinks about Vincent in a cheap casket in a near-empty room. "Oh, jeez," she says, and she immediately feels terrible about it.

"I'm sorry," Diane says, leaning against the window. "I don't want to burden you. You don't even really know me. I've already asked too much."

Amy sits up. "I'm sorry I said that. It was just a dumb reflex. I'm happy to help, Diane."

Diane nods against the glass. "Thank you, sweetie. There is one thing, if you don't mind. Vincent needs a suit to be buried in. I think he has one at his apartment. I bought him one down at Kohl's a few years ago for a wake we had to go to. If he didn't sell it, I'm sure it's still in his closet. I have his key. Would you mind going? Only if it wouldn't be too much trouble. I just don't have the energy."

"What about the cops?" Amy asks. "Won't they be there?"

"They don't even know about his apartment. They think he lived with me."

"That's right." A slight thrill runs through Amy at the prospect of being alone in Vincent's apartment, at the thought of going through his things and getting a better sense of who exactly he was and what exactly he was hiding. "I'd be happy to go."

The driver agrees to take Amy to West Eighth and Highlawn. From there, she'll pay him and let him go, because she's not sure how long it'll take in Vincent's apartment. They stop at Diane's, and Diane runs in to get Vincent's key. She tries to give Amy money to pay for the car service, but Amy refuses. She doesn't have a ton of money left, but it feels extra wrong to let Diane pay. Diane thanks her again, lets them know the address and that he lives—*lived*—in the downstairs apartment, and disappears back inside.

"Wow," Vincenzo says, heading down the block. "Tough situation."

"You can say that again," Amy says.

"You don't even know her that well, huh?"

"Just from church."

"I mostly pieced it together, but what happened exactly, you don't mind me asking?" He turns left onto Bath Avenue and then makes another quick left onto Bay Thirty-Fifth.

"Her son was killed. Stabbed. They don't know who or why."

"This was over by Kings Highway? I read about it."

"Where? What'd it say?"

"Not much. Just a stabbing. Looking for information, that kind of thing. I can't remember where I read it. Maybe the *Post*?"

"Just terrible," Amy says, again channeling how someone like Mrs. Epifanio might react.

Vincenzo takes a right under the El on Eighty-Sixth Street and then a left onto Twenty-Fourth Avenue. They're quiet now. Another left on Stillwell Avenue. A quick right onto Highlawn. Amy shudders as they pass West Tenth. She catches a quick glimpse of some yellow crime-scene tape strung up between a telephone pole and a tree, but nothing else to indicate what happened. Vincenzo takes a right on West Eighth, headed toward Avenue S. More row houses, very similar to the block where Vincent was killed. He pulls up at a hydrant across from a house with a tin awning and an American flag on a crooked pole in the front yard.

"This is the address she said, I think," Vincenzo says.

Amy looks out at the little house with green aluminum siding. It's not lost on her that Vincent lived in a basement apartment, just like her. She wonders if his landlord is nosy, too. If she will be pounced on by an old man or woman watching from behind the blinds upstairs the moment she puts the key in the door. She believes the possibility is very high. "Thanks so much," she says to Vincenzo, passing thirty bucks up to him, the fare plus a good tip.

"I'm sorry about all of this," he says. "Give the lady my condolences. And here's my card with my cell. You need a ride anywhere, just give me a call." He passes back a plain white business card with his name and phone number. She pockets it, thanks him again, and gets out of the car.

9

Amy opens the front gate. A laminated piece of paper that reads NO SOLIC-
ITING hangs from the fence post. A row of eight empty Cento tomato cans,
their yellow labels peeling, are lined up going to the front stoop of the
upstairs apartment. Three cement steps lead down to Vincent's. She can't tell
much of anything from the outside. It's a typical door, white paint chipped
away, sad brass knocker. A mailbox to the right of the door is overflowing
with circulars and Chinese menus. The blinds are drawn in the front window
of Vincent's place. Two slats are broken. A deck of cards is propped against
the window on the sill. She takes out the key. She thinks of Diane coming
over here to clean like a maid.

"Hey!" a voice above her says. "Who are you?"

Amy hadn't even heard the window of the upstairs apartment slide open.
A woman is behind the screen. She's old, grizzled, with whitish-blue hair.
Sitting down. Dragging on a cigarette. "Hi there," Amy says. "Vincent's
mother asked me to come here and get a suit for him."

"Dumb shit got himself killed, huh? I'm surprised the cops haven't been by yet."

"He was killed, yes." Amy omits the fact that the cops don't seem to know about this apartment.

"He's paid up through the end of the month, but tell the mother that his stuff will need to be out by then."

"She's got a lot going on right now. I'm sure she'd appreciate just a little bit of extra time."

"I'm not running a charity. I've got people lining up for this joint. Vincent was a bum. I don't even know how he scraped the rent together most months. Place is a disaster, you'll see. I had to pull inspection on him here and there, so we didn't get roaches or rats. What's your name?"

"Amy."

"You knew this bum?"

"I didn't. I know his mother from church. I'm just helping her out."

"A churchgoer. That's nice. Vincent should've gone to church. I used to, but I stopped going years ago, when my daughter moved to Long Island." She takes a puff. "Vincent's got a suit? That's a shocker."

"His mother says she bought him one for a wake."

"That I believe. I'm Marie, by the way. You need anything, let me know. Matter of fact, you want to come up and have a cup of coffee first? I'll put on a fresh pot."

"I'm sorry, Marie. All that's going on, I'm in a little bit of a rush."

"I get it. Good luck down there." Marie blows a line of smoke out through the screen and slams the window shut.

The key in Amy's hand feels slick. She looks around. She hasn't been thinking clearly. Vincent was friends with the killer. She's sure *he* knows where Vincent's apartment is even if the cops don't. They had to be headed back here when the disagreement between them—or whatever it was that sparked the attack—happened. If she was just being paranoid earlier, she has good reason to feel like she's being watched now. Maybe the killer has already been inside. Maybe he's looking for something. Maybe he found it. Maybe he *is* inside.

She thinks about walking away, going to Kohl's or somewhere and just buying Vincent another suit to be buried in. Too late. She doesn't know his size. But she can just call Diane and tell her the suit wasn't at the apartment. She can ask his size then.

But she goes in, turning the knob and pushing open the door. Is part of her hoping to confront the killer? Or is she merely hoping to untangle the web of Vincent's life, just a little?

The apartment is a hidey-hole. The front window is the only one she sees. A dirty sofa is strewn with clothes, as she'd imagined, and the cushions are pulled out. A small flat-screen TV is on the floor, a video-game system hooked up to it. A blue beanbag chair is close to the TV, Vincent's shape still dug into it. A bright yellow, diamond-shaped traffic sign that reads CAUTION MANHOLE hangs from the wall to her left over a ratty bureau plastered in holographic Giants and Yankees stickers. The rug is clumpy with dust.

There's a small kitchen nook at the back of the apartment. A laptop sits on a table, its screen cracked. A mini fridge, just like hers, is nudged into the corner on top of a small counter. The cabinets are all flung open, everything inside tossed around. Drawers hang out, too, heavy with junk. She walks to a door at the back of the apartment and sees that it leads into a small bed-room. A twin bed on a cheap metal frame. Bare walls. Clothes everywhere. Some DVDs. A bathroom the size of a closet in the corner. She can see a disposable razor and a tube of toothpaste on the edge of the sink.

The smell in the air is musky. Man funk: unwashed clothes, unwashed sheets. The place hasn't been vacuumed. Vincent hasn't sprayed Febreze on the sofa or bed. There's probably week-old garbage in a skanky plastic bin under the kitchen sink. If she pokes her head in the bathroom, she's sure she'll see a scummy toilet and get a heavy whiff of old piss.

She opens a narrow closet right inside the front door. A snow shovel slides out. Bag of rock salt next to that. Snow boots. She guesses that

Vincent would go around the neighborhood to shovel for a few extra bucks when there was snow. The closet is full of jackets and sweatshirts drooping from cheap hangers. She feels around and finds a suit wrapped in dry cleaner's plastic. She pulls it out. A Post-it note is stuck to the plastic: *Vincent, I had this cleaned for you. It's not just for wakes. Wear it to your next interview. Mom.* Diane must've really tried hard with him. Amy imagines that he was uncommunicative and ungrateful. That's got to be a tough thing to carry. And to know now that there's no growing out of it, no getting better.

She folds the suit over the arm of the sofa. She doesn't want to leave. She's not sure what she expects. She guesses she expects to find porn open on the laptop when she presses the power button, or drugs under the bed, or just ketchup packets in the fridge, traces of a life lived in the gutter.

But there isn't anything like that, as far as she can tell. The computer powers on to a game of solitaire. The fridge is full of cold cuts and orange juice and Bud Light. The DVDs in his bedroom are action movies: *Out for Justice, Hard to Kill, Drug War, Bad Boys, Breakdown,* and *Hard Target.* She goes through the kitchen cabinets and finds some broken plastic bowls and plates. In a drawer next to the sink, she finds a notepad, a Ziploc bag full of loose change, and some hair ties. She wonders if he had a girlfriend who left those behind. She looks for other signs of a girlfriend, but nothing points in that direction. A few dishes are heaped in the sink. The drain is clogged with soggy, ballooned pieces of elbow macaroni, the kind that comes in boxes of mac and cheese. She finds a few cans of corned beef hash stacked in a dish basin under the sink. She can't believe that a man under seventy would eat food like that.

Next to the basin, leaned up against the pipes, is something wrapped in striped dish towels. She takes it out. It's heavy. Her mind is stuck on the shape—rectangular. Maybe it's some kind of case, and when she opens the case, she'll find a gun or drugs.

She pulls back the towels. It's a cardboard box with red marks all over it. The flaps are gluey with packing tape residue. She peels them back. What she sees first is knots of Bubble Wrap. She sticks her hand in to feel around. Metal tubing and pipe fittings, that's all that's in there, probably not even Vincent's.

Back in the bedroom, a fuzzy blue robe is crumpled on the floor on the far side of the bed. She can't picture Vincent wearing it. She picks it up and feels around in the pockets. In the first one, she finds only lint. In the second, there's a small, unopened packet of Extra Strength Tylenol—the kind you pay too much for at a deli—and a crumpled receipt in faded black print.

She notices something then. The rug in the corner is curling, like someone has pulled it up. Everything could be something now. She goes to the corner and falls to her knees. She yanks the rug back as far as it will go, a Velcro crackle echoing through the apartment. Again, she expects drugs, or an envelope full of cash. Again, there's nothing—just an unfinished wood floor covered in rings of mold. She pushes the rug back into place as best she can.

She sits on Vincent's bed. The sheets are filthy. She wonders if he ever even washed them. She pictures him bunching them up and putting them in a laundry bag and bringing them over to 3 Stars, drinking across the street at Homestretch while he waited.

She goes back out to the living room. It occurs to her then that someone else has definitely been here. The open cabinets and drawers. The cushions pulled out. The rug yanked up like that. A creeping sense that the things she's touching have been touched by another person not too long ago.

She's thinking also how she'd always wished she had the guts to go into Bob Tully's garage and do this very thing. Hunt around. See if there was some trace left behind of the man he'd killed—a wallet, a ring, a watch.

The thrill again. She's enjoying this. She should be looking over her shoulder, afraid that the killer will pounce from a closet or jump out from the shower stall and attack with a longer knife, but she feels okay. Content, even.

On a final pass back to the door, she opens the top drawer of the bureau under the traffic sign. It's filled with paperback books. Westerns and horror and some sci-fi. She opens the bottom two drawers. One is loaded with underwear and socks. The other is empty except for an old telephone with its cord wrapped around the receiver. She goes back to the top drawer and starts flipping through the pages of the books.

In one of the books, *Silhouette at Sundown*, its edges green, library-stamped, a black *X* on the fragile spine, she finds a four-by-six envelope sealed with Scotch tape. No writing on it. She turns the envelope over in her hands and picks at the tape. She hears Marie's footsteps upstairs and a door opening. She guesses that Marie is starting to be suspicious of her. What could be taking her so long? Maybe she's not who she says she is.

She tears open the flap of the envelope. She can see that there's a picture inside. Just as she's about to withdraw the picture, there's a knock on the front door. She shoves the envelope inside her hoodie and picks up the suit. Another knock.

From the other side: "It's Marie. You okay in there?"

Amy opens the door, holding up the suit, her elbow pressed against her side to keep the envelope in place. "Took me a second to find it."

"I'm sure," Marie says, stooped over like a witch. "Real pigsty, huh?"

"Pretty bad, I guess."

"I should go digging around. All the crap I put up with, I deserve a reward." Marie laughs.

Amy forces a smile. "I'll be on my way."

"Tell me, you been hunting around, you find anything good?"

"Corned beef hash and some action movies. That's about it."

"Sounds like Vincent. The other guy who was here, you know him?"

"What other guy?"

"The friend. I let him in. Don't remember his name. Every once in a while, I saw his face around here. Nice guy. Jeweler's kid. He should've been my tenant."

"You don't know his name?"

"What I said. You know, I never saw Vincent bring a girl over. Not a young one anyway." Disdain in her voice. Contempt. "A fruit, I bet, and that's what did him in."

Amy pushes past Marie, ignoring her.

"You tell the mother everything needs to be cleaned out by the end of the month, otherwise it all goes to the curb," Marie calls back over her shoulder, already into the apartment.

Amy hustles away down the block, the suit hanging over her arm. She turns right onto Avenue S and stops in front of a barbershop, leaning up against a black soda machine that has COLD DRINKS painted on its side in blue. She hangs the suit on the machine. Diane's Post-it note falls to the sidewalk.

She takes out the envelope and withdraws the picture. There's just the one. It's from Homestretch. A party, with people hoisting drinks for the camera. Vincent's there with his arm around a woman. She's older, in her fifties, wearing a tight black top, sipping from a pint glass of what looks like gin-and-tonic or vodka-and-soda with a striped straw. She's flush, dreamy-eyed, dark-haired.

Beyond them, standing close to Bernie at the bar, Amy recognizes the man from the bench in his softball shirt. Next to him is a man with a long nose and a square chin. He's wearing a BROOKLYN VS. EVERYBODY T-shirt. He's looking at Vincent and the woman. And he's clearly Vincent's killer, the one whose knife she has hidden in her freezer. Amy's a hundred percent sure.

Amy flips the picture over. On the back, written in blue curlicue script, is a note: *My love is true. Let's run away.*

She stuffs the picture back in the envelope and places it under her shirt, tucking it into her waistband.

On the walk to Diane's, she sees a dead dog in the middle of Stillwell Avenue, cars and buses swerving to avoid it. The day eats at her senses. Her skin feels balmy. She smells exhaust, maybe smoke. Maybe there's a fire somewhere. She sees the dead dog as Vincent. She hears horns and alarms and sirens. Her mouth tastes like the dregs of bad coffee. Her tongue seems cold. Again, she feels a disquieting presence. Or is it an absence?

$$\rightarrow\!\!\!\!\longleftarrow$$

Back at Diane's, she hands the suit over, trembling. Diane cries at the sight of it. She's probably thinking about his lifeless body filling it out. She's probably remembering the time she saw him in it for someone else's wake. Amy can imagine that his whole life is playing before her eyes. She knows what death does to you. She remembers seeing a dress that belonged to her mother a week after they buried her and breaking down. Diane hangs the suit in the hallway closet. Amy puts a hand on her shoulder.

"Thank you for going to get it," Diane says.

"It's nothing," Amy says. She wonders if she's being suspicious. *It's nothing.* Is that an appropriate response? She knows she can't mention the picture. She knows she can't take it out and point to the killer. Not being quiet has its consequences. Bob Tully trained her early to that way of thinking. It bumps up against her very idealistic notion of being a helper. "What else can I do?"

"Sit. Please. Stay with me a bit longer."

"Of course."

They go into the living room. The TV is still on, blasting a talk show. People on couches facing each other. Close-ups. Audience reaction shots. Lots of clapping. Diane has dragged a plastic crate into the center of the room. It's full of photo albums and shoe boxes. Amy sits on the recliner in the corner, her hands on her thighs. She can feel the envelope bending against her waist, but there's not much she can do to fix it. She's terrified that Diane will somehow realize she's carrying it and wonder what's going on.

"I've been going through some things," Diane says, dropping to her knees beside the crate. She coughs into her hand.

"You should rest," Amy says. "Maybe go lay down?"

"I can't lay down. Look at this." Diane takes a picture out of one of the shoe boxes. It's in a frame made of Popsicle sticks. It's Vincent as a kid in his school uniform, at a desk, pretending to write, smiling. "Vincent in second grade. They did this as a project one day. Made these little frames. Cute, right?"

"So cute."

"That was his best year of school. He was so happy. He'd come home excited about something every afternoon. He had this teacher he just loved, Miss Krauza. She was a sweetheart. I wish life could be that year over and over again. He didn't need anything else. He was happy to come home to me after school and watch TV and eat dinner. I'd sing him to sleep. He loved when I sang 'Que Sera, Sera.'"

"Very cute," Amy says.

Diane lugs out a clunky black album and brings it over to Amy. She sits on the arm of the recliner, propping the album on her lap. She flips through the pages slowly and shows Amy Vincent's grade school pictures, pictures from birthday parties with Vincent hunched over Carvel ice-cream cakes, pictures from bowling alleys and circuses and baseball games. "Such a happy kid," Diane says. "See? I have all this proof." On the verge of bawling.

"I'm so sorry, Diane," Amy says. She thinks again of the picture she's holding under her shirt. Her stomach turns over. She puts her hand over her mouth. "Can I use the bathroom?"

Diane stands up and dumps the album back in the crate. "Oh God, are you feeling sick? I'm so sorry. I hope you don't have the flu."

Amy rushes into the bathroom. She latches the door behind her and then slumps in front of the bowl. She sticks two fingers down her throat. Her fingers are sandpapery on her tongue. She can feel them rattling against the roof of her mouth. She forces herself to throw up. When she's done, she flushes and then sits back against the tiled wall and takes the envelope out of her waistband. It's all bent up.

Diane knocks on the door. "You okay in there?" she asks.

"I'm fine," Amy says.

"You don't sound fine. I involved you in all of this, and now you're sick."

Amy puts the picture away. She tucks the envelope into her waistband. She scooches in front of the bowl and tries to throw up again. Nothing this time.

"Poor thing," Diane says.

Amy stands and unlatches the door. Diane is looking at her with such sad eyes. This woman who just lost her son has sympathy for *her*. "I'm sorry, Diane," Amy says. "I should really go."

"I hope you didn't catch this from me."

"I think it's just anxiety. I know that's a stupid thing to say. You're the one, I mean, Vincent's not my . . ."

"I understand."

"I just sometimes get these anxiety attacks. I'm sorry. I wish I could do more for you."

"You've done so much already. I don't know what would've happened if you hadn't been here."

Amy goes into the kitchen and writes her number down on a dry-erase board that hangs on the side of the refrigerator. "I have your house number, but I don't have your cell," she says. "This is my number. You need anything, please call me. Okay? Anything at all."

"Thank you," Diane says, her chin trembling.

Amy tries not to think of her alone with the terrible knowledge of her son's murder. Alone at the table. Alone as she trudges around the house. Alone in bed. Alone in the shower. A new brutality to her aloneness. "Take care of yourself," Amy says.

"I will."

"Call Monsignor Ricciardi. He'll be happy to help however he can, I'm sure."

"I will. I hope you feel better."

"I'm fine. I'm sorry to add to everything." Amy touches Diane on the shoulder again and then rushes out of the apartment.

10

Back at her apartment, Amy considers the knife. It could've been bought anywhere, probably at one of those shops on Eighty-Sixth Street where they have glass shelves full of windproof lighters and cheapo knives and cigarette cases. She often wonders how those stores even stay in business, now that most people shop online.

She opens the knife and presses the blade against her palm. Taking the knife was the single worst idea she's ever had. But she couldn't stop herself. It's an artifact of her curiosity. But if she'd just left it where Vincent dropped it, the police would have a lead. Maybe they'd have fingerprints. Was the killer wearing gloves? She tries to call up his hands in her memory. In any case, she swiped those fingerprints away into a sad toilet at the Roulette and then doubled down on erasing any trace of them here at her apartment. He must've been wearing gloves. He must've planned to stab Vincent. Why else leave the knife?

And now she's got the envelope with the picture, too. It's as if she's planting evidence on herself. She takes out the envelope and looks at the picture again, its edges creased now. The woman, the killer, the note. She drops the knife into the envelope and stuffs the envelope into the ice pop box in the freezer compartment.

When Mr. Pezzolanti knocks on her door, it's to tell her that Connie Giacchino and Monsignor Ricciardi had come around about twenty minutes earlier to see if she was okay. Amy asks whether her father has been back. Mr. Pezzolanti says he hasn't seen any sign of him. He asks if she's heard about the stabbing, and she's struck dumb for a moment. She realizes that soon everyone will know she was with Diane, because that's how word travels in the neighborhood. She's sure that Diane has already made calls to people from church, letting them know how lucky she was to have Amy there when she received the news and to accompany her to the morgue. In fact, she's betting that's why Monsignor Ricciardi and Connie came around in the first place.

Amy spills about going to pay Diane a visit, saying that Mrs. Epifanio was worried sick about her. Now it's occurring to her what a tangled web this is. If anyone talks to Mrs. Epifanio, they'll know about the Vincent situation. And then they'll be able to connect Amy and Vincent directly. She feels light-headed. She keeps telling herself she hasn't done anything wrong, and yet she knows she's done so much wrong. She's thankful, at least, that Mrs. Epifanio doesn't leave the house and doesn't have many visitors. She just has to be sure that she's the one to bring communion next week as usual, not Immacula. She has to be back to her normal routine by then. She wonders if Mr. Pezzolanti can see her sweating.

"Just terrible about that kid," Mr. Pezzolanti says, bouncing on the balls of his feet. "Young guy, whole life ahead of him. Who knows what it was about? My guess is he got involved with some bad people. Drugs, probably. Johnny Zap's son says this Vincent hung around that dive Homestretch a lot. That's what you would've called a TB joint in my day. You know what that means? You get tuberculosis drinking from the dirty glasses. Who knows what kind of lowlifes he got tied up with there? You look around—here, anywhere—on a nice day, you think there's no bad people. Well, all you've got to do is scratch the surface. Nice lady like Diane, she winds up with a son like that. But you, you're such a sweetheart, Amy. A time like that, you go and help Diane out."

"I just happened to be there," Amy says.

"Sure. But you stayed. You didn't run away. You comforted her. You don't mind me saying, you look worn-out. Why don't you try to get some rest?"

"Thanks, Mr. P. I'm going to try to do that."

"You need anything, let me know. I've gotta go move my car. It's been parked around the corner all week. Figured I'd run some errands. I'm running down to BJ's later." He pauses and rubs his temples. "Guy offered me three grand for the Caprice the other day; you believe that? I should've taken him up on it. It's nothing but a headache at this point."

When he leaves, she goes inside and sits on the bed. She expects Fred to knock on the door and listens for sounds from outside. She thinks about Vincent's apartment. She gets up and checks every corner to make sure that nothing's been disturbed, that no one has been inside rummaging around.

She pulls down her egg crate full of old stuff from the closet. She takes out an outfit she hasn't worn in years, gray swing trousers and a blue Catalina cardigan with a cherry motif. Both from the forties. Both smelling of mothballs now. She also has some cute All Hope Abandoned sugar skull flats that she's tucked away in the crate. And a red bandanna for her hair. She lays it all out on the bed. It's as if a former version of herself is there suddenly, sprawled on the bed like a ghost.

"Fuck it," she says.

She changes into her old favorite clothes and ties the bandanna in her hair and puts her makeup on in the bathroom. This version of her former self is there in front of her in the mirror now. Except for the hair color, she's pretty much the same. Maybe a little thinner. A little stiffer. Being dressed like this gives her a good feeling, one that allows her to shed some of the worry and fear that's haunted her the last day.

She stands there. She puts on her flats. She paces. She thinks about what she would've done when she was twenty-five or twenty-eight. She would've gone out. She would've headed straight to the bar. Shots. Beer. Music. She wouldn't have felt intimidated or regretful. High school had taught her that, and everything with Bob Tully. No way was it wrong to chase a feeling, to be unhinged, to act out of fear and fascination. How did she lose that knowledge? Whatever she'd gained had led to so much lost.

"Fuck it," she says again.

She leaves her apartment as someone else. Or someone she used to be.

<hr>

"What's it, Halloween?" a fortyish guy in a sauce-stained white uniform says to Amy as she enters Homestretch. He looks like he's just gotten off a shift at a pizza joint. Dark hair, olive skin, flour under his fingernails. He's standing at the bar, a Bud Light in his fist. "Who you supposed to be? Rosie the Riveter or some shit? Rosie, how about you let me buy you a drink?"

Bernie is behind the bar. He doesn't recognize her from her last visit. "What can I get you, doll?" he says, as she settles at the bar.

Her instinct is to say club soda again, but beer seems to come more naturally now. "Bud draft," she says.

Bernie goes to the taps with a mug. She can feel eyes on her. The guy in the sauce-stained whites. The others around the bar, too. Three big-bellied dudes in Rangers jerseys who seem pretty wasted. An old woman in the corner eating peanuts out of a Styrofoam cup and slurping vodka on the rocks. Amy looks around and gives them all a half smile. She'd gotten lots of attention on the walk over, too. Boys howling, Russian women stopping to stare, someone asking if she was an actress and what they were filming in the neighborhood.

"Don't mind them," Bernie says, bringing back her beer and sloshing it on the bar. "They just never seen such a pretty gal in here. You're really classing the joint up."

She goes to pay, but Sauce Stains clears his throat and raises his hand. "That's on me, Bernie," he says.

"Thanks," she says, taking a drink. It's the first beer she's had in a while. It tastes terrible.

Sauce Stains sidles up next to her, swigging from his beer. "I'm Lou," he says. "And me buying you that drink means you owe me at least four minutes of conversation."

"That's the way it works?" she says.

"Tell me about this little outfit."

"Tell me about *your* little outfit."

He steps back and does a runway-model walk toward the bathroom, turning drunkenly on his heels, and then zooming back to her. The dudes in the Rangers jerseys bust up laughing. "This old thing?" Lou says, motioning to his uniform. "Armani. Soak it in."

Amy almost laughs, the guy's so ridiculous.

"You want to dance with me?" Lou says.

"There's no music."

He starts singing "Damn I Wish I Was Your Lover," dancing up close to Amy, grinding against her leg.

"Lay off," she says.

"Lou, leave the fucking girl alone," Bernie says.

Lou settles down and steps back. "You know that song? Sophie B. Hawkins. Big fucking hit in '92. That's the year I started working at Bad Boys. You know the place? I was a senior in high school. Twenty-four fucking years I been slinging pies. That year, '92, I was finger-banging Bishop Kearney girls in my old man's Chevy Nova. I thought working at a pizza joint with my uncle was the be-all and end-all. I was on top of the world."

"Nobody gives a shit about your story," Bernie says. "You ain't learned that yet? You got regrets? Get in line. You think I wanted to spend thirty years bartending at this fucking dive?"

"Bernie, Bernie, Bernie."

"Lou, Lou, Lou."

"Let's get back to our new friend's outfit, huh?" Lou says. "Where's the party? *What's* the party? Can I come? I'd like to know the origins of such glamour."

The door to the bar opens. The man who walks in has a long nose and a square chin. It's the killer, the guy from Vincent's picture. He's wearing the same Timberland boots and drooping jeans and sweatshirt from the night before. His hood is down. She's shaken out of performing the role of her former self.

"Oh!" Lou says. "Look who's here! I saw where your buddy Vincent got himself stabbed, Dom. He always was a dumb piece of shit, wasn't he?"

"Indeed," Dom says.

Dom. Probably short for Dominic. The killer has a name, and it's so simple. The way Lou says it is like a threatening sound in a subway station at three in the morning. If Dom knew the Other Her as a witness, he doesn't seem to know the version of her sitting there. He gazes at her, but only in the typical horrible-guy way, his eyes drifting from her ass on the stool up to her chest. Amy looks into her beer and leans on the bar, crossing her arms under her chin. She should go outside and call the police, that's what she should do.

Dom sits a few stools down from her and orders a Jack and Coke.

Bernie mixes the drink for him. "You get the scoop?" he asks.

"No word," Dom says. "Mugging, I guess."

"Mugging for what purpose?" Lou says. "What'd the guy ever have on him?"

"Who the fuck knows?"

Bernie puts the drink in front of Dom and then pours himself a shot of rack whiskey. "Well, here's to Vincent. I never had any hard feelings toward the kid. He took me that one time on the Super Bowl pool. That was dirty. Aside from that, I mostly just felt sorry for him."

They drink up.

"How're your folks doing, Dom?" Bernie asks. "Ain't seen your mother in here in a few weeks. Her and Vincent were tight, no?" He winks. "And Tony, he called me and I called him and, ah, fucking phone tag pisses me off to no end."

"They're how they are," Dom says, looking away. "You know."

Amy hadn't intended on coming here as a spy. Or maybe, subconsciously, she had. She couldn't have planned it this way, and it couldn't have worked out any better. She's nervous, but she feels protected by her costume. She's safe in the arms of anonymity. Even if Dom had seen her on West Tenth, he hadn't seen this Amy. No one has seen this Amy in a long time.

"Let's not talk about that loser Vincent anymore," Lou says. "Or Dom's folks. No offense. Let's get back to me hitting on Rosie the Riveter over here. Rosie, you were about to spill about your getup."

"I'd like to hear about your outfit, too," Dom says.

"Can't a broad just come get a drink without being assaulted by you douchebags?" Bernie says, whipping a dish towel at Lou.

"You know better than to throw that towel at me, Bern," Dom says, laughing.

"There's no story," Amy says. "It's just the way I dress."

"Fair enough," Dom says. His phone goes off in his pocket. His ringtone is "Eye of the Tiger" from *Rocky III*. He takes out his phone—it's in a gaudy blue Yankees case—and says a couple of abrupt things to whoever's on the other end.

When the front door opens again, Amy is shocked to see Fred standing there, hands in his pockets. He comes over and takes the stool next to her. Lou backs away.

"What are you doing here?" Amy says.

"This bum giving you trouble?" Lou says.

"Mind your own business," Bernie says, pelting Lou with a handful of ice.

Lou laughs and puts up his hands, almost dropping his beer. "I get it. Rosie likes the old-timers."

Bernie asks Fred if he can get him anything. Fred just shakes his head, sullen.

Amy leans close to Fred. "You followed me?" she says.

"I'm sorry," Fred says, barely audible.

"What the fuck, Fred?"

"Can I just say, I didn't realize it was you at first. I thought, *That looks a little like Amy*. I thought, *That can't be Amy*."

"Jesus." Amy takes a long pull of her beer.

"You're drinking again?"

Amy can see that Dom is listening in on their conversation. Lou, too. And the dudes in the Rangers jerseys. "Let's go," she says to Fred, getting up and grabbing him by the arm.

Outside, she sits on the bench, staring across at the yellow 3 Stars sign, where Other Her stood just the day before and watched Vincent. It's dark out. She'd be afraid that someone was watching now from that same spot, if not for the fact that the man who might be watching her is in Homestretch drinking a Jack and Coke.

Fred hovers over her, dancing nervously in place. "I know it's not right," he says, "me following you here. I'm sorry. I wasn't thinking straight."

Amy looks over her shoulder through the neon Budweiser sign at Dom. He's working on a scratch-off with a nickel. He blows the black scrapings across the bar, and Bernie scolds him.

"You know him?" Fred says.

"Who?" Amy says.

"This guy you're staring at."

"I'm not staring at anybody. I thought I left something on the bar."

Fred motions to the bench. "Okay if I sit?"

"Do what you want."

Fred sits next to her. "So, you live a double life or something?" he says.

"This is just the way I used to dress," Amy says. "I felt like being who I was for a little while tonight. I don't know why."

"I get it. But the drinking."

"I'm not in AA. You're not my sponsor."

"True. How'd it taste, the beer? I miss it."

"Tasted like shit. It was Bud."

"I had a friend named Whitey used to drink Bud by the pitcher at this one joint we frequented. He'd just walk around with this pitcher, swilling from it, beer blotted all over his shirt. His beard always smelled like beer. Some point in the evening, he'd throw an arm around you and start singing an Irish song and he'd have the pitcher over your lap, splashing you."

"I don't want to do this," Amy says. She's worried again. She stands.

"I'm sorry," Fred says again.

Amy rushes away down Kings Highway, looking over to make sure Fred's not following. After a couple of blocks, she cuts a quick right on West Seventh. She knows she can catch the N train right before Highlawn, not far from Vincent's. No sign of Fred behind her. She starts to wonder if maybe Dom is toying with her, if maybe he knows who she is and he's just testing her.

She ducks into the station and buys a MetroCard at one of the machines. She goes through the turnstile, getting the once-over from the lady in the glass booth. She notices a poster that says Manhattan-bound trains aren't stopping here until the spring. She'll have to take a southbound train and switch in Coney Island for one heading into the city. She doesn't care. Her only desire now is to be on a train into the city and away from her life here as she's known it, away especially from the various mysteries and horrors of the last thirty-six hours—or however the hell long it's been—since Vincent and Fred and Dom and Diane jumped out from the darkness.

She runs down to the southbound platform, still watching over her shoulder. The station is lonely and sad. Not underground and not the El, it's one of those ground-level N-line stops she doesn't know the name for.

Open-cut, maybe. Concrete walls. Blue columns. Graffiti. Tracks that seem extra desolate. Yellow lines to keep you from standing too close. Garbage overflowing out of cans. Noise like silence. She can look up into apartments with torn shades and child safety bars on the windows. She can see clotheslines and telephone wires. She's sure she heard a story, not that long ago, of a man hanging himself here. She can't help but wonder where. From which exact beam? She stands and waits for a southbound train. When it comes, she feels relieved that she can go be her old self in the place where her old self existed once, even if it'll take a while to get there.

11

Switching in Coney Island isn't that much of a pain. She feels immediately more comfortable and less watched, less observed. In the middle car of the northbound train she's on, there are hipsters headed back to wherever from a day spent in Coney, eating hot dogs and probably drinking forties on the beach or going to the freak show. This time of year, there's not much else to do. But there's always the allure of taking pictures on the Boardwalk, of saying you've spent the day in Coney. Truth is, she lives so close by, and she's hardly ever been. Alessandra dragged her there a couple of times. They went on the Wonder Wheel and rode the Cyclone. They'd been there for the Mermaid Parade only once. She heard that good bands used to pass through MCU Park and play the now-defunct Siren Festival, but nothing like that seemed to happen anymore. Not that she was paying much attention.

She can't sleep. She feels wired to the rumbling of the train. She watches the faces of the people around her. They don't care who she is or where she's going. Even this one kid who looks kind of like Morrissey, he could give two shits about her and how she's dressed, and it's a fucking relief.

In the city, she gets off at Prince Street and Broadway. Everything feels alive. *She* feels alive. She walks down Prince and makes a left on Lafayette. It's been a few years since she's been here, but the route is etched in her memory. People walk with their heads down, looking at phones. Cabs zoom by. Right on East Fourth. Left on Second Avenue. Right on East Seventh.

Seven Bar is where she left it, between Second and First Avenue. Tailor across the street. Cupcake place next door; that's new. *Cupcakes.* Unbelievable. New frozen yogurt place on the other side with two sidewalk tables. The exterior of Seven Bar has changed. The old hand-painted sign is gone. Now there's a lit blade sign, SEVEN BAR printed in a bubbly white font.

The inside's changed more. First thing she notices is that the jukebox is gone. Music plays over the house speakers, a Sirius nineties grunge station. The little nook of a bar has given way to a gleaming horseshoe. Used to be there was a big chalkboard with the prices of everything up over the dusty bottles. That's gone, too. You used to be able to get a cheap pitcher. The Dirty Hipster Special was big. A shot of Jäger and a PBR. The bartender wears a vest and a bowtie. His hair is in a bun. He claps his hands together and smiles, holding out a laminated cocktail menu.

"How're we doing today?" he asks. The rest of the place is empty. The pool table is gone. The shitty old Naugahyde booths have been switched out for the sorts of sleek wooden booths found in airport steakhouses.

"I used to work here," Amy says.

"Excellent," the bartender says.

"Yeah," Amy says. She takes the menu and scans it. The Dirty Hipster is now a fifteen-dollar cocktail that includes egg whites. All the cocktails range from fifteen to twenty bucks. Amy laughs reading through them. One worse than the next. The Seven Sweet, the St. Mark's Place, the Joey Ramone, the Coney Island High, Kim's Underground, the East Village Eraser, Sympathy for the Strawberry. It feels like a foul joke. "Can I just get a beer?"

"I just tapped an Eppinger's Pumpkin Stout. I highly recommend it."

"What's the cheapest shit you have?"

"We have pony bottles of Miller High Life for two dollars."

"Perfect."

He brings her one, and she pays and sits at the bar, looking all around. A lot of nights in this place. Meeting Alessandra here. Merrill, too. A lot of ghosts. A lot of memories. Totally antiseptic now. She's guessing the place has been taken over by new owners; "keep the name and change the vibe" being their guiding principle. Make it more of a theme park dive than an actual dive.

"How long's the place been like this?" she asks the bartender.

"Only about six months," he says.

She nods.

"I know," he says. "I just work here."

She downs her tiny beer and leaves. She stands out on the sidewalk near a tree. More people on phones. A bad painting leaning against a nearby garbage can. Now the city feels slumped with sadness. What she'd mistaken for electricity is actually more like a buzz of destitution. Everything's changing all the time. She'd half expected to walk back into *her* bar, to see *her* regulars. She thought wearing these clothes might be a key into that old life. It's nothing like that.

A coffee shop up the block that she used to frequent, Holy Grounds, is still there and appears unchanged, with its red awning and flyers for shows and readings in the window. She wonders if any of the same people still work there. Gwen, Troy, Leesa, Liz, any of them will do. She doubts it. Probably just some NYU kid with a hangdog look.

The door clangs when she walks in. A few people sit scattered at the little round tables, working on laptops and tablets. Gwen is behind the counter. She hasn't changed much. Dreadlocks. Black lipstick. Nose ring. She notices Amy and smiles. "Holy shit," she says.

"You're a sight for sore eyes," Amy says.

"Tell me you didn't go into Seven Bar."

"I went in."

"You believe it?"

"Pretty horrible."

Gwen comes out from behind the counter and gives her a hug. She smells like kush oil. "I get off in an hour," she says. "Hang out, and then we'll go get a drink somewhere real."

"That sounds great."

Amy sits at a table while Gwen dances over to the espresso machine. She checks her phone. It's after eight. Two missed calls from Diane. One from Mrs. Epifanio, probably calling because the news about Vincent has made its way to her. One from Connie Giacchino. No voice mails. She powers it down and considers tossing it in the trash. It feels like the only link to anything that's happened.

Gwen brings her back a mug of coffee. "Americano with an extra shot," she says. "Still your drink?"

"Exactly what I wanted," Amy says, wafting her hand through the steam.

"Nice flip phone."

"Don't make fun of my phone."

An hour later, Amy leaves Holy Grounds with Gwen, and they walk down the block to International Bar on First Avenue. It's the same place Amy remembers. It had reopened under new ownership in 2008, but they'd done it the right way. No TV. Long, narrow scuffed bar. Purple walls. Movie posters. Dark as shit. Smells like a bowling alley. Gwen orders a Schaefer and a shot of well whiskey for five bucks. Amy gets the same. The bartender's cool. He's wearing a Gun Club *Fire of Love* T-shirt. The Shaggs play on the jukebox. A dude is passed out at the bar. Amy used to come here after getting off at Seven Bar a lot of nights. Mostly she remembers the killer jukebox. Amy goes over and punches in three songs: Nina Simone, Lou Reed, R.E.M. There's a little patio out back, but they sit at a table inside and clink their shot glasses and down the whiskeys. They work on their beers slowly, playing catch-up.

Gwen fills her in on what's changed and what hasn't. Most things have. The city sucks. Everything's closing. Rents are out of control. Chain stores spread like a virus. Whatever good places stick around, it seems like a miracle. She lives in Williamsburg, shares a place with these guys Mike and Danny. She broke up with Michelle two years ago. She's in a band called A Woman Under the Influence, after the Cassavetes movie. She had a little heroin problem, and then she kicked it. Now it's just booze all the way. She has a blog and an Instagram with her pictures of old NYC signs and storefronts, stuff that's fading away. She just uses her iPhone, nothing fancy, but she's discovered that finding places to photograph has given her some purpose.

Gwen checks her phone. She responds to a couple of texts. She scooches over next to Amy and holds out her camera and takes a picture of them with the flash on. The whole place seems to flash white for a sec. They look at the picture together. Amy's eyes are half-closed. They try again. This time, a better one. Gwen posts it on Instagram.

"Leesa's gonna go crazy," she says. "She always loved you." Within a minute, she shows Amy that Leesa's already commented on the picture: *Amy Falconetti!!!! Holy shiiiiiiiit!!!!*

Gwen asks about Alessandra. She says she follows Alessandra on Instagram, so she knows she's back out in Los Angeles. Do they keep in touch? She says she used to really like Alessandra, but it bums her out that her whole Instagram page is pictures of her doing yoga and all these cute little dogs and salads she's made or smoothies she's drinking. That's a lot, she says. One of those three is deadly, and she does them all constantly. Amy tells her they're not in touch since they split and leaves it at that.

"Tell me all about Amy," Gwen tries next. "You look the same. Except for the hair. I like it."

"There's not much to tell," Amy says. She guards her recent life fiercely. She doesn't lie, but she doesn't give anything up. Not that Gwen would believe her.

They get another round. And then another. Amy's songs have come and gone on the jukebox. They talked through them. She plays three more by Nina Simone and sings along. They go out to the patio so Gwen can try to bum a smoke. She succeeds. Amy watches her smoke and smiles dumbly. The world feels slowed down and almost pleasant.

"What?" Gwen says.

"I'm drunk," Amy says.

"Good."

"I haven't been drunk in a while." Her thoughts go back to Dom. There's no concrete threat yet hanging over her about reporting the murder, but she's conditioned to avoid talking. She imagines Bob Tully putting an apple slice in his mouth and telling her that she could wind up in a tree.

"What are you thinking about?"

"I don't know. Nothing. I don't want to go home."

⁂

They walk to Essex Street and take the J train back to Williamsburg, getting off at the Hewes Street station. Gwen's apartment is on Marcy Avenue. Her roommates, Mike and Danny, are up, dicking around on guitars, when they get there. It's a dump of a place. Smells like wet towels and Febreze. Lots of empty pizza boxes and records and overflowing ashtrays. Gwen gets them cans of PBR and they go into her room, which is pretty small. Her bed's on cinderblocks. The wall is full of show posters and drawings by Leesa. It feels like the bedroom of a teenager. Five Styrofoam wig heads are lined up on the dresser. Only one holds a wig, golden peroxide blond. A bob cut. Like something a character in disguise would wear in a spy movie when they're dropping off a briefcase or a secret key: this wig, trench coat, dark sunglasses.

Gwen puts music on her laptop. It's low enough that Amy can't really make out who it is that's playing. Still, she misses being around music all the time like this.

"You okay?" Gwen says. "You look worried or something."

"Do I?" Amy sits on the bed. She takes a long pull of her beer and leans back, the can between her legs. The bed is so much more comfortable than hers. It's memory foam. The sheets are black. The comforter is soft and cold.

"You tired?"

"A little. I haven't really slept in a while."

"What's going on, Amy?"

"It's nothing. I'm just tired, I guess." Amy closes her eyes. She can feel Gwen's hand between her legs, plucking up the can. She hears Gwen put down the can on the bedside stand. She hears Gwen's fingers on her phone. The sounds of typing. Of texts being sent. The phone buzzing when she gets a message. Amy's not asleep yet, but her head feels swimmy and she feels something that must be close to contentment. She fades off to sleep.

She wakes up in darkness a few hours later, her mouth dry and her throat achy. Gwen is asleep on the bed, wearing only striped underwear and a plain yellow T-shirt, her dreadlocks spread on the pillow. She hadn't moved Amy, had just let her stay the way she was on the bed, only angling her body so they both had room enough to sprawl out. It's a pretty big bed, maybe a queen. Amy's head is pounding. A few beers and a few shots, nothing in the old days, has her feeling like she'll never be the same.

She takes out her phone and turns it on. The same missed calls from before, but now a text from Alessandra. She hardly ever gets texts. Alessandra is the only person who's ever texted her regularly. When they were together, anyway. Mostly they'd send each other messages about where to meet for food or drinks.

Amy rubs her eyes now and reads the text from Alessandra: *saw your pic on G's insta. i'm in bklyn. call me.*

Without hesitation, she goes to her contacts. ALESSANDRA is the first name there. The name she's hit ENTER for the most. By far. It'll be nice to hear Alessandra's voice. Something to reel her back in from this very strange present.

"Amy?" Alessandra says, picking up after two rings.

"Hey," Amy says in a whisper. "Sorry to call so late."

"It's okay. What is it, three? I'm up. I'm always up. I don't really sleep well ever."

"Same here. I got a little drunk and passed out at Gwen's."

"How's Gwen?"

"She's good. She's asleep."

"I'm in Brooklyn for a couple of days. Going to auditions."

"That's nice."

"You want to meet up for lunch tomorrow?"

"Sure."

"Where you living these days?"

"Still in your old neighborhood."

"Really?" Alessandra laughs. "That's fucking crazy, dude. I thought you'd be out of there in a flash. Go live in Williamsburg or Greenpoint or Astoria with everyone else."

"I got a good deal. Where you staying?"

"This hotel called Brooklyn Way or something. Right near Green-Wood Cemetery. Not far from Prospect Park. You know it over there?"

"A little."

"Pretty cheap. Got it as part of a package deal on Priceline."

"Thrilling."

Crazy how easy they fall into their old rhythms.

"I wasn't gonna call you," Alessandra says. "I didn't think it was a good idea. I didn't want to put you out. I don't know what you've got going on. Then I saw Gwen's picture, and I thought, *What the fuck?* We've got a lot of history, good and bad, and we can be fucking adults. When'd you make your hair dark, by the way?"

"I don't remember. It's been a while."

"You know Tom's Restaurant on Washington Avenue?"

"Yeah, of course."

"Want to meet there at one? Lemon ricotta pancakes and egg creams, that's what the fuck I'm talking about."

"They've got cherry-lime rickeys, too."

"Okay. One, then?"

"One."

They say hushed byes to each other, and Amy closes her phone. She'd leave if it wasn't the middle of the night. She goes out to the kitchen and gets a glass of water from the sink and drinks it in one big, sloppy gulp, water running down her chin onto the cherries on her sweater. She can't remember the last time she drank water like this. She goes back to the bedroom and sits down on the bed and rubs her temples. She'll leave at first light. Who knows when Gwen will get up? She'll probably sleep until noon. She still lives that life.

Amy's not sure what to do until she meets Alessandra at one. She doesn't want to go back to her apartment. She doesn't want to check in on Diane or Mrs. Epifanio. She likes having Alessandra to focus on now. Lunch with Alessandra means remaining in character.

The sun doesn't rise until seven. Amy's been unable to sleep and has spent her time flipping through a pile of photography books that Gwen keeps stacked on the floor near the bed. She's had to strain her eyes to see the pictures. Three of the books are by Camilo José Vergara. Pictures of ruined buildings and cities in decline. Amy's almost cried a few times looking at them.

She gets up and writes a note for Gwen, then attempts to leave the room as quietly as she can. As she's walking past the dresser, the blond wig catches her eye again. It's the same blond she was before she went dark. A different cut, though. She likes the idea of putting it on, of furthering her costume. She takes the bandanna out of her hair and stuffs it in her pocket. A little package of bobby pins is on the dresser between two of the heads. Amy knows enough about wigs to know that she has to put her hair up and try to find a wig cap if she wants to wear this. She wonders why Gwen even has it, if it's some kind of cosplay thing. She wonders what Alessandra will think. She'll know it's not her hair. She saw the picture on Gwen's Instagram. Maybe she'll think she's sick. She starts to put her hair up with the bobby pins.

"There's a wig cap in the top drawer," Gwen says, dry-voiced.

Amy turns to her. "I'm sorry if I woke you up," she says. "This reminds me of the color my hair used to be. I just wanted to try it on."

"Go for it." Gwen gets up and stretches. She comes over and helps Amy find a black nylon wig cap in the drawer and then takes over pinning her hair. She stretches the cap out with both hands and puts it on Amy's head.

Amy looks at herself in the mirror over the dresser with only the cap on, her hair tucked away.

"I wear this at shows a lot," Gwen says, removing the wig from the Styrofoam head. "I used to have a few others. When I'm drunk, I like to take them off and throw them into the crowd." She fits it over the cap. She tells Amy she has to kind of reach in between the wig and the cap on both sides and click two little clips into place. Amy does that. Gwen adjusts the wig and smooths it down.

Another look in the mirror. Amy in the wig is Amy unknown. Her former self mixed with her new self. A woman in trouble. A woman in hiding. She smiles like an actress.

"Wear it," Gwen says. "Keep it, if you want. You look fucking badass."

Gwen invites her to brush her teeth and stay for coffee, and Amy takes her up on it. She has no reason to go home. She'd change for Alessandra, but she doesn't want to risk going back to her apartment. Her clothes reek slightly of mothballs, but maybe she can bum some of Gwen's oil.

Mike and Danny come out, yawning. They get back to work on their guitars. Mike gives her a thumbs-up for the wig. Danny hardly seems to notice the difference.

"You're meeting Alessandra, huh?" Gwen says, pouring water from a measuring cup into an electric kettle.

"I'm sorry about being on the phone in the middle of the night like that," Amy says.

"I wasn't eavesdropping."

"I know, I know."

Gwen gets two mugs and fits a pour-over dripper on one. She scoops Holy Grounds dark roast into the filter. When the kettle boils, she pours the water over the coffee in a slow circular motion. She hands Amy the first mug and then repeats the process for herself.

"Maybe I shouldn't have posted that picture?" Gwen says. "I know you're not really on social media or anything."

"It's okay."

"You know, it's been good hanging out with you again after so long, but you've managed to tell me nothing about yourself. Where you live. Work. Who you're seeing. Nothing."

"Sorry."

"No apology necessary. It's actually pretty impressive. That wig really completes the picture. A mystery woman."

Amy laughs this off but still manages not to talk about herself. She wonders what her life would be like if she'd stayed who she was. If she'd kept working at Seven Bar and moved here to Williamsburg with Gwen. If she'd kept her records. If her heart hadn't been shaken by faith, by the strange desire to help.

A couple of coffees later, Gwen's given her the rundown on just about everything and everyone she can think of. What's become of Nix and Edie. A quick story about the guy they used to know who kept a bottle of aspirin taped to his hat. Norma the painter's success. Jill and Sylvia's move to Vancouver. The Ukrainian's disavowal of the Lower East Side. Raised rents, broken people, cashed-in chips. Mike and Danny improvise an instrumental piece that casts a melancholy feeling over the apartment.

Since Amy's phone is practically useless, she maps the walking route to Tom's Restaurant on Gwen's iPhone. Then she goes into the bathroom and brushes her teeth with her finger, using Gwen's minty toothpaste. The kush oil is out on the counter. She dabs her wrists with it.

When Amy finally leaves, it's after ten. She doesn't even think about taking off the wig. It's part of her. Gwen gives her a big hug and pecks her on the cheek and says she should come back soon, don't let it be years again. Amy nods. Gwen says next time she wants to hear all about *her* and she's going to try to talk her into moving to Williamsburg, assuming she doesn't live here already, mystery woman that she is. She says that Danny's moving to Portland in March, and they'll have a room opening up. Amy says she'll think about it, for sure.

Outside, the sky is gray and it looks like rain, but the temperature hasn't dropped much. Up the block, on the corner of Marcy and Hooper, is Trans-figuration Roman Catholic Church. She's heard about it. Read about the history of the church and the good work they do in the parish. The South-side Mission. But she's never been.

Truth is, she's spent very little time in Williamsburg over the years. Her biggest memory is being here with Merrill at some party. They were on a roof. This was before Williamsburg got to be what it is now, this gentrified hipster wonderland. It had a dangerous edge to it then. You felt like you could get mugged at any time. Merrill was wasted. She was standing on the ledge of the roof, swaying, a can of Busch in her hand, moonlight reflecting off her face piercings. Amy had to pull her in. She can't believe she ever dated someone like Merrill.

What she's thinking she remembers reading about Transfiguration is that it has Tiffany windows. She wants to go in. She wants to see the beautiful stained glass windows. The church mostly serves the Latino community here, she knows. She wishes there was a Mass now. In Spanish. She wishes she could go in and kneel and pray. This church is far more beautiful than St. Mary's. It's old. It's seen the way the world changes. It's proof that maybe certain things *don't* change. She remembers that there's a Transfiguration Church in Queens, too. Maspeth. She's never been there either.

A large statue of the Virgin Mary looms in the garden behind the gate. She has a white wooden fence built up behind her, like a grotto. Amy sees that the gates are closed. She imagines herself walking into the church. The smell of myrrh. Those gorgeous windows. She imagines feeling light-headed, having to sit down in a pew. It's as if she knows the inside of the church, never having seen it. She imagines Fred slipping into the pew next to her.

She doesn't even try the gate. She crosses the street and presses on.

It's about a two-and-a-half-mile walk to Tom's. Pretty straightforward. Right on Rutledge from Marcy, Classon for a long stretch, right on Sterling Place, and then come out on Washington Avenue and the restaurant will be right there. She's got the route memorized. She likes keeping maps in her mind. Only about an hour at a normal pace. She'll take it slow. She'll get there a little early to secure a table. She's nervous to see Alessandra. And she's happy. She's happy to feel a little happy. Everything else that's happened feels far away. Until she looks across the street and is sure she sees Dom watching her from an alley between two apartment buildings.

12

There's no way it could be Dom. There's no way he'd know it was her if it was him. Not with the wig. But he'd probably at least realize she was the same woman he saw at Homestretch the day before. She's in the same clothes. Another possibility enters her mind: he's not after her because he thinks she witnessed him killing Vincent; he's just a psycho stalker who decided to follow her when she walked out of the bar.

Probably it's just her eyes playing tricks on her, like at the Starbucks with Fred. She's reluctant to go back and confirm what she thinks she saw. She moves faster.

Just off Classon, on Myrtle, she ducks into a coffee shop and orders an Americano. She sits at a table and watches out the window, waiting to see if Dom appears on the sidewalk outside. No sign of him. She checks her phone. No messages from Alessandra. Nothing else from Diane or Mrs. Epifanio. She wonders if Mr. Pezzolanti will call, worried sick that she didn't come home last night.

Time passes. She's shaky from all the coffee and hungover from the
booze and tired from getting up in the middle of the night and afraid at
the possibility that Dom is on her trail. She taps her foot against the floor.
The coffee shop's nice. Spare. Quiet. She's anxious, watching people pass on
the sidewalk through the letters on the window. Every face could be Dom's,
but none are yet. She wants to shake some of this returned paranoia before
meeting Alessandra. A copious amount of coffee probably isn't the best idea.

She leaves the coffee shop and walks aimlessly for a while, passing Tom's
Restaurant once and walking through Prospect Park a little before doubling
back. By twelve forty-five, she's got a table at Tom's and more coffee. It's
been a long time since she's been here. Back in the early days at Seven Bar,
her friend Abby had dragged her over on a Saturday morning and they'd
waited on a long-ass line to get in. Abby thought it was the place that
Suzanne Vega sings about in "Tom's Diner," but she had that wrong. Later,
they found out a lot of people get that wrong. Amy's never been here with
Alessandra. They wouldn't have had many reasons to hang out in Prospect
Heights.

She tears open a sugar packet and pours the sugar on the tabletop, pushes
her finger through it, and looks around. Pictures and signs on the walls. A
few people at tables around her with big plates of pancakes. She feels like
they know about the wig and they're laughing at her. She looks at the menu.

Alessandra arrives, and Amy's heart jumps. All that black hair. She's
wearing shoes that make her a little taller. Super skinny high-waisted jeans.
A white chambray shirt with no wrinkles. Dark aviator sunglasses. She
didn't have fifteen pounds to lose, but she's lost at least that much. She's
the actress. Memories flood in. Kissing that neck. Listening to records, legs
entwined on the couch. Drinking. Showering.

Amy stands. They hug. Alessandra's wearing perfume that smells like the
beach.

"Nice wig," Alessandra says.

"It's Gwen's," Amy says. "I look stupid?"

"I like it. You okay? You look upset."

They sit across from each other. Amy plays with the handle of her coffee mug. Alessandra takes off her sunglasses, sliding them into her breast pocket. The waiter comes over and interrupts. Alessandra orders a coffee.

"I'm fine," Amy says, finally responding to the initial question, trying to perk up. "How are you?"

The waiter brings back Alessandra's coffee. She empties in a packet of Splenda and stirs with her butter knife. "I'm okay. Crazy. Just had an audition in the basement of a church. It's for this low-budget boxing movie. The role's a boxer's wife who gets raped by her husband's opponent. I mean, Jesus Christ. This is the kind of shit I keep auditioning for. One worse than the next."

"I heard you were just in a horror movie, but I haven't seen it."

"It sucks. Don't see it. It's called *Hair Trap*. I get killed by a guy in a wolf mask. But I met my friend Phoebe on it, and she's a genius. She's trying to make this movie she wrote called *Accomplice*, and it's gonna be really fucking good. She wants me for one of the leads. So, there's that."

"You're doing pretty okay?"

"I'm fine. Los Angeles is fine. I don't know. I'm a dog walker. It's fine. Everything's fine."

"Dog walker, huh?"

"Pays the bills. I'm one of those dumb bastards you see walking around with eight little rich people's dogs on leashes. I take them to the park, and I consider the shitty choices that led me to where I am. Some of these dogs, their assholes are bleached. I'm not even kidding."

Amy laughs. "And I heard you do yoga? Gwen gave me the full rundown on your Instagram."

"I have the pants and the mat. I go sometimes. The life I present on social media isn't real. I don't like dogs. I don't like yoga. It's just another way of auditioning."

The waiter comes back, and they order food. Alessandra gets the lemon ricotta pancakes and an egg cream. Amy gets a fried egg sandwich and a cherry-lime rickey. They work on their coffees. Amy's not sure where to go with the conversation. She has the overwhelming desire to come clean with Alessandra. To tell her about church and about bringing communion to shut-ins. To tell her about Vincent and Dom and Fred and Diane. To hold up her hand and show her how it's shaking. To ask if she saw a sketchy guy outside on her way in. Alessandra, of all people, would understand her twisted motives, her private fears. She knows about Bob Tully. She's the only one who knows.

"Tell me what's been going on with you," Alessandra says.

"Nothing much," Amy says.

"You're still around the old neighborhood, huh? I really can't believe that. And you're still not on Facebook or anything? I've got all these people I don't give a shit about, and I know what they do, where they live, where they work, what they're eating, how many dogs they have, when they're sick, what their ugly kids had for breakfast. You, I'm actually interested, and I don't know anything anymore. It's 2017, and there's no real trace of you online. That's why I was so excited to see Gwen post that picture." She pauses to take a breath. "I'm rambling, I'm sorry. I miss you."

"I miss you, too."

"You should come to LA sometime."

"When do you go back?"

"Tomorrow morning."

"You're here just for the auditions?"

"I had to meet up with my Aunt Cecilia yesterday. She owed my father a thousand dollars before he died, and I guess she wanted to feel okay about herself, so she scraped it together and gave it to me. She lives out on Long Island now. I took a fucking Uber there. Stopped at the cemetery to visit my folks. That sucked. Holy Garden's so sad and ugly. Everything here's sad and ugly to me. The money came at the right time, though. I didn't know how I was gonna pay for this trip. I've got, like, six hundred bucks in my checking account right now." Alessandra takes a sip of coffee. "You're stalling. You're not telling me shit about yourself."

"I work at a bank. I live in a little basement apartment. I still have a flip phone. I've been pretty happy." Two truths and two lies. She's not sure what the bank lie is all about. Alessandra won't be impressed. It just seems like a good, easy cover. She had a crush on a Russian girl who worked as a teller once. And of course she wants Alessandra to think she's been happy. That's natural when talking to an ex, even in the throes of a crisis.

"You seeing anyone?"

"No. You?"

"Not now."

"You were?"

"This EMT. Sid. He was nice. I wreck everything. I wrecked that one good." Alessandra pauses, motions between them. "I wrecked us."

Their food comes. Alessandra digs in. She downs half her egg cream in one long slurp. Amy picks at the edges of her sandwich.

"I can tell something's wrong," Alessandra says, her mouth full. "You forget how well I know you. You forget what it's like to be around someone who knows you so well."

Amy takes a bite of her sandwich and then spits it out into a napkin, nearly retching.

"It's not good?" Alessandra says.

"It's good," Amy says. "It's just me."

"Tell me."

"I saw something I shouldn't have seen."

⟸⟹

From Tom's, they go to Prospect Park. Amy is harried, anxious, looking all around for Dom. She opens up to Alessandra. Tells everything there is to tell. Where she lives and what she does and how she really dresses these days. The ordeal with Vincent at Mrs. Epifanio's a couple of mornings ago. Following him. Homestretch. The murder. Vincent's apartment and the picture she found in the book. Her fear that she's being followed. Diane. Identifying Dom as the killer and then running off to the city.

"You're fucking with me, right?" Alessandra says.

"I'm not," Amy says.

"So, not only do you not usually wear a wig, you're telling me that you normally dress like you teach kindergarten at a Catholic school and you go to church all the time and you just pretty much hang out with old people. Amy Falconetti, is that really you?"

"You're making fun of me. You think I'm being paranoid."

They sit on a bench near the Picnic House. The park is beautiful around them, but Amy can't take it in or think about it.

"I was afraid for a while after I saw that kid get killed," Alessandra says.

Amy remembers her first days with Alessandra, how they met at Seven Bar and went back to her place in Queens. How Alessandra almost got chased away by Merrill the next time they met up. And how, that third time, Alessandra came to her a mess after having witnessed Ray Boy Calabrese's nephew, Eugene, get gunned down on the subway tracks. It was in all the papers. Alessandra's name wasn't, though. She was worried about the Russian who'd killed the kid coming after her. He'd told her to keep quiet. She told Amy about all of this at Seven Bar that very night over beers and shots. They wound up back in Queens, tangled in her bed again. They were inseparable after that. Alessandra trusted her. Amy kept quiet about it. No one else knew what Alessandra had seen. When Amy moved to Gravesend to live with Alessandra, it was as if none of it had ever happened. One of those things from the past that feels like it must have gone on in an alternate reality. After a month together, Amy told Alessandra about Bob Tully. And now there's Vincent. Their history has linked them in this way. Both witnesses. Both with secret knowledge of the other.

"You keep your head down, that's all you can do," Alessandra continues. "Don't report it. Go throw the knife in the water. Just mind your own business. The things you did and saw that you shouldn't have done and seen, just forget them. I don't have to tell you that. I remember what you told me about that neighbor of yours in high school."

"I know," Amy says.

"You can drop this new church life if you want, Amy. You can drop the act."

"It's not an act." A beat. "I don't think it's an act."

"You following this Vincent, that was you subconsciously wanting out of this corner you painted yourself into. That's all religion does, paints you into a corner. You got out young when your mom died, but you got tempted back, because you were looking for something to fill the void. There's nothing to fill the void."

"Jeez, Al."

"I don't think this guy's following you. You're imagining it."

"I witnessed a murder."

"You already have a membership in the club. You know what not to do." Alessandra stands. "Let's go to my hotel room."

Amy nods. "Okay."

She gets up, and they walk south. Some of the quiet trails through the park make Amy feel extra uneasy. Alessandra grips her arm. "There's no one but us," she says.

A long walk to the hotel. Probably two miles. It occurs to Amy that she's walked almost five miles today—walked off her hangover, at least. And if anyone's following her, she's giving them one hell of a workout.

She feels safe with Alessandra. It feels good to be with her, natural, even in this part of Brooklyn, which feels so unfamiliar. This big, beautiful park that she couldn't imagine living near. A neighborhood she'll never be able to afford. Families wandering around with carriages and snacks, hopeful, happy-seeming.

Once out of the park, they make a right on Fifteenth Street. They're quiet now. Amy is listening to the sounds of the street. They're passing plenty of good bars along the way. One dark little dive called Zito's that looks like a fine place to hide out and drink a day away. Amy almost suggests it. She's nervous about going back to the room. She's not sure what's going to happen. She hasn't been with anyone since Alessandra. Alessandra's probably been with lots of people. Women and men. Amy isn't sure she wants to sleep with her. She isn't sure it's right or if she's capable of it with all that's going on. But she is in disguise. She tells herself there's *that*, at least. Maybe she can continue to channel her old self, even if only for a couple of hours of pleasure. Alessandra's leaving the next day. There's no future here, no past to bring back to life for more than one night. Returning to what's familiar for solace isn't a crime. It's human.

On Fourth Avenue, they make a left. The sky is getting darker. It looks like rain's on the way. The hotel is on Fourth between Twenty-Fifth and Twenty-Sixth, close to the train. The building is modern, bright red brick, almost looks like a new wing of a hospital. Alessandra had called it Brooklyn Way, but a yellow-and-blue Best Western sign hangs over the front door. Brooklyn Way is probably just an alternate name to make people feel better about booking a stay at a Best Western. Next door is a C-Town supermarket. The Gowanus Expressway is one block west. Green-Wood Cemetery is one block east.

Amy's been over here a couple of times, because Our Lady of Czestochowa–St. Casimir Church is right around the corner on Twenty-Fourth Street. Another beautiful old church. She went to Mass in Polish there once with Monsignor Ricciardi. She doesn't remember noticing this hotel.

Alessandra's room, on the third floor, is clean, small, and spare. Nondescript landscape painting on the wall. An unmade queen bed. The TV on. Heavy smell of that beach perfume she's wearing. Towels crumpled on the floor. A bra hanging from the bathroom doorknob. Amy's trying to remember the last time she even stayed in a hotel or motel. Probably that time she and Alessandra went to Atlantic City for the weekend. They stayed at a Howard Johnson a few minutes' walk from the Steel Pier. They'd gambled a little at the Showboat. They'd had a big fight that weekend and slept in separate beds.

"I've got booze," Alessandra says, locking the dead bolt and then snapping the door guard into place. She goes into the bathroom and emerges with a half-full bottle of Seagram's gin.

Amy sits on the bed. "I don't know, dude. I tied a pretty good one on last night. I haven't been drinking the last few years."

Alessandra unscrews the cap and takes a pull. She passes it to Amy. "Come on. Don't make me drink alone. I drink alone way too much. I drink with the dogs. No shit. I keep a little pint of gin with me. That I don't post on Instagram."

Amy takes a sip, wiping her mouth with the back of her hand. "My father also showed up."

"Your father? I thought he was dead."

"I thought maybe he was. I didn't really know. I just knew he was gone."

"What'd he want?"

"Just to talk. To try to make things right."

"And?"

"I couldn't deal with him."

"I say, fuck that." Alessandra reaches out and grabs the bottle back, takes a drink. "Guy can't just waltz back into your life and expect to make amends."

"I know."

"Shit, you've had a lot going on the last couple of days."

"And now here you are."

Alessandra sits next to her on the bed. "Take off the wig. Let me see your hair."

Amy removes the wig, dropping it atop a tangle of sheets.

Alessandra laughs at her in the cap.

Amy swats her leg and plucks the cap off. Her hair, pinned up, is messy.

"So dark," Alessandra says. "Almost as dark as mine."

"I just wanted a change."

"It's pretty."

Amy looks down at the carpet. "I haven't dated anyone since you. I haven't been with anyone."

"No one's touched you in all this time?" Alessandra says.

Amy shakes her head.

Alessandra puts her hands on Amy's neck, her fingers curling up into her hair, dislodging a couple of bobby pins. "I can't believe that."

"No one," Amy says.

In the shower, their old rhythms return. Same bodies, under water. Same ways of touching. Same lips. Same ways of reaching for the gin in the caddy hanging over the nozzle. Same ways of passing the bottle back and forth and laughing. It feels like six years ago. It feels new. Alessandra touches Amy's tattoos, as if she's surprised they're still there. Amy knows this won't last. The joy she's feeling is countered with melancholy. Tomorrow, Alessandra will go back to Los Angeles. Tomorrow, Amy will have to reckon with reality. But it's not tomorrow yet. She's lost in the nowness of now. She's trying to convince herself to be happy. She *is* happy. Her arms are around Alessandra's waist, her head buried in her neck. Alessandra's hand is between her legs, moving. The heavy sound of the water. The water running into her mouth. The smell of that beach perfume. Amy missed this.

Afterward, lying naked on the bed, they watch whatever movie's on TV. Something with Anna Kendrick. Amy watches old movies now and then, but she hasn't watched anything new in a while. She doesn't have cable at her place. She doesn't even have Internet, so she doesn't stream movies on Netflix like everyone else. Alessandra talks about how much she likes Anna Kendrick. She says she just read her memoir; her friend Lucy let her borrow it. She says there's this one movie with her—not this one that's on now—called *Happy Christmas* that she loves. Anna Kendrick plays a character named Jenny she really relates to. She says she wishes she could land a movie like that.

Amy gets cold and pulls the blankets up over them. She settles her head comfortably on Alessandra's chest. Alessandra strokes her wet hair. Amy puts her hand on Alessandra's belly.

"You should come to LA for a bit," Alessandra says.

"I don't have the money to make a trip like that," Amy says.

"I know."

"You don't ever think about moving back?"

"I can't. Not again."

Amy's feeling woozy, relaxed. Her eyes close. She's slept very little in the last few days, but she doesn't want to sleep now. She wants to talk to Alessandra. She wants to just be naked with her. Alessandra's fingers in her hair are a drug.

"You're falling asleep," Alessandra says. "Poor baby. You must be so tired."

Amy sits up and shakes her head, holding her eyes open. "But I don't want to sleep."

"Rest. You need it."

Amy leans over Alessandra, nestling her head against her neck again. She kisses her chin. She kisses one shoulder and then the other. She kisses down her body. Such warm skin. She slides to her knees on the carpet, pulling Alessandra to the edge of the bed, hugging her legs, the sheets pushed away. Alessandra puts her hands on the back of her head. Amy flutters her tongue in the fluttering place. Alessandra is moving beneath her. Amy thinks of taking communion on her tongue. There's laughter from the TV. Alessandra's soft noises are making Amy want to cry. *Not now*, she tells herself. *Not while doing this.* Still, the tears come. Down her cheeks into her mouth. Their saltiness mixing with the taste of Alessandra.

⟨═══⟩

Another movie, legs entwined now. Amy's afraid of saying the wrong thing. She's afraid of letting Alessandra know how much this all matters.

"Tell me more about your father," Alessandra says.

"It didn't sound like you were interested," Amy says.

"Of course I'm interested. I'm just wondering how he has the balls to strut back into your life like this. What's he look like? I want to visualize the fucker."

"He's pretty sad-looking."

"I'm sure."

"He's got that look that old alcoholics and stray dogs have. Like you just caught him eating out of the garbage."

"You feel bad for him?"

"I don't feel bad for him. I don't know what to think. There was a time, after my mom died, when I would've . . . I don't know, I would've at least wanted to give him a shot, I guess. I was a kid; I would've had to give him a shot."

The sound of rain comes suddenly from outside. The wind whips up. There's something about the way wind swooshes against a hotel room window. It's probably not even night yet, but with the curtains pulled and the hovering gloom from the storm, it's dark in the room, except for the light of the TV. Amy cuddles closer to Alessandra.

"That's nice," Alessandra says.

"What?"

"The rain. Listening to the rain."

"It is." Amy presses her face into Alessandra's hair. "I'm scared. I don't know why I do what I do."

"Don't be scared. You're fine. Nothing's wrong. You need to start new. I know you wanted to help people, but you're killing yourself. You were better off in bars. You were helping more people serving them drinks."

"Maybe."

"You *were*. And you followed this guy for the same reason you followed your neighbor in high school. You're in a rut. Getting close to the edge gets your blood pumping. Dating Merrill was like that, too."

The TV blips off. The room goes totally dark and still. Nothing but the sound of rain and wind.

"Did we just lose power?" Alessandra asks.

"We did," Amy says.

"That seems crazy. A little storm, and we lose power like that?"

"I don't know." What Amy wants to say is, *I hope the lights stay off. I wish we could stay like this forever.*

"Should we go out to a bar?"

"Let's stay here. You have more gin."

"Let's go to a bar. They have umbrellas downstairs." Alessandra's hands around her waist, tugging at her a little.

"I don't want to be around other people."

"You just want to be here in the dark with me?"

"Right."

"I get it."

"You do?"

"Of course. I'm desirable." Alessandra laughs. Her laugh is throatier than it used to be. Booming. Echoey. Probably from cigarettes. "Where's the gin? I don't see the gin."

"It's around," Amy says. "I can't see anything."

"If we're staying here, I need the gin nearby at all times." Alessandra separates herself from Amy and gets up. She clunks around in the dark. Her feet on the carpet make a rustling noise. She's headed toward the bathroom.

Alone in the bed, Amy stretches out. She can't remember the last time she's stretched out like this in a big bed. With fresh-smelling sheets, no less. All she ever does is curl up on her little twin mattress on the floor, resigned to discomfort.

"I found it!" Alessandra says from the bathroom. "I'm sitting on the toilet, and I'm taking a big fucking swig right now." The sound of Alessandra starting on her stream mixes with her glugging down gin.

"Come back," Amy says. On the nightstand, she sees the small light of her phone, indicating she's missed something. She picks it up and flips it open. A voice mail from Diane. She presses it to her ear in the dark and listens.

Diane's voice is cracked, broken-sounding. She says, "Amy? Please, call me. I want to ask you something about when you were at Vincent's apartment. I'm so sick over here. Just call me when you get a chance, okay?"

Amy feels a pull of guilt. *Tomorrow.* She'll deal with it tomorrow. She closes the phone and powers it down, then puts it back on the nightstand.

Alessandra stumbles back into the bed, the gin sloshing as she settles next to Amy. "Who were you talking to?"

"No one," Amy says. "I was listening to a message."

"From who?"

"The mother. Diane."

"Christ, Amy, what are you doing?"

"I don't know. You think I'm nuts?"

"Far be it from me to judge you, dude. I just want you to be careful. Say this lady goes crazy, after asking you to dig around in her dead son's apartment like that. Forget the guy you think's following you. Be afraid of this mother. She comes undone, watch the fuck out."

"Going there was so stupid."

"Have some gin." Alessandra pushes the bottle at her, the cap gone for good.

The rain lashes harder against the window. Amy takes a pull of gin and it sends shivers through her. She imagines Diane at home, sitting at the table in her kitchen with cold tea. Staring at photos of Vincent. Wondering why someone like Amy would present herself so ominously just minutes before she found out about her son's murder, linger to help, and then go AWOL.

Tomorrow, she tells herself again. *Save these thoughts for tomorrow.*

They finish the bottle, and then they sleep.

Amy jolts awake when the TV comes screaming back on. She's totally lost track of time. Alessandra is still asleep next to her, sprawled on her stomach. Black hair curtained over the pillow. Arms up. Hands cupped together near the headboard. Little wrinkles on her shoulders. A sheet covering her bottom half. Her back rising and falling with every breath.

A movie with Denzel Washington is on TV. He's trying to stop a runaway train. Amy finds the remote buried in blankets and thumbs down the volume. She presses the info button to see what time it is. Almost midnight. The power was out for a long time. It's still raining, thudding against the window. Slick sounds from outside of car tires on wet pavement. Amy's not sure what time Alessandra's flight is. Just like her to leave it a mystery.

Amy flips through the channels and settles on some nature show. An armadillo digging a burrow. A soothing voice prattling on over the action. She goes over to Alessandra's open suitcase and takes out a blue Dodgers T-shirt and a pair of black American Apparel jersey boy briefs with a white elastic waistband. She pulls the shirt on over her head and slips into the briefs. The shirt is big and loose, but the briefs are a little tight. Alessandra's clothes used to fit her perfectly, but Amy's sure she's gone down a size. She fumbles through the suitcase. More clothes. So much underwear for such a short trip. A coffee-stained script for the boxing movie; it's called *Caught Cold*. Amy flips through it. Alessandra highlighted the parts for a character named Vicki. A Ziploc bag holding some pills is scrunched into a pocket on the inside of the front shell. Amy wonders what they are. Probably something to help Alessandra sleep. She doesn't need them now. Or she took one on the sly, washing it down with gin.

Amy walks to the door and presses her eye to the peephole. Nothing scarier than looking at a hotel hallway through a peephole: ominous carpet, murky light, sad walls, the big blank door opposite them, that hum of silence. In her case, there's the added fear that Dom will show up, emerging from the elevator and rushing toward their door.

Alessandra sighs in her sleep. Amy goes back to the bed and curls up next to her. She wants to stay awake. She feels a little scraped out from the gin and all the drinking with Gwen the night before, but she also feels at peace. She doesn't want to close her eyes. She doesn't. She focuses on the TV, that armadillo. And then the ceiling. Rain against the window. Fucking rain and fucking peace. She drifts away, one arm flung over Alessandra.

⋯⇥⋯

When Amy wakes up, Alessandra is gone. She expects to hear the shower. She doesn't. Some show about the ocean is on TV, schools of colorful fish gliding smoothly underwater, soft blue light dappling the carpet and bed. Dramatic music. Amy's first thought is that it's early and Alessandra went to get them breakfast and coffee. She expects she'll be back to the room any second with foil-wrapped bagels and avocados to mash up with little plastic forks. Maybe a couple of Roma tomatoes.

Amy rises, yawning, stretching. She goes over to the window and draws back the curtain. It's light out, probably seven or eight. The rain's done, and the sky's clear. But, judging by the heavier jackets and hats people are wearing out on the street, the temperature's dropped. She expects to see Alessandra emerge from C-Town or the bodega on the opposite corner.

She's still wearing Alessandra's boy briefs and Dodgers shirt. She's cold, so she picks up the blanket and wraps it around her.

She notices then that Alessandra's suitcase is gone.

She goes over to the lamp on the desk and flicks on the switch. The light illuminates a hotel notepad. A cheap pen, uncapped, partially blocks the words on the paper. Alessandra's handwriting, sloppy and rushed. Amy reads the note:

Am,

Didn't want to wake you. My flight's early, so I caught an Uber to the airport. Checkout's 11. Stay until then. And try not to worry too much. No one's following you. Everything will be fine. Forget what you saw. It'll only bring you trouble. Start over. Gwen will help, I'm sure. Come visit me in LA sometime. I had fun last night. I have a headache from the gin. This flight's gonna suck. Still got a lot of love for you.

—Al

Amy had woken up feeling peaceful. The feeling has faded. Leaving like this is such a deeply predictable Alessandra move, she should've seen it coming. Alessandra's not into good-byes or emotional scenes. The state Amy's in, Alessandra probably anticipated things getting weird and bailed. Amy wonders if she actually has an early flight or if that's just a bullshit excuse to get away. Doesn't matter. Reality's back. She rips up the note and tosses it in the trash can.

Amy watches a little TV. Morning news. It makes her sick. She shuts off the TV and takes a shower, putting the door guard back on before she gets in. She stays in the shower until her skin starts to get pruny.

When she gets out, she dries her hair and pins it back up. She finds the wig cap and wig on the chair next to the bed and puts them on. She likes the idea of staying who she is now. Without the wig, she fears drying up, retreating. She stands in front of the mirror, wearing only the wig. Her tattoos are still there. She remembers that she'd dreamed they'd disappeared. She puts on Alessandra's shirt and underwear. She's wearing them because they'll keep her close. She gets dressed in the swing trousers and cardigan. The underwear she wore the day before, she just throws into the trash can with the torn note. She wishes she had makeup. Aside from that, she feels prepared. She has a plan.

13

Her plan is that she'll go home and grab a few things and then leave her sad life behind. The life where she's Mr. Pezzolanti's tenant, where she delivers communion to old folks, where she eats Chinese food and has a crush on a woman who has no interest in her. She'll leave it behind for something new, something truer to who she used to be. Maybe Alessandra's right. Following Vincent was a cry for help from a version of her that once existed. *You don't have to live this way. Go back to the edge. Here's a map.*

A happy by-product is that Fred will also lose her trail.

What she thought she saw yesterday, Dom following her after she left Gwen's, that can't be. It's the paranoia. Alessandra's right. Alessandra's right about everything. Whatever else someone can say about her, she knows how to survive. Amy wants to call Alessandra. She wants to see if she really got on that plane or if she's off having breakfast somewhere, waiting for a later flight, afraid to deal with Amy's shit.

She takes out her phone, powers it on, and calls Gwen. It goes straight to voice mail. "Thanks again for letting me crash," Amy says. "It was great seeing you. I'm sorry I didn't tell you anything about myself. What I'm stuck with right now, I'm not happy. I want to start over. I come there, you think I could stay for a week or two until I get a room and a job somewhere? Would your roommates mind?" She pauses. "This is Amy Falconetti, by the way." She folds the phone and stuffs it in her pocket. She was trying not to think about it too much, but she noticed there weren't any new voice mails from Diane.

Before leaving the room, Amy searches for any traces of Alessandra. She knows very well that she's the kind of person who forgets jewelry, floss, socks. But she's left nothing behind. Amy shuts off the TV. She leaves the room and lets the door thump closed behind her. The hallway is quiet. She gets chills.

She leaves the hotel and hustles across to the Twenty-Fifth Street station. She thinks she can catch the D there. It should only be about a twenty-minute ride back to her apartment. Or what she's now thinking about as her former apartment. She hopes she can get in and out without running into Mr. Pezzolanti. She wants to pack a few things, that's all. Mostly the contents of her egg crate.

She's glad it's such a short walk to the station because it's much colder now. The streets are wet, gutters thick with puddles.

She remembers that the D only stops here late nights and waits for the Bay Ridge–bound R. She can take that one stop to Thirty-Sixth and then switch for the D.

When the train finally comes, she gets on and decides not to sit, to stand and hug a pole. A man in a black tracksuit, a big plastic bag at his feet, stares at her. He's got grimy features. His sneakers are new. She looks through the scratched glass at the station wall's mosaic tiles as they pull away.

"You like that pole, huh?" the man in the tracksuit says.

She ignores him.

"You heard me?" he says. "You like that pole, and I like your costume."

"Fuck off," Amy says through gritted teeth.

"Oh, she bites."

Amy fumbles along to the other end of car, hovering over an old woman reading a Chinese newspaper. She rushes off at the next stop and watches to make sure the man in the tracksuit doesn't follow her. He doesn't.

The D train rumbles into the Thirty-Sixth Street station. She gets into a near-empty car, and a woman skitters in behind her. Amy sits down in a center-facing seat and crosses her legs. She looks down at her lap. Out of the corner of her eye, she sees the woman, diagonally across from her, readying a stack of cards. The woman is young, maybe in her late twenties, and she's wearing a ratty green sweater and men's jeans. She comes over and puts a card on the empty seat next to Amy. Amy looks at it: *I have a one-year-old daughter at home. Anything will help.* The woman heads down to the other end of the car where four other people are clustered close together. Amy watches as she puts cards on empty seats next to them. They don't look up. They don't acknowledge her. She collects the cards quickly and heads back to Amy. Amy takes out five dollars and gives it to her. The woman nods and picks up the card. She gets off at the next stop and moves on to another car.

Back in her neighborhood now. *Former* neighborhood. It feels good to think about it that way. Amy watches the tops of buildings: graffiti, wet brick, dramatic roof puddles. Old signage that always catches her eye. Fire escapes, pigeons on windowsills, drawn shades.

She gets off at Bay Parkway and walks down to street level. It occurs to her that she doesn't have a bag at home. She's not going to bring much, but she should get a backpack. She stops at one of the little Chinese gift shops selling paper dragons and striped NYC caps and umbrellas and weird little dancing dogs. Everything's three bucks. She walks in and finds a cheap blue backpack that looks like it will hold everything she needs it to hold, some clothes and tapes. Everything else, she'll leave behind.

Except the knife. She's going to do just what Alessandra said, walk down to Gravesend Bay and throw it out into the water. The picture, she'll rip up and throw out in one of the overstuffed cans on Eighty-Sixth Street.

She pays for the backpack. Three dollars. The zipper's a bit frayed, and it'll probably fall apart in a week, but that doesn't matter much.

As she leaves the store, her phone dings. A text from Gwen: *yeah!!!!!!!!! come live with me, motherfucker!!!!!!!!*

Amy laughs. She's definitely making the right decision.

When she turns onto her block, she sees that Mr. Pezzolanti is standing outside the front gate, half blocking it, looking nervous. She approaches him, the backpack slung over her shoulder.

"Help you?" Mr. Pezzolanti says.

Amy says nothing. She considers for a second how she should play this. She doesn't have the guts to pretend to be someone else. Say a long-lost twin.

"Amy?" Mr. Pezzolanti says.

"It's me," she says.

"You had me fooled. You okay? I was worried."

"I'm okay."

"That's a wig?"

"It is."

"You hiding out from your old man?"

"Something like that." She wonders if she should be straight with him. Tell him she's moving out. Moving on. She can't deal with that now, though. He'll tell her don't worry about the money. Stay for nothing, he'll say. It'll probably be too hard to refuse. She'll agree right on the spot, go in and change back into her other clothes. She'll think about Mrs. Epifanio and Monsignor Ricciardi, and she'll resume living this dead-end life, the last however long being nothing but a weird blip.

"You need anything?"

"I'm good."

"Well, you need anything at all, you let me know. Okay? I like the look, I do. You remind me of how the girls used to dress back in the fifties. You're not careful, I'm gonna invite you out for dinner and a show." Mr. Pezzolanti pauses, fondles a spike on the gate. "I haven't seen your old man around, that's what you're worried about."

"I don't think he'll come back."

"Chased him off, huh?"

Amy nods and squeezes past Mr. Pezzolanti, a move she wouldn't usually make. In the past, if he was blocking the gate, she'd wait for him to finish his small talk and step aside before moving in toward her apartment.

Surprised by her forcefulness now, Mr. Pezzolanti stammers a little and says, "I like the backpack. You going to school?"

"No," Amy says, not turning to look back at him.

She walks down the steps and keys open her apartment door. It's the one time since Vincent's murder that she's truly let the paranoia slip away. She enters the apartment with her head down, closing the door behind her. When she looks up, she sees that the killer is there waiting for her.

⊰⊱

A good scream will bring Mr. Pezzolanti running. He's not that far away, after all. Fifteen feet. Less. Amy doesn't scream. Dom is just sitting on her bed, drinking a venti Starbucks coffee with his name written on the side in big black letters. He's wearing a satin Jets jacket with snap buttons and the same jeans and boots. He doesn't have a weapon—that she can see. She thinks of the knife in the freezer. If she could just get to it, she could use it to fend him off. He looks calm, relaxed.

"How'd you get in here?" Amy says.

"I'm not good at much," Dom says, "but I'm good at stuff like that."

"My landlord will call the cops. He's right outside. All I've gotta do is yell his name."

"Don't do that. Just don't."

"Or what?"

"I want to talk to you, that's it."

"About what?"

"You know who I am?"

Amy treads lightly. "The guy from Homestretch."

He laughs and slurps down some coffee. "I like the wig. It's a good addition. But you're going to a lot of trouble for nothing. I know what you know. I know what you saw. I'm not worried about it. I believe that if you were gonna do anything, you would've done it already. I believe you're smart. A city girl. You know how to keep your mouth shut. You don't need to get dressed up and run away from me. Let's get that out of the way right now. Okay?"

"I'm not running away from anything," Amy says.

"When I saw you at the bar, it took a second to register you were the same girl."

"Same girl as what?"

"Sweetie, drop the act."

"Don't call me sweetie." She should be more scared than she is. She was right. He *knows*. He's been watching her. She wonders if he realizes she has the knife.

"What's your name? Tell me your name."

"I didn't see anything. I don't know who you are. I just know you were at Homestretch yesterday."

"I saw you. Without the wig. In your normal clothes. I saw you go to Vincent. I know you saw me stab him. I believe you didn't know it was me until I walked into the bar."

"Have you been following me?"

"I followed you here from the Roulette afterward. Other than that, just a little. You're hard to keep up with." He stands up and comes over to her. He drinks more of his coffee. He's standing close to her. Almost toe-to-toe.

The coffee on his breath is strong. "Can I tell you what I want? Let me start with a question. I know you've been to Vincent's place. What's your aim? You looking for something?"

Amy swallows hard. Nothing to do but tell the truth at this point. He has her pegged. "I don't know why I did it. I'm not looking for anything."

"Okay," Dom says. "Okay. Now we're talking." He takes two steps back, his coffee breath a whisper in the air now. "I want you to know something. I'm not a bad guy. That's why you don't have to be scared of me. Vincent, he was a bad guy. What I did to him, I did because he was a bad guy. You don't have to be afraid of me. That's straight? Even if you wanted to go to the cops—and I know you won't—I wouldn't do anything to you."

"Are you looking for something?" Amy says. All she can figure is the knife. It can't be the picture.

"Something belongs to me, yeah."

"What?"

"Tell me your name first. I'm Dom, but you already know that."

She hesitates. "It's Amy."

"Amy, you and me are gonna be fast friends, I can tell."

Dom sits on one of the folding chairs at the little table, the same seat Fred occupied when he showed up that first time. She's had no one in this apartment other than Mr. Pezzolanti for years, but now Fred *and* Dom have been here in the same week.

"Sit," Dom says, motioning to the other chair.

Amy scrapes the chair out and sits on the edge of her seat, setting down the backpack at her feet.

"You don't look comfortable," Dom says.

"I'm not," Amy says. She feels for the phone in her pocket. It's as if Gwen's message is getting further away. Amy's being sucked into something else altogether. It was stupid to come back. She's stupid for not trusting her instincts about Dom. She's stupid for tempting fate. And yet, she feels oddly at ease. This moment with Dom has purpose; she's playing her part.

"You're making me nervous, sitting like that."

"Like what?"

"On the edge. Like you're gonna try to bolt any second."

"Tell me what you're looking for, and I'll tell you if I've seen it." Her eyes dart to the refrigerator again. She's thinking about the knife, how she can pull it on him and chase him away. Maybe he's just gutless. Maybe Vincent *was* a bad guy, and Dom reacted that way because he was scared and dumb. Scenarios play out in Amy's mind: Vincent was bringing Dom somewhere to kill him, and Dom cut it off at the pass; Vincent had stolen something valuable from Dom and wouldn't give it back; it was over a woman, drugs, guns, money, all of the above. Could be anything. Vincent remains a mystery. Dom's one, too.

"I can see your brain's working overtime, trying to figure this shit out," Dom says. "What's most important is you understand I'm a decent person. What happened, it happened because of Vincent. We're clear on that, right? You've gotta take me at my word. Did you know this guy at all? I've known him a lot of years."

"Tell me about him," Amy says, and she's surprised by her own words.

Dom sits back. "Well, for starters, he killed a guy in high school and got away with it. This Ecuadorian at the park in Dyker Heights. No shit. I go back that far with him. We were at Our Lady of the Narrows in Bay Ridge together. We'd get off the B1 on Thirteenth Avenue every day after school and hang out in that park. There were all these Mexicans and Ecuadorians who'd started hanging out there, a lot of them old guys, in their forties. Playing soccer, drinking out of brown bags. Kept to themselves."

Amy's trying to picture these younger versions of Vincent and Dom. She knows Our Lady of the Narrows. Alessandra went to its sister school, Bishop Kearney, and they often joined forces for dances and plays. She knows the uniform: blue shirt, tie with a gold emblem, dark slacks. She always sees boys from the school waiting for the bus at Twenty-Third Avenue.

Dom continues: "One afternoon, this is junior year, Vincent gets a bone up his ass about these guys. He goes over to them. 'You don't belong here!

Get the fuck out of this neighborhood!' The guys don't really give him the time of day. Vincent rallies a couple of other guys, John and Cal, and they disappear for fifteen, twenty minutes. I'm still there with my buddy Iggy. Vincent comes back, charged up. He's got the fucking leg of a table. John's got a bat. Cal's got a two-by-four. Vincent starts again, waving the bat around. 'Get the fuck out of this neighborhood!' A few of the foreigners, they get the message and get the hell out of there. One of them—Manuel, his name was, I'll never forget, because I read it in the paper the next day—he's drunk, and he kind of staggers in Vincent's direction and says something. I don't even hear what. But Vincent clocks him right across the fucking head. The guy goes down. Vincent just keeps pounding him. John and Cal take off. They were thinking threats; they weren't thinking 'beat an old drunk to death.'"

"Jesus Christ."

"I'm just sitting there. I can't fucking believe it. People are watching. It's obvious he's killing the guy. Nobody intervenes. Not me. Not nobody. You know the deal. You walk away, you don't get involved. When Vincent's done, the guy's limp. Blood everywhere. Vincent books it out of the park. I walk away, go straight home. A little while later, I hear sirens. Everybody around knows it was Vincent. Nobody's gonna rat him out. Somehow, it doesn't get back to the cops. This poor Manuel guy was homeless. It's all forgotten in a week. You were ever out drinking with Vincent, he'd brag about it. He'd tell you what it felt like swinging that table leg."

"How come you didn't say anything to anyone?"

"My parents would've killed me."

"Why are you telling me this?"

"Just, you know, so you know that this is who Vincent was. This is the kind of shit he carried around with him. I did the world a favor."

Amy tries to reconcile this Vincent with Diane's grade-school darling. Same kid who made that frame out of Popsicle sticks killed this homeless guy with a table leg, maybe ten years between those two things.

She catches herself. Who's to say Dom's not lying? Maybe he's the one who killed the guy in the park and got away with it, just like he killed Vincent and got away with it. Maybe he sees an opportunity to put that on Vincent, to put everything on Vincent.

"You don't believe me?" Dom says.

"Why should I?"

"I'm a good guy, I'm telling you."

"I don't think guys who keep insisting they're good can be very good."

"That's not nice," Dom says, looking down at the floor. "Can I tell you a story?"

"I got a choice?"

"You're free, Amy. Come on. Don't do that. You're free."

"I'm so free, why do I feel like a prisoner?"

"We're all prisoners to an extent, right?" He sips some coffee. "I'm getting too philosophical. Fuck it. You don't mind, I'm gonna tell you this quick story. Short one. When my grandma was in hospice, I'd go see her every day. I'd get off work—I was working construction then—and I'd go over and I'd sit with her. She was half-dead. I'd just hold her hand. Sometimes I'd read to her. I'm not a very good reader, but she seemed to like it. She didn't say much to me. A few words here and there. *Water. Nurse.* I don't remember what else. Right near the end, I was with her, and she looked at me and somehow managed to say, 'Get out of here. Get away from everything.' She knew me. She knew how trapped I felt by my old man. That's what she wanted for me. That kind of freedom. I'm telling you this because I want you to understand. Vincent got in my way. I was close. This fucking close." He pinches his thumb and index finger together.

"I don't get it."

"Let me backtrack. To understand, you gotta understand my old man. Tony Mescolotto, that's my old man. You heard of him?"

"No," Amy says.

"He's kind of well-known around these parts. He's a big-shot jeweler, but he used to play piano in a lot of clubs in the city and whatnot. I don't know shit about piano, but I've always been told he's great. Anyhow, you wanna talk bad guys, my old man's a bad motherfucker. Drunk. Gambler. Womanizer. Beat the shit out of me all growing up. Especially on Sundays." Dom stops. "I can see what you're thinking. You're thinking I'm gonna talk you to death. I'm not trying to, I swear. I just got a lot to put in context in terms of the whys and hows. You're bored?"

"Just tell me what you're gonna tell me."

"I can be honest with you, Amy. It's a good feeling."

They sit there in silence for a few seconds. Dom seems to be chewing over where the story's going. A sort of white noise feeling has settled in Amy. A knock on the front door shakes them.

"Who's that?" Dom says in a whisper. "Your landlord?"

"Probably," Amy says.

"What's he want?"

"I don't know. He likes to check up on me."

"What do you want me to do?"

She parrots the line back: "What do you want *me* to do?"

Dom stands. "You're not my hostage."

Another knock. Harder this time.

"I'll go in the bathroom," Dom says. "How's that? I'll hide in the bathroom." He raises his finger, as if he's warning her of something, but he doesn't say anything else. No threats. No directions to not reveal he's there. He closes the door behind him, and she can hear him sit on the toilet.

Amy goes to the door, playing through her options. Let Mr. Pezzolanti know she's in trouble? Or just push him out of the way and take off, away from Dom and the whole mess? Forget what little stuff she wants—just go to Gwen's. But Dom would probably know to look for her in Williamsburg. She has to remind herself that he actually was following her, at least for a while.

Amy puts her hand on the knob and slowly opens the door. Mr. Pezzolanti's there, but he's not alone. Diane is standing next to him. She's red-eyed, sniffling. A handkerchief dangles from her closed hand. She's in the same clothes and smells stale. "Amy?" she says.

"Looks different, huh?" Mr. Pezzolanti says. "I didn't even recognize her."

"What's going on?" Diane asks.

"I'm sorry I missed your calls."

"I was worried about you."

"Poor lady," Mr. Pezzolanti says. "I was just saying how sorry I was about Vincent. A tragedy. I hope they get the bastard who did it."

"Can I talk to you?" Diane says to Amy.

Amy doesn't say anything. She's stuck on thinking about Dom in the bathroom.

"If it's a bad time, we can talk later," Diane says.

"It's fine," Mr. Pezzolanti says. "Right, Amy? You can talk to Diane."

"Of course," Amy says.

"I think that blond hair's turning you a little ditzy." Mr. Pezzolanti forces a laugh.

Amy's about to step outside. "Let's go get some coffee somewhere," she says to Diane.

"You mind if I just come in?" Diane says. "I'm not in any condition to go anywhere. I can't stand on lines. I can't be around other people. I keep seeing Vincent everywhere."

Amy moves aside to let Diane in.

"I'm here, you two need me," Mr. Pezzolanti says, retreating toward the gate.

Amy closes the door.

"Nice little place," Diane says.

"It's not much," Amy says, trying to keep her eyes away from the bathroom door. She's sure she can hear Dom breathing. She's sure Diane can hear him breathing.

Diane sits down at the table, the seat probably still warm from Dom. Amy notices that the venti coffee is right there in front of her, his name on the side of the cup. Diane must know Dom. He said that he went to high school with Vincent. They might've even gone to grade school together. The name is facing Amy. Diane doesn't see it. Amy scoops it up and drops it in the garbage even though it's half-full of lukewarm coffee.

"Thank you again for being with me during such a hard time," Diane says.

Amy sits across from her, rubbing her hands together. She's sure Diane can tell that she's on edge. Then again, she's probably too preoccupied thinking about Vincent. "I'm just so sorry you're going through this," Amy says.

"Thanks." Diane leans forward on her elbows. "Can I ask you to do me a favor? It might be strange. It's probably not a decent thing to ask."

Amy, interest peaked, leans in, too. "What is it?"

"Can you take the wig off? I know we don't know each other well, but I don't even feel like I'm talking to you."

"Sure. Of course." Amy unfastens the clips and takes off the wig, setting it in front of her and clutching it like a bouquet of shiny fake flowers. She leaves the wig cap on, bobby pins poking through the nylon. She feels like an actress again, sitting in a trailer, about to be made up or taken apart.

"You don't mind me asking, what's that all about?"

"The wig?"

Diane nods. "And the clothes."

"I was with a friend of mine," Amy says. "She's a musician. She likes wigs. She put it on me, and I liked it. It reminded me a little of the way I had my hair years ago. And the clothes, well, they're mine. This is the way I used to dress."

"You had a whole other life, huh? Vincent had a friend in high school who went through a—whaddayacallit?—goth phase. Like that?"

"I guess."

"What I said in my message, I wanted to ask you about when you were at Vincent's to get the suit."

"Right. I'm sorry I didn't get the chance to call back. I got swept up with my friends."

"It's okay. It's just my brain won't stop working. Who would do this? I'm going through every possibility. I can't accept it's random."

"Sure. That's natural. You've gotta believe the police are doing their job."

"I went down to the precinct. I didn't like that captain. I've seen enough shows; I know the way these things end. 'We tried everything, ma'am. No murder weapon. No witnesses. No leads. Zilch. We're sorry for your loss.'"

Amy thinks of the murder weapon, right there in the freezer, just a few feet away. Diane so close to it that Amy's amazed she can't feel some magnetic pull to it. Forget the fact that the man who stabbed Vincent with it is also so close Diane can probably smell his breath if she tries hard enough.

"They'll turn up something," Amy says.

"When you were over there," Diane says, "did you see anything weird? I remembered that the last time I saw Vincent, he was on the phone with someone and he was agitated. I didn't get what they were talking about. Vincent never liked to think I was eavesdropping on him, so I tried to tune out. But did it look like anybody else had been in there? Did you see anything out of the ordinary at all? I know you weren't looking for anything other than the suit, but you never know."

"You can go over there," Amy says. "You can see for yourself."

"I did that."

"And?"

"That landlord of his, Marie, she'd been in there. Cleaning the place. Piling his stuff up in one corner, getting it ready to go. You believe that? If there was any trace of anything, it's gone now. She even threw things out, things *she'd* determined to be trash. I can't get over the gall. I was in my right mind, I'd sue her."

"Jeez, that's awful."

"I've got your memory to go on, that's it."

"I don't remember anything out of the ordinary. I got the suit, and that was all." Dom was in Vincent's apartment; Dom's in the picture she found of

Vincent and a strange woman; Dom's in her bathroom right now. All these choices she's made, they've led her to protecting Dom.

"I figured it was a long shot." Diane slumps in the chair. Defeat after defeat.

"Did you tell the police about his apartment yet?"

Diane nods. "They were with me when I went. They didn't do anything about Marie."

"You want something to drink? Tea?"

"I'm fine."

"You're taking care of yourself? You feeling any better?"

"Trying. I think I'm just about over this flu."

Dom's phone rings in the bathroom, "Eye of the Tiger" blasting through the door. Jesus Christ. To Dom's credit, he doesn't make any additional noise. He doesn't even silence the ringer. Amy's sure she can play it off as no big deal. *Just left my phone in the bathroom, Diane, that's all.*

"What's that?" Diane says.

Amy remembers that Diane saw her basic little old-school flip phone when she was over there. She borrowed it in the My Way car to call Andy Capelli. She'd probably be able to guess that this ringtone couldn't possibly match that phone. "Just the phone," Amy says, not specifying *which* phone. "I left it in the bathroom."

"You can answer it."

"It's okay."

The song stops. Silence.

"Vincent's wake is today, four to six," Diane says. "At Capelli's. I decided on the one visitation. I don't know who's going to come. Maybe more people than I thought since it's been in the news. Will you come?"

Amy nods.

"And the service is at St. Mary's tomorrow morning at ten."

"Can I do anything?"

"I don't think so. I've got to figure out how to get dressed. I don't even have anything to wear. Probably I'll have to go down to Kohl's. My son's funeral, and that's what I'm thinking about."

"I can come with you, if you want."

"That's kind. But it's okay. I'll be okay." Diane gets up, leaning against the table. She's a little unsteady.

"I'm sorry, Diane," Amy says. "About all of this. If I remember anything from the apartment, I'll let you know. The cops will get this guy." She stands and accompanies Diane to the door. When she opens up, she sees that Mr. Pezzolanti is still out by the front gate. He catches a glimpse of her in the wig cap and seems scandalized.

"I'll try not to bug you anymore," Diane says.

"You're not bugging me at all," Amy says.

Diane leaves, stopping to talk to Mr. Pezzolanti. Amy closes the door. She lets out a sigh of relief. Dom stirs in the bathroom. He comes out, iPhone in hand, tapping the screen. He looks up when he's done writing. "What the hell was that all about? Vincent's mother? You went to see her?"

Amy nods. "Jesus Christ, your fucking phone."

"Whoops."

"What if she knew that was your ringtone?"

"She doesn't. No way. Why'd you go see her?"

"I don't know. Guilt? I didn't say anything to her about you."

"I appreciate that, I do. Maybe we're on the same page."

"We're not on the same page. I was just thinking what a bad position that'd put me in." She tunes her voice to a whisper. "Vincent's killer in my fucking bathroom."

"You know, one time I watched her shower. Diane. No shit. She used to be nice—to look at, I mean, before the years beat her down. I was over at Vincent's. We were in his room, playing *Grand Theft Auto*, me, him, and our friend Mikal. I go out to the kitchen to get a soda. I pass the bathroom twice. On the way there, the door's closed. I can hear the shower running. Way back, the door's open a crack and I can see in. Damn right, I take a peek. She's under the water. I can see in because she's got one of those see-through shower doors. It's steamy, but I'm looking real hard through that steam. I always figured she opened the door. She wanted me to see her."

"We done yet?" Amy says.

"Not yet. You went to Diane's place, what else did you do you didn't mention?"

"What are you looking for?"

Dom goes back to the table and sits down. "You threw out my coffee? I like that shit cold."

"Your name was right there on the side. Diane sees that, then what?"

Dom shrugs. "Vincent stole a purse full of jewelry from me."

"You had a purse full of jewelry?"

"I told you, my father's a jeweler. He's got so many pieces he made for my mother and grandmother, diamonds, pearls, gold, you name it. He has this closet in the attic of our place where he keeps it. We live a couple of doors down from that Jewish high school. Big old house He's got my mom's old purses and shoe boxes filled with shit. Ziploc bags stuffed in jacket pockets. You ever went in there, you'd just think it was a closet of nothing. Clothes in plastic, old bags, shoes. You dig around a little, *bam*."

"And?"

"I snagged a couple of the purses, figuring he wouldn't miss them. I hate my old man. He never gave me a thing. Never taught me his trade. Never taught me to play piano. Just beat the shit out of me and yelled and acted all disappointed. He thinks I'm uncultured. Low. He's ashamed I'm my age and still live at home. I figured this was my ticket out, sell all the shit for some good bank and go down to the Caribbean. I had a guy in Borough Park was gonna buy everything for what I considered a good price. I had a Russian in Coney was gonna hook me up with papers and a new ID. I was gonna start over. Date a waitress, hang out on the beach, drink beers with limes on the rim, like in those commercials. No more Homestretch."

"Start over, just like that?"

"Right. But I learned the hard way what I should've known all along: talking gets you nothing but trouble. I was drunk off my ass one night and I mentioned it to Vincent, and his little cockroach brain started doing backflips. I told him I'd stashed the purses in my trunk since I couldn't keep them in the house. He wanted that dough. He wanted out. Three nights before what happened, my car was broken into. Nothing missing but the jewelry. Not my radio, not my piece in the glove compartment, not my Jordans on the floor in the back. I knew it was Vincent. Who else?"

One thought crosses Amy's mind: Vincent was hiding the jewelry in Mrs. Epifanio's bedroom. Had to be. And Dom, somehow, doesn't know Vincent went there three days in a row—the three days right after the jewelry was ripped off. It's the perfect hiding spot, with Diane having the key and the room mostly unvisited and untouched.

"What is it?" Dom says.

"*You* learned talking gets you nothing but trouble?"

"I'm telling you because I can sense you've got a code. You're no thief. Help me find the jewelry, and I'll cut you in."

"Didn't you say your father had more up there? Why not just go after that?"

"The truth is, I want to be done with him. I want to get this stuff—*my* stuff—and go." He scratches his jaw. "I got a limited window of opportunity here. With Vincent dead, who knows what becomes of all this jewelry if I don't find it soon? And if my old man gets wind of what I've done, he'll fucking lock me in the basement and chain me to the boiler. He did that to me once, you know that? When I was nineteen and conned a guy I didn't know was Paulie Lo Biondo's kid out of the keys to his motorcycle and a five-hundred-dollar bottle of Scotch. Help me out here, Amy. Please. I'll give you five grand."

The way Amy figures it, she's got three options: (1) She tells Dom, and they go and get the jewelry at Mrs. Epifanio's. The purses are probably just stuffed behind the dresser or in one of the drawers. Easy. She gets Dom off her back that way, and she's got five grand for her troubles with which to start over in Williamsburg or maybe even LA. (2) She doesn't tell Dom, and she keeps the jewelry to herself, if it's there. That'd make her something else altogether, something she never saw herself capable of being. It'd also open up a world of logistical problems. Who would she sell the jewelry to? How do you make contacts like that in this world? (3) She gets Dom out of her hair right now and reports everything to the police. The murder, the jewelry, whatever else. It means coming clean about her own strange behavior, but that's the cost. She might have to spend the rest of her life trying to understand why she's made the decisions she's made in the last few days, just as she's always been hung up on her high school years. Being with Alessandra again made her remember what desire was, all the things she's sought to control and tamp down in her religious life. She's desperate. Maybe she's always been desperate.

After a moment of hesitation, she says, "Can you give me the five thousand now?"

"I can probably scrape it together."

"Go get it. I think I know where your jewelry is."

14

Dom says he trusts her. He's going to borrow the money from Bernie at Homestretch and then he'll pay Bernie back when he sells the jewelry to the Borough Park guy. Amy wants the money first because she doesn't want to wait on him. Waiting on him means not leaving. It also means another avalanche of potential problems—things falling apart for Dom, his father catching on, the murder coming to light. The money's not much, but it's more than she has now, and she desperately needs something to start over with. She's not a criminal. She's not greedy. A chance has fallen into her lap. The God-fearing side of her could make a case that this is all meant to be.

But Dom doesn't trust her *that* much. He wants her to come with him to get the money from Bernie. And then he wants to go with her to wherever she thinks the jewelry is. She hasn't yet told him where exactly she believes it's hidden. He makes a couple of veiled threats. "Don't do anything against me," he says. "Be a good girl, okay?"

Amy puts on the wig and packs her backpack. There's not much she wants or needs, just what's in the egg crate in the closet: sketches of her tattoos and more old clothes. The bag's not big enough to fit the few records she held on to. She doesn't care. She gets her toothbrush and makeup from the bathroom. Her Walkman and tapes. She leaves the library books and everything else. When Dom's not looking, she grabs the envelope with the knife and picture in it out of the freezer and stuffs it in the front pocket of the backpack. She looks around. She's not coming back. It already feels like an apartment where no one lives.

Dom says his car is parked in the St. Mary's lot. They need to get out of the apartment without Mr. Pezzolanti seeing them. Amy devises a plan to distract him: she'll go out and ask him if he has batteries she can borrow for her Walkman. He won't think twice. She could easily run over to Eighty-Sixth Street and grab a package, but he won't think of that because he'll be flattered she's asking him for help. When he goes in to get the batteries, Dom can escape to his car. Amy will wait for the batteries and then meet him there.

"How do I know you won't just take off on me?" Dom says.

"I haven't yet," Amy says.

"True enough."

The plan goes off without a hitch. While Mr. Pezzolanti skitters inside, Dom rushes to his car. Amy waits for the batteries. Mr. Pezzolanti brings back ten double As in a sandwich bag fastened with a stringy green twist tie.

"I only need two, Mr. P," Amy says.

"Take them all," Mr. Pezzolanti says. "I won't use them."

Amy takes the bag. "You sure?"

"Of course, of course."

"Thanks, Mr. P." Amy's tempted to hug him and say thanks for everything, but she knows that'll make him aware that something's off.

"I really do like the hair."

Amy walks up the block and turns into the St. Mary's lot. Dom is sitting behind the wheel of a red Dodge Daytona that must be from the eighties. The trunk is open a bit, the lid kept in place with a frayed length of bungee cord. She's about to get in the passenger side when she hears someone call her name.

She turns. Monsignor Ricciardi is sitting on the bench at the far end of the lot closest to the rectory. He's wearing jeans and a Fordham sweatshirt, and he's got a brown bag in his hand. Crumbled bread is scattered at his feet, a few pigeons pecking at it on the wet pavement. "Amy, that's really you?" he says, rising and walking over to her.

"Monsignor, I'm sorry, I'm in a rush," Amy says.

"You look so different."

"I know. It's nothing."

"Is everything okay?"

"Fine."

He leans down and looks at Dom in the car.

Dom raises his hand from his thigh, giving Monsignor Ricciardi a nervous little wave.

"Is that Dominic Mescolotto?" Monsignor Ricciardi says.

"Hey there, Father," Dom says.

Amy is stunned into silence. She was hoping not to be seen with Dom here. She was hoping not to be seen at all. She would've also guessed that there was no way Monsignor Ricciardi could know Dom, who clearly isn't a churchgoer. But she always underestimates how tangled the wires of the neighborhood are.

"How's your mother?" Monsignor Ricciardi says to Dom.

"Just terrific," Dom says.

Monsignor Ricciardi explains to Amy: "Dom's mother helps out with flower arrangements at Emilio's on Bay Parkway. We go way back, though she no longer attends Mass. Every time there's a funeral, I talk to Mrs. Mescolotto." He pauses. "In fact, I'm sure I'll talk to her later today, because of Diane Marchetti's son."

Amy looks away, over the roof of Dom's car, at the row houses across the street. An old woman she doesn't recognize sits on an overturned egg crate, shining a pair of men's shoes with newspaper and black polish.

"How do you two know each other?" Monsignor Ricciardi asks.

"We don't, really," Amy says.

"I'm just selling her something on eBay, that's it," Dom says. "One of them old Casio keyboards. It's in good condition. I'm taking her to look at it now."

Monsignor Ricciardi nods. "You're taking up keyboard, huh, Amy? Gonna give Katrya a run for her money? With the outfit and the hair, maybe you're joining a band?"

"Maybe," Amy says, aware that she's being short with Monsignor Ricciardi in a way that she's never been.

Monsignor Ricciardi's face tells her he recognizes her tone: someone who has no interest in him or what he's peddling. "Can I talk to you a sec before you go?" he says.

"Sure," Amy says, stepping reluctantly away from Dom's car.

"Privately, if you don't mind?"

"Like I said, I'm in a rush."

"To buy a keyboard? Just come feed the birds with me a minute."

They sit on the bench, Amy keeping her backpack between her feet. Monsignor Ricciardi opens his bag and takes out a piece of stale Italian bread, hands it to Amy. She accepts it. She looks across at Dom in the Daytona. He's antsy, jerking around under the wheel, pawing at his phone. Amy crumbles the bread and tosses some on the ground.

"I met your father," Monsignor Ricciardi says.

"You what?" Amy says.

"He came and introduced himself to me."

"He shouldn't have done that."

"I understand how hard this must be for you. If I may speculate, I think Fred coming back into your life like this has been real tough for you. He told me everything. Must be quite a shock to the system. Things like this, they can cause us to slip back into old bad habits. I can't help but notice that Fred's arrival has coincided with you abandoning your responsibilities."

"*Abandoning* is a strong word. Just . . . stopped. Out of necessity, at first. I was helping Mrs. Epifanio. Other things have gotten in the way."

"People depend on you. They look forward to seeing you. We've gotten several concerned calls. 'What happened?' 'Is Amy okay?'"

"I'm sorry. I can't do it anymore. I can't do any of it."

"This is about your father?"

"It's about me."

"Talk to me, Amy. I'm here to listen, to help. We don't want to lose you, that's all. A lot of people around here love you. A lot of people are awfully grateful you're in their lives. I'm one. You've made this parish better."

"That's nice of you to say."

"It's true. I'm not just saying it."

Amy crumbles a bit more bread and tosses it in the direction of the pigeons. If word gets around, especially if Dom is found out, she knows how this will look to Monsignor Ricciardi, in retrospect. Like she's an accomplice. And he doesn't even know she's got the murder weapon in her bag and that she's on her way with Dom to pick up the jewelry that Vincent stole. She thinks about decisions, how all these lines cross at once. Vincent steals from Dom; Dom stabs Vincent. Mrs. Epifanio. Diane. Fred and Alessandra thrown back into her life in the middle of this mess.

"Thanks for your concern, Monsignor," she says. "I'm fine. Everything's good."

"Your father wants to reconnect with you. I want to help him do that. I think he deserves your forgiveness," Monsignor Ricciardi says. "I think that's a good place to start."

"I didn't ask your advice," Amy says. She gets up and walks back to Dom's Daytona.

Dom hits the gas, and they scream out of the lot, Monsignor Ricciardi left scratching his head on the bench, pigeons pecking around at his feet.

Amy feels unsure about trusting Dom. She'd have to be stupid not to doubt him. One thing she knows is that he killed Vincent, whatever the circumstances were. He could be bringing her anywhere. She certainly doesn't believe he's honest, and she sees the holes in his story, but she *does* believe what he told her about the stolen jewelry, and she believes they're headed to Homestretch to get five thousand bucks from Bernie. And that money is where her mind is at right now. She's tried not to let her mind get consumed by money, but she's in a jam, and money's what you need when you're in a jam.

"A keyboard?" Amy says.

Dom shrugs. "You know what I heard about that guy?" he says, turning onto Twenty-Third Avenue.

"About Monsignor Ricciardi?"

"Yeah, who else?"

"What'd you hear?"

"I heard he eats his macaroni with maple syrup."

"What?"

"I'm not shitting you. Macaroni with maple syrup. My mother told me that."

"Who cares how he eats his pasta? He's a nice guy. He's always been nice to me."

"I know, I know. My mother likes him, too. That's just weird, right? What's he, Canadian or some shit?"

They're at Homestretch in no time at all. Dom pulls up right out front and leaves the car idling. "Bernie says we're good," he says. "I texted with him while I was waiting for you to get done with Father Whatshisname. You wait here." He climbs out and hustles into the bar.

Amy just sits there, more time to consider how absolutely goddamn crazy this situation is. Vincent's blood is probably still on the sidewalk just up the block. She opens the glove compartment. Earlier, when he was telling her about how Vincent stole the jewelry from his trunk, Dom had mentioned the other things Vincent didn't take from the car. A gun in the glove compartment was one.

It's here, and the exact kind she'd imagined. Something bought at a pawnshop or from a van in some alley. Dirty. Probably hot. She thinks this is a good opportunity to get rid of the knife. To put it right there next to the gun. She takes the envelope out of the front pocket of her backpack and empties the knife onto her leg. She wipes it down with her shirt. She scoops it up with the envelope and deposits it in the glove compartment behind the gun. She closes the glove compartment, wiping down the latch with the sleeve of her cardigan. She's relieved. That's one inexplicable bad decision adjusted. The knife's back where it belongs. The picture she's keeping for now. She tucks the envelope back into her backpack.

The door to Homestretch claps open, and Lou comes bounding out. The guy in sauce-stained whites who hit on her relentlessly when she was here. He motions for her to roll down her window.

She doesn't.

He talks through the glass. "You're in the same clothes and I'm in the same clothes," he says. "How about that?"

She doesn't respond.

"I saw you through the window. I like the hair. A lot. Tell me it's a wig. I'm fucking fascinated by wigs. Had a teacher in grade school I was in love with, wore a wig. Found out later she was sensitive about a bald patch she had over her ear."

"Leave me alone," Amy says.

Lou's breath is fogging the glass, his voice only slightly muffled. "Tell me one more thing. You're not with Dom, right? Can't be. Come on. How'd that happen? Beautiful girl like you? He's a fucking caveman. You want a drink? Have a drink with me. Forget Dom. One time, I saw him eat a dead cockroach off the bar on a dare. He won't give a shit. He's used to losing."

Amy takes out her phone. She opens her contacts and clicks ENTER for Alessandra. The phone rings five times and goes to Alessandra's voice mail.

Amy doesn't say anything. Lou's still standing there, like an animal in a zoo waiting for her to throw him a handful of food. He bangs on the glass as Amy closes the phone. She entertains the idea of taking out the gun and showing it to Lou, but that'd be dumb.

A bald man in his sixties, toothpick clenched between his lips, turns the corner from West Tenth and notices Lou. The man's in a nice suit, wearing a purple flower on his lapel. Fancy watch. Gold rings on both hands. His head is shiny. The wispy hair on the back of his head is greasy and curly. Amy watches him in the rearview mirror first and then turns to watch through the glass as Lou's attention is diverted to the man.

"Lou, where is he?" the man says, raspy-voiced, ballooning his chest out.

"He's inside with Bernie, Mr. M," Lou says.

It takes Amy only a second to ascertain that this is Dom's father. Tony Mescolotto. Trouble.

"Bernie's the one who called me," Tony says, and then he takes a good long look at Amy. "Who's she?"

"Just some broad from the bar," Lou says.

"How do you know my son, sweetheart?" Tony says, leaning close to the glass.

Amy looks straight ahead, ignoring Tony.

"Sweetheart, you hear me?" To Lou: "She deaf?"

"She's not deaf. She's just a tough nut. She likes me, Mr. M."

Dom comes charging out of Homestretch, one of those white Priority Mail envelopes from the post office folded under his arm, Bernie fast on his heels. "Jesus Christ, Bernie, I thought I could trust you here," Dom says.

"What do you need five large for?" Tony says to Dom.

"I'm sorry, Dom," Bernie says. "I figured you were in trouble."

Dom's headed for the car. Tony gets in front of him and puts a hand on his shoulder. Dom swats it away. "Get out of here, Pop," Dom says.

"Out of here?" Tony says. "What's going on? You're in trouble? Bernie says he thinks you're in trouble."

"I'm not in trouble."

"What then? Tell me. You got this broad knocked up?"

"Fuck off, Pop."

"Oh, that's no way to talk to your old man," Lou says. "That's Mr. M right there. The majestic Mr. M. Made my mother's favorite ring."

"I tell your mother you talked to me like that, she'll break down," Tony says. "You want to kill your mother, that's what you want?"

"Yeah, my mother's got other things on her mind," Dom says, and he runs around to the driver's side and gets in under the wheel. He looks at Amy and shakes his head, makes a face like he's disgusted. He hands her the envelope. She unfolds it and opens it and looks inside. A big stack of crumpled twenties. "There's your money," he says.

Bernie and Tony conspire together by the front of the car. Amy can't hear what they're talking about. Lou winks at her. She stuffs the envelope full of money in her backpack.

Dom puts the car in gear, and they lurch away from the curb. He pulls a quick U-turn on Kings Highway, just missing a beer truck that's grinding to a stop outside 3 Stars. A couple of cars beep at him. He pounds the wheel. "Fuck Bernie," he says. "Calling my old man like that."

"Your father didn't seem like the guy you described," Amy says.

"Never mind," Dom says. "Tell me where I'm going."

⇥

Now it's Amy's turn to tell Dom to wait in the car. They're parked outside Mrs. Epifanio's. She hasn't pointed out the house or told him who lives here yet. Guiding him here, she started to feel a creeping sense that this was definitely the wrong road to go down. Beyond the pale. Epic as fuck, in terms of how stupid she's being.

"No way," Dom says, throwing the car into park and yanking the key from the ignition. "I'm coming with you. I'm gonna be there when we find where this fucker hid my shit."

"Your father's not a bad guy at all, is he?" Amy asks.

"Forget about my father."

"What else are you lying about?"

"You got your money, right?"

"The house where we're going, the woman who lives there is very fragile."

"I'm smooth. I'll be smooth."

"You know what? Forget this. I can't."

"Which house? This one right here?" He points at Mrs. Epifanio's.

"This is so fucking stupid. What am I doing?" She pulls her backpack up into her lap. She takes out the Priority Mail envelope and shoves it at him. "Keep the money. I don't want it."

"It's too late, Amy. You're close. This is almost over. Don't make a mistake. You don't want to regret anything." He takes the envelope and sets it on the dashboard.

"You're threatening me?"

"It's not a threat. I'm talking smart. You and me, we're a team here."

"We're no team."

"Do me a favor and open that glove compartment."

She ignores him.

He reaches across and unlatches the glove compartment. It falls open. He points to the gun. "You see that? You want me to use that? I can force you to do this, or we can walk in there as a team. What do you say?" He doesn't pick up the gun. He just lets it sit there as an object of possible doom.

Amy knows the score. Once a gun enters the picture, it doesn't just go away. What she's more worried about now is that he'll notice the knife she planted— though thinking about it that way makes it sound like she's the murderer, like she's got something to hide. Whatever happened between them, however it really went down, he stabbed Vincent in the throat with that knife.

"What the fuck is that?" Dom says, leaning across her, realizing her worst fear. He pushes the gun aside and grabs the knife. He holds it up in front of her. "Where'd this come from?"

"I don't know," she says.

"It wasn't there before." He flicks it open and studies it. The burnt bone handle. The steel blade. "You took this from the scene? Why would you do that?"

"I don't know what you're talking about."

"You know what this is, right?" He presses the blade against her neck.

Amy pulls back in her seat.

"You took it," Dom says. "Why?"

"I don't know."

"But you took it?"

"Yes."

"And you put it back here?"

"I just wanted to get rid of it."

He takes the knife away from her neck and snaps it closed. "I didn't want to do that, but you freaked me out. Bad." He pauses. "Listen, things are going awry here. Bernie calling my old man threw me off. He gives me the money *and* calls my old man. That's Bernie for you, a complex individual. I didn't lie about Vincent; everything I said about him was true. Killing the homeless guy with the table leg, ripping me off—all true. I lied a little about my old man just to spruce things up, you know? Take me to where the jewelry is and then we'll be done. I'm not mad about the knife. I'll take care of the knife. You did the right thing giving it back to me. The more I think about it, the more I think you did the right thing. I believe you don't know why you took it. That's human. A lot we do as a species, we don't understand."

Amy is rattled, breathing in heavy bursts.

"Settle down, okay?" Dom says. "I'm not a bad guy. Give me a do-over." He glances out the window. "You want to go across the street? I saw a deli. I'll buy you an AriZona Iced Tea. I love that shit. Ever since I was a kid, my big treat to myself was to go buy an AriZona."

"I'm good," Amy says.

"Let's get this over with then, okay? Look, I'll put the knife back." He tosses the knife behind the gun and punches the glove compartment shut.

"Gun's staying right where it is, too. We'll be fast. This is an old lady, I'm guessing. You said she's fragile. She'll love me. Old ladies love me. I'll turn on the charm. We'll be in and out."

What choice does she have at this point? She's come this far. Let him get what he's after and then she'll be free of it, of this, of everything. She's thinking beyond Gwen now. She's thinking she can just go to the airport and buy a ticket to L.A. and find Alessandra.

Dom takes the envelope off the dashboard and hands it to Amy. "Here's your money. Put it in your backpack, okay? It's yours."

Mrs. Epifanio opens the door, in a different housedress than the one she was wearing the other day. "Amy?" she says.

It takes Amy a few seconds to remember that she's got the wig on. Dom nudges her. "It's me, Mrs. E," Amy says, clutching her backpack to her chest.

"I was so worried about you," Mrs. Epifanio says. "I tried calling. I heard about Vincent. Just terrible. I was worried I'd involved you in something."

"I'm okay," Amy says.

Mrs. Epifanio smiles and aims a thumb at Dom. "Is this why you haven't been answering my calls? You've got a boyfriend? And the hair? I love it. You look like an actress. Introduce me to your boyfriend."

Amy's about to correct her, but Dom puts out his hand and offers it to Mrs. Epifanio. She takes it in both hands, as if testing the heft of it. "My name's Dom, Mrs. E," he says. "I've heard all about you. Amy's pal. It's a big honor to meet you."

"A real charmer. And such a sturdy handshake."

"Talk about actresses. You must've been in movies. Am I right? Were you in movies? You're a true beauty. Tell me what movies you were in. Maybe one of those song-and-dance ones with Bing Crosby and Bob Hope?"

"Oh, stop. Would you listen to him? I'm starting to blush over here. I wasn't expecting company. If I was dressed nice, I'd really knock you off your feet."

"I'm sure. So, you gonna tell me what movies you were in?"

"*Dom*, you're so bad." Mrs. Epifanio swats at the air, flashes a big smile. "Come on in, the both of you. You'll get sick. It's damp out today. Come in."

At the kitchen table, Mrs. Epifanio sits in her normal padded chair. Dom sits next to her, and she grips his hand. Amy sits across from them, her backpack in her lap, fidgeting with her phone, hoping Alessandra will call or text back.

"I want to hear all about you," Mrs. Epifanio says to Dom. "The man who's finally good enough for my Amy."

"I'm just a lucky guy, that's all," Dom says. "Right place, right time."

Mrs. Epifanio leans close to him: "You know about her tattoos?"

"Of course."

"This day and age, I guess, it's no big deal."

"She's the best woman I've ever met. Inside and out." Dom winks at her.

"Listen to the way he talks. A gentleman, Amy. You've got a good eye."

"I'm a lucky gal," Amy says, going along with it. There's no plan. She's not sure how they'll get in the bedroom without upsetting Mrs. Epifanio. She's lit up with anxiety, a crawling feeling under her skin. She's nervous that doing the wrong thing will wreck Mrs. Epifanio. Her plan, since she's leading the way, is to hang out and wait until Mrs. Epifanio needs to take a nap. She hopes that Dom can hold on until then.

"What's your line of work?" Mrs. Epifanio says to Dom.

"Construction," Dom says, without any hesitation.

Mrs. Epifanio cups her hand over her mouth and turns to Amy. "Very nice, dear. Construction's good."

Amy nods.

"And what's your line of work?" Dom asks Mrs. Epifanio. "If you're not an actress, what is it? Beauty consultant?"

"Job? This guy, I'll tell you. I'm ninety, Dom."

"Ninety?" Dom rubs his eyes with the heels of hands. "Pardon my language, but you've gotta be shitting me, Mrs. E. You don't look a day over sixty-five."

Mrs. Epifanio laughs. "I was born in 1927, you believe that? A lot of life I've seen."

"I'm sure," Dom says. "Incredible. God bless. You give me hope."

"Such a sweetheart you are. What can I get you two? Coffee? I've got Entenmann's. Elaine brought it yesterday."

"Elaine came to visit?" Amy says. "That's nice."

Mrs. Epifanio waves it off. "It'd kill her to come here more often? My daughter, Dom, she's caught up in her own life. She's already got me dead and buried. I bet you take care of your mother."

"I do love my mother very much," Dom says. "I can't imagine going a day without seeing her."

"You see your mother every day? That's wonderful. She's a lucky woman, your mother. And, Amy, let me tell you, good sons make good husbands. The ones who walk away from their parents, they're trouble." Mrs. Epifanio gets up and trudges over to the fridge. She takes out a box of Entenmann's crumb cake and puts it on the table between Dom and Amy. She opens the box. A little red plastic knife is lodged in the cake. Next she goes over to the stove and fiddles with the percolator, scooping Folgers into the basket, running cold water from the sink into the pot. "I'm making coffee. You'll have coffee, right?"

"Sure we will," Dom says, keeping his eyes away from Amy.

Amy finds herself thankful for his patience. He's clearly not the same as Vincent. He's able to control himself. "Can I help you, Mrs. E?" she asks.

"Not at all," Mrs. Epifanio says. "Sit, sit. Have some crumb cake. Okay?"

"Don't mind if I do," Dom says. He pulls the cake box close to him and cuts off a jagged little corner, scarfing it down over his palm, wiping the crumbs he's made on the table into a neat little pile afterward.

Mrs. Epifanio turns on the gas under the percolator and comes back to her chair. "Can I tell you what I heard about Vincent?" she says. "I take it Amy's told you, Dom, about my issue with Vincent Marchetti, who was just murdered on West Tenth Street. His mother, Diane, she sat with me four days a week. Helped a little here, a little there, whatever I needed. I feel so bad for her. Anyhow, her son comes in her place a couple of days in a row. Says she's sick. I'm thinking he killed her. Amy, did you tell Dom all of this?"

"A little," Amy says.

"A *little*? This is the most drama the neighborhood's had since Eugene Calabrese. This Vincent, he was no good, you could just tell. Shifty. Right, Amy?"

"Right," Amy agrees.

"He came here," Mrs. Epifanio continues, "he did nothing to help. He disappeared into my bedroom. God knows what he was doing in there. Probably trying to rob me blind. Joke was on him. I don't have much."

Now Dom looks at Amy, as if he finally gets why they're there.

"You've heard about the murder, at least?" Mrs. Epifanio asks Dom.

"I read something about it," Dom says.

"God knows what Vincent was mixed up in. Immacula came over to check up on me, which was nice of her, considering I haven't had many good things to say about her in the past. She told me Vincent was caught up in this Mexican kidnapping scheme."

"What's that?" Dom says.

"Who the hell knows? She also said she heard from Mary Magliozzo that Vincent was"—she lowers her voice—"*gay*. And that this was maybe a jilted boyfriend who stabbed him. Backward world we live in now. When I was young, things made sense, things were easier to understand."

"Simpler times."

"Anyhow, I don't want to be a dirty gossip. I feel terrible for Diane, but I can't say I'm surprised about her son. My husband used to say, 'You mess with the bull, you get the horns.' That's right, isn't it, Dom?"

"Very true. Your husband was a smart man."

The sound of coffee perking fills the kitchen. Dom devours another piece of cake.

"I like a man who can eat," Mrs. Epifanio says.

"I *love* to eat," Dom says.

"What's your favorite food?"

"My mother's meatballs."

"Of course. Let me ask a sensitive question." Mrs. Epifanio tilts a thumb at Amy. "Can she cook?"

Dom makes a so-so gesture with his hand. "*Mezza mezza.*"

Mrs. Epifanio laughs again. "You want some lessons, Amy? I'll give you cooking lessons. We can start with meatballs. They'll never be as good as Mama's, right, Dom? But we can try. Chopped meat, good Parmesan, Italian bread, salt, pepper, garlic powder, parsley, an egg. That's all there is to it."

"You're making me drool here, Mrs. E," Dom says.

"How's that sound, Amy?" Mrs. Epifanio says.

"Sounds good," Amy says, and for a minute this almost feels like some alternate reality where Dom is her boyfriend and she would be absolutely fucking thrilled to take cooking lessons with Mrs. Epifanio, because she's sick to death of takeout.

"Just a few more minutes on that coffee," Mrs. Epifanio says, getting up again and aiming herself at the refrigerator. "How do you take it? Sugar? Milk?"

Dom rises. "Sit, sit, I can get anything we need."

Mrs. Epifanio falls back into her chair. "Such a gentleman."

Dom goes to the refrigerator, opens the door gently, and pulls out a half quart of Farmland skim milk and a full-to-the-brim sugar bowl. "Me, personally, I take lots of sugar and lots of milk. That's the way I am. Amy?"

"Just black," Amy says.

"You don't know how she takes her coffee?" Mrs. Epifanio says.

Dom shrugs.

"Men." Mrs. Epifanio shakes her head. "So unobservant. My husband was the same way. All those years married, and he couldn't tell you how I take my coffee."

"Uh-oh," Dom says, bringing the sugar and milk back to the table. "Your opinion of me is declining."

"Not at all. Just trying to impart some wisdom. Pay attention to what Amy likes."

A smirk from Dom. "Will do, Mrs. E. That's sound advice."

When Mrs. Epifanio indicates that the coffee has perked long enough, Dom tends to it, taking it off the gas and setting it to the side on a battered Christmas potholder. She points him to the mugs in the cabinet over the sink, and he gets down three. He pours their coffees and puts the steaming mugs on the table. Amy takes hers, hungrily slurping some coffee. Mrs. Epifanio fixes hers with a dash of milk. Dom goes to town on his. A hefty dose of sugar, and so much milk that his coffee turns the color of the sidewalk.

Mrs. Epifanio sips her coffee and then cuts herself off a hunk of crumb cake. After she's done eating it, crumbs flaking her chin, she turns her attention to Amy. "I've gotta ask," she says. "That's a wig, right?"

"It is."

"You like it?" Mrs. Epifanio says to Dom.

"Of course," he says.

"I like it, too."

Amy's phone rings in her pocket. She takes it out and looks at the screen. Alessandra. She mutters an apology to Mrs. Epifanio, then flips the phone open and says, "Hello?"

"It's me," Alessandra says.

"I know," Amy says.

"Who's that?" Dom says.

"A friend," Amy says.

"You're with someone?" Alessandra says.

Amy stands and ducks into the living room with its green shag rug, carrying her backpack with her. "I'll tell you later."

Dom's right behind her, listening to her conversation.

She shushes him, motions that it's got nothing to do with him, but he's not getting that. He takes it as a threat.

"I got drunk and missed my plane," Alessandra says.

"Really?" Amy says.

"I'm sorry I left that way. I didn't want to. I was so pissed at myself, I started drinking as soon as I got to the airport. I had a couple of hours before my flight. This guy was buying my drinks, and I must've had about six mimosas. After I left the bar, my head was spinning. I sat down at the wrong gate and passed out. Woke up about an hour after my flight had taken off."

"Where are you now?"

"Still at LaGuardia."

"Can I call you back in a bit?"

"Sure."

Amy closes the phone. "Can't you just give me a sec here?" she says to Dom.

"Who was that?"

"Just my friend, okay?"

"You told her about me?"

"I didn't tell her anything."

Dom peeks back into the kitchen at Mrs. Epifanio to make sure she can't hear. "What are we doing here? How long's this gonna take?" He pauses and gives her a sly grin. "I'm doing good, right? I told you I'm good with the old ladies."

"I just don't want to unnerve her."

"Where's my stuff? In the bedroom?"

"I think so. He was in the bedroom doing something when he was here. I went in there, but I didn't see anything."

"I can be patient. Let's continue to finesse the situation. I'm enjoying being your boyfriend for the afternoon. Maybe we can get her to take a rest. They love to take rests, these old ladies. Put on the TV, they're out like a light in five minutes."

Amy, hugging her backpack, returns to the table. Mrs. Epifanio is eating more crumb cake. Dom lingers in the living room, looking into the adjoining bedroom, but then he comes back out.

"Everything okay?" Mrs. Epifanio says.

"Fine," Amy says. "Just a friend. I told her I'd call her back."

"You know what I was thinking? I'd like to go to Diane's son's wake. Pay my respects. For Diane. I feel bad for her. Something must've been off in his brain. I think it's this afternoon. Four to six, Immacula said."

"You think that's a good idea, Mrs. E?" Amy asks.

"This guy—Vincent, his name was?—sounds like he really upset you," Dom says. "Maybe it's best just to let it be."

"Maybe," Mrs. Epifanio says. "I get sick of being in the house, you know? Wake's a social occasion. I thought with you two here, maybe we could all go together." She pauses, considering it. "Forget it. Not going's for the best. I'll send a Mass card."

"I can't go anyway," Amy says, thinking of Alessandra kicking around LaGuardia, drinking coffee, buying a little packet of Tylenol to push back against the champagne, wearing her dark aviator sunglasses. "I have to be somewhere around then."

"For the best. I don't want to see Diane like that, anyway. I'm sure she's a wreck. You haven't seen her, have you, Amy?"

Amy knows that eventually the role she played the day Diane got the news about Vincent will be public knowledge, but she's guessing Mrs. Epifanio doesn't know yet. If Immacula didn't know about it, Mrs. Epifanio can't know. "I haven't. She was sick, too, wasn't she?"

"That's what Vincent said. The flu. Terrible. What a world. You get the flu, and then your son winds up dead. At least he didn't kill her, like we thought at first."

"There's a silver lining right there," Dom says, smiling.

"Mrs. E, you want to go into the living room and watch a little TV?" Amy says.

"You two don't want to waste your afternoon just sitting around watching TV with an old bag like me," Mrs. Epifanio says.

"We want to visit," Amy says. "I know you like to sit down around now and watch a movie."

"I love the old movies," Dom says.

"Oh, me too," Mrs. Epifanio says. "Channel two-fifty-six."

"What's that, Turner Classic?"

"That's it. Last night, I watched one with Elizabeth Taylor and Montgomery Clift. *A Place in the Sun*. I hadn't seen it in, I forget, probably sixty-five years."

"Elizabeth Taylor. What a lady."

"Let's go see what's on," Amy says, maybe pushing a little too hard. "We can bring our coffees."

They sit in the living room, Mrs. Epifanio slumped in her leather recliner, Amy and Dom next to each other on the plastic-covered orange velvet sofa. Decorative brass plates hang on the walls. Amy nudges her sugar skull flats into the green shag. Amy and Dom sip coffee as Mrs. Epifanio studies an extra-large remote control, trying to figure out which buttons do what, as if it's all brand-new to her.

"This channel changer gives me such heartache," she says.

"You need some help?" Amy says.

"I've got it. Here we go." She narrates her discoveries as she makes them. "Power. Input. Two. Five. Six."

Turner Classic Movies clicks on. A Western.

"Here we go with the bang-bang shoot-'em-up," Mrs. Epifanio says. "I can't stand these pictures."

"You don't like Westerns?" Dom says.

"I like a love story." But she doesn't change the channel. She didn't bring her coffee along. She leans back in the recliner and kicks up her feet.

"Can I get you anything, Mrs. E?" Amy says. "A pillow? A blanket?"

"I'm great," Mrs. Epifanio says. "It's so nice having company."

Amy and Dom watch the movie.

"This is special," Dom says.

"Fuck you," Amy says under her breath.

When Mrs. Epifanio nods off, five minutes into the movie being on, they slink into the bedroom. Dom takes it in. "You look around at all?" he asks.

"Not really," Amy says. "It looked undisturbed. But Mrs. E said Vincent was back here a bunch, so I think this has gotta be where your stuff is. I wasn't thinking he'd hid something. I was thinking he was maybe stealing from her, if anything."

Dom nods. He yanks out the top left dresser drawer and sifts through a pile of silky underwear and bras. He takes a pair of underwear out. "Jesus. These must be fifty years old. You want them?"

"I'm good," Amy says.

He sniffs the crotch. "Just the faintest whiff of a young Mrs. E."

"Stop talking."

"Trouble in paradise. The lovers are on the ropes."

"Find your stuff, okay? Find it fast."

"I'll find my stuff after you sniff the underwear." He comes over and presses the underwear against her face.

She swats his arm away. "Fuck off."

"Come on, that's small potatoes. I'm just having fun." Dom goes back to digging through dresser drawers. He finds handkerchiefs that belonged to Mr. Epifanio. Pajama bottoms, too. Old bedsheets and pillowcases. Mrs. Epifanio hasn't gotten rid of much.

Amy helps. She looks under the bed and behind the sewing machine.

After going through all the drawers, Dom pulls the dresser away from the wall. "Bingo," he says, reaching back behind the dresser. "There's one." He comes out with a basic knockoff designer purse, maroon, the kind that hangs from the racks in the little shops on Eighty-Sixth Street. He feels around in the bag. He takes out a Ziploc bag full of diamond necklaces and shows it to her.

"How many more?" Amy says.

"How many more what?"

"Purses."

"Should be another." He pushes the dresser back into place.

Amy helps him shut the drawers.

"Where are we not looking?" he says, getting down on his knees and sniffing around by the sewing machine table. He stands and peels the chenille spread off the bed, hurls the pillows to the floor. The sheets are wispy. There's nothing under them.

Mrs. Epifanio stirs in the living room. She chokes on a snore. Amy goes in and lowers the TV volume.

Back in the bedroom, Dom is lifting the mattress. It's soft and misshapen, difficult to hold up easily. Amy grabs one end.

There, between the mattress and the ancient box spring, the rest of the jewelry is laid out. No sign of the purse. Some of the smallest pieces are in sandwich bags. The rest is simply spread there like something that's been dug up or discovered. They push the mattress off to the side.

"More brains than I ever gave him credit for, that Vincent," Dom says. "Pretty solid spot."

He starts scooping up the pieces and dropping them into the first purse. They won't all fit. He zips it, then swipes the rest of the jewelry into his arms and piles it on top of the dresser. He asks Amy to make the bed the way it was. She should be the one, after all, who cares that things look right.

She does it, getting the mattress back on the box spring, straightening the sheets. She smooths down the chenille spread and puts the pillows back in place.

Dom opens the drawer with the extra sheets. He pulls out a yellow pillowcase and fills it with the rest of the jewelry. "I can tell you're looking at me," he says to Amy. "You got a better idea?"

Her bag would be a better idea, but she's not going to give it to him.

He knots the end of the pillowcase. "Okay, let's go."

Amy smooths down the remaining sheets and pillowcases. Just as she's about to shut the drawer, she notices a sterling silver chain coiled in the corner under bunched-up floral-print sheets. She pinches it between her thumb and index finger and draws it out, dropping it into her other palm. A small silver medal is latched to the end of the chain, its blank back looking up at her. She flips it over: Joan of Arc. A simple, plain, beautiful medal. She wonders if Mrs. Epifanio's first name is Joan. She has no idea. She remembers that Alessandra's favorite painting is the one of Joan of Arc at the Met. She can't remember the painter's name, but it's a wildly gorgeous painting. They went to see it together several times. The medal is not worth much, she bets, but she really likes it. She'd like to give it to Alessandra. She thinks Alessandra would appreciate it, because it's beautiful and because Joan of Arc is the patron saint of strong women, even though Alessandra isn't into things like patron saints. She drops the medal into the pocket of her cardigan and closes the drawer as quietly as she can. Dom winks at her.

15

Amy feels terrible about leaving Mrs. Epifanio like that. She was in pretty good shape—alert, not confused, genuinely happy to see Amy and to meet Dom—and Amy wonders if she'll wake up disoriented, trying to figure out if it was all dream. But then she'll see the coffee mugs in the dish drain and know it really happened. She'll probably think how strange it is that they left the house without waking her to say good-bye. She wonders what Mrs. Epifanio's reaction would've been if she'd introduced her to Alessandra instead of Dom.

They're sitting in Dom's car. She's itching to call Alessandra back.

"See," Dom says, tossing the purse and the pillowcase on the back seat. "Easy-peasy. I knew you were a good egg."

Amy's thinking about the Joan of Arc medal in her pocket. She's wondering what Alessandra would do. Alessandra's belief is that sometimes you've got to burn the fucker down, do what's best for yourself, scratch an itch until it bleeds. Maybe she hadn't listened to Alessandra enough during their time together. Alessandra has guts. She can be cold and detached, but she always seems in control.

"Let me drop you somewhere," Dom says. He turns to look at her. "Or you could come with me. We could go over to my guy in Borough Park and sell all this shit and then get on a plane to the Caribbean. I'm thinking the Bahamas or Saint Croix. I'd like to see you in a bathing suit."

"You disappear down there, won't people start to suspect it was you who killed Vincent?"

"Why? They'll just think I ripped off my old man, that's all."

"You've known Vincent for years. You don't go to his wake and then you just up and leave the country?"

"No one's surprised about Vincent. He's been marked for this kind of end for a long time."

"That's not the impression I get from Diane."

"Diane? Come on. What's she gonna say?"

Amy knows she should've walked away and gotten on the train with her five grand and called Alessandra. But she followed Dom to the car. She can feel heat from the bags of jewelry. Amy's realizing that she hasn't transformed back into old Amy but into a totally new one. She's got a romantic notion in mind: Alessandra's hungover and stuck at the airport. How great would it be if she showed up at the airport to pick her up in Dom's car with all this stolen jewelry? "Hop in, Al," she'd say, the car rumbling at the curb behind a taxi, Alessandra rubbing the champagne buzz from her temples. Then they could hit the road, drive all the way to Los Angeles, staying in motels and kissing on sad beds with the heater humming and the TV playing movies they've never heard of. Roadside motels with kidney-shaped pools, the kinds of places people take pictures of because they have beautiful old signs and seem like they're from another time. They could probably sell the jewelry in Los Angeles. Seems like the kind of place you can sell stolen jewelry without too much effort.

But this is the new Amy thinking. And it's dumb. There'd be so many practical obstacles in the way of her winding up with the jewelry. Dom, for one. If she ever managed to get away with it—the jewelry being the thing that he fucking killed Vincent over—she'd have to live her life looking over her shoulder. Her only advantage would be that he wouldn't know where to look.

"What are you thinking about?" Dom says.

"What?"

"You think you're gonna steal all this shit, don't you?" He laughs. "You just got that big idea in your mind, didn't you? You're seeing dollar signs, just like Vincent."

"I'm not a thief."

"I know you're no thief, but you're feeling temptation. Temptation's all it takes."

"I'm leaving." Amy goes for the door handle.

Dom stops her. "No, wait." He reaches across her and opens the glove compartment. "Here, I'll give you a chance." He takes out the gun and hands it to her. "Point it at me. Tell me what you want."

She holds it in her lap. It's a little heavier than it looks.

"Aim it at me," Dom says. "Let's see what you're made of."

"It's loaded?" Amy says.

"Should be."

Her hand is shaking. She can't even lift the gun. She's looking at it in her lap. She doesn't know anything about Dom, not *really*, other than the fact that he killed Vincent, and she wonders what else he's used this gun for. She's never even held a gun before, but she can feel that this one's got a history.

"Aim it at me," Dom says. "Come on!"

Amy looks around. Mrs. Epifanio's not peeking out from behind her blinds. No one's walking by. The cars that are parked around them seem like they've been parked there for days and that they'll never leave. Amy tries to imagine herself as the kind of person who could lift a gun and point it at another person, even out of fear or in jest or in some kind of threatening way.

"You don't have it in you," Dom says. "Fucking shame." He snatches the gun back from her, reaches across, and yanks the door handle, pushing open the door and shouldering her out onto the sidewalk.

Amy lands curled over her backpack.

"Stay quiet, stay alive," Dom says, leaning out of the car on the passenger side and then pulling the door shut. He gets back under the wheel, revs the engine, and busts away from the curb, his tires smoking.

The day is now eerily still. Pigeons. The breeze. A bus off in the distance. Amy crawls over and sits against Mrs. Epifanio's fence, the sidewalk cold and gritty against her bottom. She takes out her phone and dials Alessandra. She's not sure what she's going to say. *I have five thousand dollars, and I'll meet you at LaGuardia. Can I come to Los Angeles and live with you?*

Alessandra picks up. "I'm headed to you right now," she says. "My new flight's not until tomorrow. I got an Uber. You said you're on the same block as St. Mary's, right?"

"What?" Amy says. "You hate it in the neighborhood. Don't come here."

"Too late. I'm headed there. What's your address?"

"We can meet somewhere else."

"You okay?"

"Things have been pretty crazy."

Alessandra drifts away from the phone, talking to her driver, telling him something he shouldn't be doing. "I'll be there in fifteen minutes," Alessandra says.

"Okay," Amy says.

⇥⇤

Mr. Pezzolanti is waiting at the gate when she gets back to her apartment. She wasn't expecting to see him again, and that casts a new sort of melancholy over their encounter. "Those batteries work out okay?" he says.

"Great, Mr. P.," she says.

"I just walked over to the dollar store and bought another pack. You need more, I'm your man."

She smiles and rushes into the apartment. She hurriedly unpacks some fresh clothes—blue denim capris, a Sourpuss Beki polka-dot top—and lays them out on the bed. She takes off the wig and the cap and plucks out the bobby pins. She gets undressed. There's a faint smell of kush oil on her wrists still. She goes into the bathroom and turns on the shower. She imagines Dom squeezed in there. Her shower is hot and fast and feels good. She needed soap. She needed to feel clean. When she's done, she towels off, finds a half-empty bottle of Listerine, and swishes some around in her mouth. She gets dressed and repacks her bag, making sure to stuff Alessandra's Dodgers shirt and boy briefs in there, as well as the wig, wig cap, and bobby pins. She puts on a little makeup. Nothing fancy.

Stacked on top of the clothes in the backpack is the Priority Mail envelope. She thumbs through the five thousand dollars, as if to make sure it's absolutely real. A payoff, that's what it is. Now she's got real blood on her hands. She wonders if she should've asked for more. She waits for Alessandra, her body racked with anxiety.

Fifteen minutes was what she said. It's already been more than twenty. Maybe they hit traffic on the BQE or Belt.

Amy checks her phone.

She hears a car pull up outside. She opens the door and sees Alessandra getting out of her Uber, hair up in a ponytail, sunglasses on, the driver dragging her bag out of the trunk. Mr. Pezzolanti is standing there between them.

"I can already feel the neighborhood pressing down on me," Alessandra says. "You can get away, but you can never *really* get away."

"This your friend?" Mr. Pezzolanti says to Amy.

"Yes," Amy says, tucking her wet hair behind her ears.

"Busy few days around here," he says.

"'Friend,' wink-wink," Alessandra says. She thanks the driver and wheels her bag over the wet sidewalk up to the front gate, introducing herself to Mr. Pezzolanti.

"You're Zeke Biagini's kid, aren't you?" he says. "Back before your mother passed away, I used to play cards with your old man. You know, I don't even know his real first name. I called him Zeke as a goof. It stuck."

"That's me."

"The actress, right? How do you and Amy know each other? She was looking like an actress herself with that hair earlier. Back to normal now, huh, kid?"

"Why'd you leave the hotel the way you did?" Amy asks Alessandra, ignoring Mr. Pezzolanti.

"You know me," Alessandra says, walking through the gate as Mr. Pezzolanti holds it open for her. "I suck at good-byes."

"Excuse us, Mr. P," Amy says.

"Sure thing," Mr. Pezzolanti says. "You need any more batteries, just let me know."

Alessandra walks past Amy into the apartment. Amy looks out at the street, half expecting to see Dom perched behind the wheel of his Daytona, letting her know that she's not in the clear yet. But he's nowhere that she can see. She closes the door on a gawking Mr. Pezzolanti.

"Hell of a place you got here," Alessandra says, parking her bag by the table, taking off her sunglasses, and then collapsing on the bed. "You believe what a fuckup I am? Who the fuck gets drunk and misses her flight? Such an Alessandra move."

"Al," Amy says, giving Alessandra serious eyes.

"What's going on?"

"He was here."

"Who?"

"The guy I told you about. The guy I thought was following me. He was here."

Alessandra sits up. "No shit?"

"No shit."

Amy spends the next twenty minutes filling in Alessandra, telling her everything from Dom's history with Vincent to her big daydream of making off with the swag in Dom's car and living from motel to motel across the country. Alessandra's digesting the information—Amy's plans, Dom's threat—with glee.

"You don't have to look so happy that I'm in the middle of this crazy situation," Amy says.

"I'm here with you," Alessandra says. "Besides, he would've killed you if he was gonna kill you."

"Jeez, thanks."

"What about your dad?"

"What about my dad what?"

"How's he fit into all this?"

"He doesn't." Amy sits next to Alessandra on the bed. "I really thought for a second there about stealing that jewelry. I can't believe myself. I can't believe the last few days. What the hell have I been doing?"

Alessandra leans on her elbow, plays her fingers through Amy's still-damp hair. "You were just dreaming of taking something back. It's natural, imagining what it'd be like if things were easy."

"But that's just a dream," Amy says. "All that stolen shit, that's what Vincent died over. It would only make things hard."

"Would it, though?" Alessandra says.

"What do you mean?"

"Listen. We've never had much. Wouldn't it be nice to have enough money to live without worry for a while? This neighborhood will trap you and murder you slowly, and if you don't leave now, you'll end up like all these old people you take care of, miserable and alone."

"We'd be looking over our shoulders forever."

"Not if this Dom is out of the picture. You said he's a bad guy."

"I said he's *probably* lying about everything, and he's *probably* a bad guy. And now you've got us adding murder to the daydream."

"It's all the champagne. Sorry."

Amy laughs. "How would we do it?"

"I don't know. From all you've told me, the guy sounds like a fucking moron. Maybe we just get him to cross the street in the wrong place and a bus does our dirty work for us."

"Then we swoop in and pick up the bags," Amy adds. "*Nothing to see here.* He's probably on his way to Borough Park to sell the stuff right now. And then he's going to go down to the Caribbean to live like a king. I bet he gets away with it."

"How long's that last? A few months, maybe? He'll either blow all the money or someone'll take it. I had this line in a script I read for once, a Miami crime thing. Part was a prostitute, of course. The line was something like, 'There's people, that's their whole job, to watch for guys like him advertising a big score.' Applies here, right?"

Amy goes for her bag on the floor. "I got you something," she says. "I almost forgot."

"A present?" Alessandra says, scuttling to the edge of the bed on her elbows.

Amy digs around in her bag and unfurls the cardigan she just changed out of. She reaches into one of the pockets and finds the Joan of Arc medal she took from Mrs. Epifanio's bedroom. She lets the chain dangle from her hand.

Alessandra takes it and holds it close to her face.

"Because of the painting you love," Amy says.

"It's really pretty," Alessandra says.

"I found it in Mrs. Epifanio's bedroom when we were looking for the jewelry."

"You stole it?"

"It's not stealing."

"It *is* stealing. And it's romantic as hell."

⟞⟝

They sit at the table over steaming cups of black tea, the water slowing from a boil in Amy's electric kettle. The Joan of Arc medal is in front of Alessandra. She fiddles with the chain. "When I went back to LA after I left you," Alessandra says, "I took up with this woman named Sadie. She dealt drugs, mostly to rich kids. Business was booming. She had a garbage bag full of cash in her closet. We'd only been dating a couple of months, and she didn't care that I knew about it. She was really confident. She was also pretty nasty. I stayed with her because I didn't have any options at the time."

"You had options," Amy says.

"You know I couldn't stay in the neighborhood. You know what this place does to me."

"You're here now."

Alessandra, smiling, does a little Michael Corleone: "'Just when I thought I was out . . .'"

"Go on," Amy says. "Tell me about Sadie. What she smelled like. Looked like."

"There's a moral to the story. This isn't just a memory lane thing."

"Okay."

"But, now that you mention it, she always smelled like she just came from a campfire. She had dreadlocks and a little triangle tattoo on her chin. She called herself a 'script consultant.' She had six cats. I still remember their names."

"Shoot."

"Edgar, Rifle, Rye, Bessie, Mr. Turner, and Neil Young. Bessie was a little bitch. She scratched me on the thigh once. I thought it was gonna scar. Anyhow, Sadie not only dealt drugs, she was pretty heavy into them. Mainly heroin. Every night just about, I'd lose her. She'd be shooting up. In the bathtub. On the toilet. In bed. I got to thinking she was gonna OD and I could just let it happen. Don't call the cops. Just get that garbage bag full of cash, leave some food for the cats, and walk out."

"What happened?"

"She never overdosed. I just kind of took off one day. She was pretty boring, actually."

"So? What's the moral of the story?"

"The moral of the story is, I should've stolen some of that fucking cash. She probably just blew it or lost it or whatever. You think you're a good person, and you go around *thinking* you're a good person, and you miss all these opportunities. That cash, even some of it, could've changed my life."

"But that's not you. You're not a thief."

"Why's it not me? It could be anybody. The thing that separates successful people from unsuccessful people is that unsuccessful people are suckers. They don't pounce. They float the fuck away from opportunity."

"Al. Come on."

"I'm serious, dude. Before you know it, we're gonna be forty. No money in the bank, no house, no family left. Just a fucking graveyard of missed opportunities behind us."

Amy leans close. "What are you saying?"

"Okay. Forget the Dom guy for now. Let him go. He sells the jewelry, escapes to the Bahamas or wherever, and he gets away with killing this nobody. Who the fuck cares? Not our problem. But what you said to me was that *he* said his old man had more jewelry in that attic closet. And you said this guy, the father, didn't really seem like the guy that Dom described."

"And?"

"Well, maybe we've got a pushover with a closet full of jewelry he doesn't give a shit about."

"That's stretching. The dad still seemed like *someone*, you know? We're not talking about a scaredy-cat here."

"You know where they live?"

"He said right near that Magen David High School."

"Easy to find out where, exactly."

"And we're gonna, what? Break into this house and steal some jewelry? You want to go to Eighty-Sixth Street and get ski masks and water guns?"

Alessandra laughs. "Maybe."

"You're joking, right?"

"Doesn't it just seem so easy? You've already got the five grand. You've gone that far. We could buy a car for a few hundred bucks at Flash Auto. Those guys loved my dad. They'd give us a deal. And then we could live out that daydream you were talking about—motels, the open road."

"You're crazy. It doesn't seem easy at all. Plus, Flash Auto's gone."

"I just keep seeing this closet full of jewelry nobody gives a shit about. Guy's got so much, he won't even notice it's missing."

"I have this five thousand. I was thinking I could come to Los Angeles with you, anyway." Amy pauses, nervously glances away from Alessandra. "Either that, or I could try Williamsburg with Gwen."

"Sure. You should come back with me, if you want. But five grand's not much. It'll be gone in a couple of months. We could have more." Alessandra smiles.

Amy thinks it through. She wants to do what will make Alessandra happy. She likes seeing that smile again. "I don't know. It sounds like a bad idea."

They get up and walk to Eighty-Sixth Street. They leave Alessandra's suitcase at Amy's apartment, but Amy carries her backpack. Alessandra stops in front of a dollar store and considers a mechanical kitten that dances in place. Amy pulls up next to her. She suddenly feels naked, out in the world without the wig. A train rumbles by overhead.

After it passes, Alessandra says, "Hear me out, okay? You think it's a coincidence that your old man showed up at the same time that all of this is going on, and that I'm here, and now you've had this change of heart?"

"I don't know," Amy says. "It's, what, meant to be?"

"Exactly," Alessandra says, plopping the mechanical kitten on its side so it dances off the edge of the gold tray it's on. "Meant to be. This opportunity."

"We can't do this. We're not cut out for it."

Alessandra nods. Bites her lower lip. "But *we* don't have to do it."

"What do you mean?"

"We get your father to do it."

"Fred? No way."

"Why not Fred? He owes you."

———⊷———

They walk up Bay Parkway to Avenue P and sit on a bench on the far edge of Seth Low Playground. Amy's aware that they've passed Magen David Yeshivah, the Mescolotto house right nearby, somewhere on Seventy-Eighth Street. She's sure Alessandra knows that, but she doesn't say anything about it yet. She throws an arm around Amy. Her idea is to make Fred the fall guy. This is a man, Alessandra insists, who let Amy down majestically. Amy was a kid, her mom had died, she was drowning in the world, and he had walked the fuck away. If he'd been around and managed to stick it out as a dad, she wouldn't have ever encountered Bob Tully. Doesn't a man like this, no matter what and who he's become, deserve her scorn? And doesn't Amy, maybe, deserve some revenge—and a reward?

Sounds pretty righteous, when Alessandra puts it that way.

"I bet he'll do anything for you," Alessandra says to Amy.

"I don't know," Amy says.

"I know. I fucking *know*. To hell with this guy. Let's use him to take advantage of this opportunity. You know how to find him?"

Amy thinks of Monsignor Ricciardi. She can't imagine going to him and asking if he knows where to find Fred. Not with this deceitful purpose in mind. The way Dom read her intentions, she's sure Monsignor Ricciardi would be able to read her intentions, too.

"Maybe," Amy says.

"You think it's a good idea, I can tell."

"I think it makes us bad people. But maybe we're already bad people."

"We're not bad people. We're just trying to find the best way to make it through. Me and you in Los Angeles will be great. For once, we'll get some breathing room."

Amy shrugs, the shrug saying *yes* more than *I don't know*. Alessandra means far more to her than her father ever has or ever will.

Fifteen minutes later, they're at the rectory. Amy sidesteps inside, opening and closing the door with a gentle touch, Alessandra right behind her. Connie Giacchino's there at the main desk, PRAY BIGGER mug clutched in her hand, tinted glasses low on her nose. She says Amy's name a couple of times, as if she's not sure she's really just walked in.

"I was hoping to speak to Monsignor Ricciardi," Amy says.

"Is that Alessandra Biagini?" Connie says, straightening her glasses.

"Sure is," Alessandra says.

"My Sonny says he saw you in a movie on his Amazon Prime."

"Oh yeah, which one?"

"*Alien Carwash Something*. You were in it for maybe a minute. Got killed."

"We don't talk about that movie." Alessandra smiles.

"The monsignor is in his office," Connie says to Amy.

They go back to his office. Monsignor Ricciardi is sitting at his desk with his legs up, watching *Columbo* on his computer. He taps the mouse to pause it when he notices Amy and Alessandra. "Alessandra, good to see you," he says. "You're back visiting? How do you know Amy?"

"We've known each other a long time," Alessandra says.

"I had no idea," Monsignor Ricciardi says.

"Do you know how I can get in touch with my father?" Amy says to him.

"You've given what I said a second thought?"

"Yes."

"I talked to her, too," Alessandra says. "I convinced her that he deserves a shot."

"Excellent," Monsignor Ricciardi says, tapping his fingers on the desktop. He takes a retractable pen out of the top drawer and clicks it a few times. He says the word *excellent* three more times.

"You know where he is?" Amy says.

"As a matter of fact, I do. He wanted to stay around, didn't want to give up on you. The possibility of reconnecting with you, of making amends, has given him new purpose. He asked me if I knew anyone renting out rooms. I pointed him to Oggie Agostino on Eighty-Third Street. Between Twenty-Third and Twenty-Fourth. Oggie takes in lodgers, like people used to. He's got about six rooms he rents out for a hundred dollars a week. Fred took one in the basement."

Amy's unnerved to hear this, that Monsignor Ricciardi essentially okayed Fred's decision to stalk her, despite her wishes that he get the hell out of the neighborhood. Given Alessandra's plan, though, it's good news. He's just a couple of blocks away. He's ready to be used. He wants a new purpose? They'll give him one.

But Amy's suddenly convinced there's no way he'll go along with it. He's clean, after all. He did plenty of bad stuff in his drinking days that he's got to atone for, and he's probably not interested in adding to the list.

Monsignor Ricciardi finds a pad of Post-its and writes down the address. He hands the top Post-it to Amy. She feels the stickiness against her fingers. "Thanks," she says.

"Good luck," Monsignor Ricciardi says. "I mean that. I hope everything works out. You're a good daughter for doing this."

"What I said to you before," Amy says, "about not wanting advice, I'm sorry about that."

He grins like a card dealer to whom she's apologized for losing so badly. "Amy, we all have our moments. I understand. Believe me."

"Monsignor," Alessandra says, saluting him as if he's military.

⇥⇤

Amy's heard of Oggie Agostino, but she's never been to his rooming house. What she's heard is that a lot of sketchy people pass through the place.

Ex-addicts. Ex-cons. Gamblers off the rails. Guys who live with their parents until their parents can't take it anymore and throw them out, and then they need to find somewhere on the quick. It's a couple of short blocks from the rectory. Alessandra's got a little skip in her step.

"What if he just flat out says no?" Amy asks.

"I guess our backup plan will have to go into effect," Alessandra says.

"What's our backup plan?"

"I don't know. We'll figure one out."

When they arrive at the address, Fred is sitting out on the stoop. The house is dumpy. Crumbling porch. Tattered siding. A roof that needs fixing. The garden is a tangle of weeds and some kind of stringy wire. Fred's wearing a plain black sweatshirt and thrift store jeans. He digs into a big red bag of SunChips, seeming pretty confused.

"You're looking for me?" he says to Amy.

"I am," Amy says.

"Really?"

"Really."

He's got tears in his eyes. "Shit, that makes me so happy."

Alessandra steps in front of Amy and extends her hand. "I'm Alessandra," she says.

Fred shakes it. "Very nice to meet you."

"Alessandra's visiting from Los Angeles," Amy says.

"That's nice," he says, then grows somber. "Listen, I hope you're not upset about me getting this room here. I'm guessing the monsignor told you where I was. I didn't mean for this to upset you. It's just I thought staying local was my only shot at connecting with you. It's not a forever thing. I was just gonna give it a week." He stands, setting down the bag of chips on the steps. "Where are my manners? You want to come inside? There's a water heater in my room and nowhere comfortable to sit, but I'd be happy if you came in."

"We can just stay out here," Amy says.

"Out here's great," Fred says. "Sit down." He moves out of the way so they can sit on the stoop, and he just looms there before them. "You want some chips? Have some chips."

"Let the healing begin," Alessandra says, clapping her hands together.

Amy rolls her eyes at Alessandra.

"Where do we start?" Fred says, taking the wisecrack seriously.

"Well, for one, your sweet daughter has a little issue, and she needs some big help," Alessandra says.

Amy and Alessandra didn't really talk about this beforehand. There's no plan for what she will or won't say. Amy's nervous.

"Yeah, absolutely," Fred says, moving close to Amy. "I could tell something was off. Just by looking at you, I could tell. I know trouble. And I'm here to help, kid. You should've asked me earlier. Whatever you need."

"See, Amy?" Alessandra says. "I told you. He's here to help."

"I don't know," Amy says. She feels terrible, suddenly, about pitching this idea to Fred. She feels almost evil.

"You don't know what?" Fred says. "I've never been there before. I want to be there now. I can't do much in terms of dough, you know that, but anything else."

"Thing is, she had some jewelry," Alessandra says.

"Some jewelry?"

"Yeah. That she inherited."

"Your grandmother's?" Fred says to Amy.

Amy nods.

"And this jewelry," Alessandra continues, "which is *super* precious to her, was stolen."

"That stinks," Fred says.

"Amy's all torn up about it."

"What can I do? You reported this? You know who's responsible?"

"We know," Amy says, almost choking on the words.

———<⸺>———

They walk over to Seventy-Eighth Street. They stop on the corner by Magen David Yeshivah High School. Alessandra says they don't know the exact house, but they know the guy lives on this block and that he's got Amy's jewelry stashed in an attic closet.

"What's his name again?" Alessandra asks Amy.

"Tony Mescolotto," Amy says.

"The attic, huh?" Fred says. "Christ, no matter what, that's up there. That means getting into the house and getting all the way to the top."

"It's stupid," Amy says. "You can't do it."

Alessandra nudges her.

"Wait a sec, kid," Fred says. "Now, I didn't say that. I'm just strategizing. How do we find out the address?"

Alessandra takes out her phone and starts pecking at the screen with her thumb. She asks Amy to spell the name for her. Amy takes a stab at it.

"I'm checking the Whitepages. Give me a sec."

"How's she checking the Whitepages?" Fred says. "The Whitepages is a big clunker of a book."

"Welcome to the future, Pa Falconetti," Alessandra says. "Here it is. Two-two-five-six."

They walk up the block on the opposite side of the street. Oak branches hang over them, darkening the sidewalk with shadows. Amy homes in on a pair of sneakers strung up from the telephone wires. The gates of 2256 are silvery, tacky, polished. The house is ordinary, yellow vinyl siding, stone steps, flowers in the window. The attic window is like a porthole. Grapevines curl around a trellis in the muddy front yard, where two statues of St. Francis and one of St. Rosalia stand. A purple Eldorado sits in the driveway under a makeshift carport. There's a big BEWARE OF DOG sign taped to the mailbox and an iron fire escape shelved on the side of the house.

"What time is it?" Amy says.

"Little after four," Alessandra says.

"Maybe they're at the wake," Amy says.

"Who died?" Fred says.

"Just some guy from the neighborhood." Amy tries not to think about watching Vincent bleeding from the neck, his tender request for help. *Call someone.* Amy tries not to think about how easily life gets forgotten in human schemes.

"We should draw up a plan," Fred says.

"We don't need a plan," Alessandra says. "Just go in. That's Amy's stuff. They have no right to it."

"Even if no one's home, it says they have a dog."

"People just put those signs up to scare off intruders."

"What about an alarm?"

"There's no alarm."

"Your friend's very confident," Fred says to Amy. "I want to help. I do. But look at me. What am I gonna do, scale the fire escape, break in through the third-floor window, and hope there're no dogs or alarms? I'll crap my pants. My thing was booze, Amy. I was never a burglar. I think you should call the cops. I'll go talk to them, if you want. Explain the situation. We'll get you back what's yours."

"No cops," Alessandra says.

"You girls hungry? Let me get you something to eat. We'll sit and we'll talk and we'll make a plan. Go to the cops is my vote."

"Let's just forget it," Amy says. "It's fine, it's fine. I shouldn't have asked you, Fred. I shouldn't have put you in this position."

"I'm sorry."

Amy remembers her conversation with Dom. If there was truly more jewelry in that attic closet, why wouldn't Dom just go after it, instead of trying to track down what Vincent had stolen? He said he was flat-out done with his old man, but that's a bullshit story. She can't believe she put faith in anything he said.

"What is it?" Alessandra says.

"There's probably nothing anyway," Amy says, shaking her head.

"What have we got to lose?"

"I feel a little clueless here," Fred says.

The heavy front door of 2256 is pulled inward. Tony Mescolotto stands at the threshold in the same suit as before, same purple flower on his lapel, mopping his bald head with a red silk handkerchief. A woman appears next to him. Mrs. Mescolotto, Amy guesses, wearing a black dress and black heels. Her hair dyed tire black, her olive skin leathery. She has cat-eye sunglasses on and carries herself like she's in charge. Monsignor Ricciardi said he knows her well—flower arrangements are her thing. Amy recognizes her from somewhere. Not church. Ricciardi said she doesn't go. And Amy's never seen her at the funerals and wakes she's been to.

"Make me this fucking late," Mrs. Mescolotto says. "You're lucky Nancy's taking care of the flowers."

"I'm sorry, dear," Tony says.

They head down to the Eldorado. Tony opens the passenger door.

"Dom's meeting us there?" Mrs. Mescolotto says.

"What he said," Tony says.

"He fucking better, Tone." She gets in the car.

Afraid Tony will look across and recognize her as he goes to push back the gate, Amy says, "Shit shit shit," and she starts walking away down the block, her eyes on the sidewalk. Fred and Alessandra follow.

"What's going on?" Fred says.

"Nothing," Amy says. "Just walk."

"That's them?"

"Forget it."

Alessandra knows the score. She keeps quiet.

"Maybe I should go talk to them?" Fred says, shuffling to a stop. "I can talk reason."

Amy tugs at his sweatshirt. "Come on."

Fred picks up walking again. "You sure?"

Amy thinks they're in the clear, far enough away from the Mescolotto house that there's no way they'll be spotted.

"They're pulling out," Alessandra says. "Let's go back and break in."

"We should just call the cops," Fred says.

"If there was more," Amy says, "why wouldn't Dom just have gone back there first? Is it worth the risk to chase a lie? He's a liar."

Alessandra clenches her jaw. "You can't know."

Amy wants to believe there's nothing else. She's not that kind of thief. Despite what she did with Dom in Mrs. Epifanio's bedroom—under duress—she really can't imagine sneaking into someone's house and going through their things. She can't imagine sending in Fred either.

"Jesus Christ," Alessandra says.

"You go back, if you want." But she hopes Alessandra will just let it go.

"I'm not going back for nothing. We're no good at this. I was stupid to suggest it."

"I'm confused," Fred says. "Let me take you girls for some food. How about that?"

As they make a left on Bay Parkway in front of Magen David, Fred out in front now, Amy feels guilt and anger and a rush of overwhelming sadness. Everything is regrets. Tears hot in her eyes. She can't look at Alessandra. Amy knows Al's slipping away. And this man, this man who is her father, what on earth's she supposed to say to him now? She'd woken up from dreams many nights and mornings, upset by encounters with him that had never even occurred. And now this dreaded door is open. Against her will, it's open. She doesn't see herself in him. Her features aren't his features. She doesn't feel the pull of blood. She wishes he wasn't being nice. She wishes he wasn't sober. She wishes he'd disappear.

⟐

Amy has never been to Chris's, a Polish restaurant on Bay Twentieth and Eighty-Sixth Street, but she's seen the blue awning before and she knows that Capelli's, the funeral home where Vincent is being laid out, is catty-corner.

She leads Alessandra and Fred there now, because she's not sure what else to do and she has the desire to see—from a distance, at least—what's going on at the wake.

"This is on me," Fred says, as they enter. "Pierogi. Borscht. Perfect."

Amy and Alessandra don't say anything to each other, but Amy can tell they're thinking the same things about the absurdity of their pipe dream, their lack of purpose and planning. Things don't just happen because you want them to happen. They of all people should know that.

As they settle down at a table by the window, Amy looks across at Capelli's. She can see the new sign they put up, black script letters on white wood, hanging against gray brick. The El is between here and there, squatting over Eighty-Sixth Street and curving away up New Utrecht Avenue. A train pulls in, its reflection dancing in the glass. Soon enough, people descend the stairs at the Eighteenth Avenue/New Utrecht Avenue station, right in front of Capelli's. A bus stops at a red light and blocks Amy's view momentarily. A beer truck, with its back door half open, pulls up behind it. More people hurtle down the stairs from the El, headphones in, collars up, serious faces on. The sky is purpling over the neighborhood. It'll be dark soon.

The light changes. The bus and beer truck zoom away up Eighty-Sixth Street, out from under the El. Amy wonders how many people are inside Capelli's. Diane, Monsignor Ricciardi, and who else? Vincent, of course, hands clasped on his chest in the suit she'd retrieved. Maybe Dom, if what his mother said about his planning on being there is true. Whatever's followed Amy has followed her this far. Or whatever needs her to see it is calling to her. She feels, again, guided by something. Spooked.

"You okay?" Alessandra asks.

Amy can't quite bring herself to nod. The waitress brings over three menus and fills their waters. She's got a soft stare, the waitress. Brown hair. Sad eyes. Fred says hello and calls her by the name on her tag, Hanna. Amy takes a menu but doesn't look at it, her eyes fixed firmly on the funeral home.

"This is my daughter," Fred says to the waitress, pride in his voice.

"Okay," Hanna the waitress says, and then she's gone.

"You're hungry?" Fred says to Amy and Alessandra.

Amy watches as the door of Capelli's opens and Dom's mother comes strutting out in her heels and sunglasses. She has a cigarette in one hand, a purple Bic lighter in the other. She leans against the gray brick and lights her cigarette. She exhales dramatically.

It takes Amy a minute, Mrs. Mescolotto's face still simply registering as familiar, before she recognizes where she knows her from—the picture. She digs around in her backpack and finds the envelope. There she is. Front and center. In a tight-fitting black shirt, her eyes showing she's wasted, pint glass in her hand. Dom's mother, Dom, and Vincent all in the same picture.

"It's her," Amy says aloud. "That's where I recognize her from."

"Who's who?" Alessandra asks.

"I told you about the picture at the bar, the one I found at Vincent's. It's Dom's mother in the picture."

"What's that mean?"

"You two are losing me," Fred says, not having noticed Mrs. Mescolotto across the street. "You know what you're gonna order? Polish Platter looks good."

Amy tries to piece together what Vincent's connection could've been to Mrs. Mescolotto, beyond his longtime friendship with Dom. She wonders if maybe they were having an affair. Maybe Vincent got started with her and Dom found out about it and exploded. Add the jewelry to that. Maybe Vincent wanted to split town with Mrs. Mescolotto. *Let's run away*, the note on the back of the picture reads. Whatever the case, there's a fuller story there, and Amy wonders if she'll ever have any sense of what the truth is or if it even matters.

The waitress comes back.

"You know what?" Fred says. "I'm gonna order for the table. How about we get a Polish Platter, an order of pierogi, and an order of blintzes? We'll split everything. Sound good?"

Amy okays him, still fixated on Mrs. Mescolotto. The waitress scurries back to the kitchen.

When Dom comes out of Capelli's, dressed in a suit that's very similar to Vincent's, leans against the wall next to his mother, and motions for a puff of her cigarette, Amy's more fascinated than surprised. Mrs. Mescolotto looks angry at her son, frustrated, like she's about to smack the shit out of him. She refuses to pass the smoke, instead dropping it to the sidewalk and stomping it out with her heel. Dom throws his hands in the air.

Amy's watching all of this through the glass with no sound.

Alessandra's watching now, too. "That's him?" she says.

Amy nods.

"Hey, that's the same lady," Fred says, finally noticing Amy staring at Mrs. Mescolotto across the street.

"Right," Amy says.

"And the guy? Where do I know him from?"

"He's nobody."

"Another nobody, huh?"

Dom storms back inside, leaving his mother alone out front.

"This fucking place," Alessandra says. "Nothing but dead ends and disappointments."

"The pierogi will cheer you up," Fred says.

Amy stands, still holding the picture of Mrs. Mescolotto in her hand, and shoves her backpack at Alessandra. "Hold this a sec."

"Where you going?" Alessandra says.

"I don't know. Across. I want to ask her something."

"Just let it go."

"What's going on?" Fred asks.

Amy leaves Chris's, the door clanging behind her. The sidewalk buzzes with life. Three women in hijabs pass. An old man on his cell phone complains about his water bill. Two dudes leaning against the newspaper rack outside Duke's Deli drink coffee from Anthora cups.

Amy crosses the street to wild honking. A minivan with plastic bal-looning over its side windows slams on its brakes to avoid hitting her. The driver yells in Chinese. She slips between two parked cars and stumbles over a knot of black garbage bags, trying to keep her eyes on Mrs. Mescolotto, who walks away from Capelli's, headed to a liquor store called Liquor One on the corner of New Utrecht and Eighty-Fourth. Amy passes in front of a decrepit law office with broken blinds in the window.

When she catches up to Mrs. Mescolotto, she's not sure what to say.

"I know you?" Mrs. Mescolotto says, putting her sunglasses up in her hair. She's prettier up close. Not as hard-looking. Probably late fifties. Brown eyes. Wearing a wispy necklace, its small charm inlaid with pavé diamonds. She's got the kind of neck that looks like it's been kissed and choked a lot. Her lipstick is candy-apple red. She's been crying. Her mascara has run into the dark creases of her crow's-feet. Her breath smells like cigarettes.

"No," Amy says.

"So, what's your deal? You selling shit? Hitting me up for money?"

"It's about Vincent." Amy holds up the picture.

16

They take refuge in Liquor One. Dusty bottles and boxes surround them. There's the sound of another train outside. A guy sits behind the counter with a sci-fi paperback, wearing a Yankees fleece and a hat that reads BARRY BROTHERS TOWING. Mrs. Mescolotto seems desperate for a certain kind of vodka, hunting through the bottles until she finds it. Russian and expensive.

"My fucking elbow itches," she says. "You ever get an itch on your elbow and it's right there on the fucking bone and you just can't get at it?" She rubs her elbow against the edge of the shelf that the vodka's on, rattling the bottles.

"How'd you know Vincent?" Amy says.

"You're a detective or what?" Mrs. Mescolotto says.

"I'm not a detective."

"What's with the fifth degree?"

"I don't know. I'm just curious. I found this picture at his place." Amy's talking ahead of her thoughts now.

"What were you doing at his place? You're a friend?" Mrs. Mescolotto's on edge, probably unnerved by Amy. She goes up to the counter and pays for her bottle with a fold of soggy bills that she plucks out of her bra.

The guy doesn't even look up as he counts the money. When he's done, he brown bags the bottle and hands it to her. She unscrews the cap and takes a slug.

"Come on, don't drink that in here," the guy says.

"Leave me alone," Mrs. Mescolotto says. "I'm in mourning."

The guy shakes his head.

Mrs. Mescolotto turns her attention back to Amy. "I know you're not Vince's girlfriend," she says.

"How do you know that?" Amy says.

Mrs. Mescolotto smiles. "Vince only spent time with one woman. He had a special sweetheart."

"And who was that?"

"You're not a detective, huh?" Mrs. Mescolotto takes another drink.

"Lady, I'm asking you nice," the guy says.

Mrs. Mescolotto waves him off. "Shush up," she says. And then back to Amy: "Vince was a sweet kid. I've known him a long time. He went to school with my Dom."

"Were you seeing him? Is that what this picture's about?"

"Who are you, exactly?"

"I'm not really anybody."

"You're just curious?"

"Right."

"And you don't work for my husband?"

"Of course not."

"Come on. 'Just curious,' you expect me to believe that shit?"

"What were you fighting with your son about?"

"You were watching me? Or you were over at the wake? Who the fuck are you?"

"I don't work for anybody."

"Tone must've hired you." Another slug of vodka. Wiping her mouth with the back of her hand.

"Okay, lady. I warned you." The guy puts down his sci-fi book and picks up the phone. "I'm gonna call the cops."

Mrs. Mescolotto holds up the bottle. "You call the cops, and I'll have this fucking place blown up with you inside. You know my father, Jimmy Long-abardi? You know that name?"

The guy puts up his hands like, *Whoa, whoa now.*

"Tell me about Vincent," Amy says.

"You didn't know him?" Mrs. Mescolotto asks.

"What was he like?"

Tears in Mrs. Mescolotto's eyes now. "No one was like Vince. He was the kind of guy who knows what flowers you like and what your favorite color is. He was shy." She pauses. "Never mind."

"You loved him, huh?"

"Never mind, I said."

They walk outside. Darkness settles on the neighborhood. Capelli's is in view, a few people in black milling around out front. One guy eats a slice of pizza over a white paper bag. Amy recognizes him as the guy who was wearing the softball shirt that first trip to Homestretch. He's also in the picture. He stuffs the last hunk of crust in his mouth, drops the bag to the sidewalk, and then walks away from Capelli's.

Mrs. Mescolotto steps out of her heels and sits down on a dry patch of sidewalk under the awning, setting the bottle between her legs. Her back is against the red brick, beer and soda ads plastered on the window above her head.

Amy sits next to her. She can't see Chris's. She wonders if Alessandra and Fred have come out looking for her or if they're just there with the food, waiting.

"I did love him," Mrs. Mescolotto says.

"That's why you're drinking?" Amy says.

"I drink. That's what I fucking do. That's what me and Vince did together. Let me see that picture again."

Amy passes it to her.

Mrs. Mescolotto laughs a little, wipes tears from her eyes with the heel of her hand. "This was the night of the Lopez–Ledbetter fight. We got so drunk. It was the first time we were dumb enough to go to Homestretch together. We'd been screwing around for a long time, but we'd always been discreet. Not out of respect to Tone. Fuck Tone. I was worried about Dom. We didn't know he was there and then, suddenly, he was, watching us." She traces her finger from Vincent to Dom. "I didn't want to upset Dom." She glances at Amy again. "Who are you? Why am I even talking to you?"

"I'm here to listen," Amy says. "I'm a friend."

"Yeah? You just come out of nowhere? You're like an angel?" Mrs. Mescolotto pushes the bottle over to her. "Have a fucking drink, angel."

Amy tilts the bottle back and lets it burn against her upper lip, but she doesn't swallow much. It's strong stuff.

"Friends are good," Mrs. Mescolotto says. "I wish Vince had more real friends."

"You know who killed him?"

Mrs. Mescolotto grabs the bottle back. "A lot of things killed him."

"What's that mean?"

"Means stop pressing. Poor Vince shouldn't be dead, but he is. That's the way of things. My father once told me, 'You either get luck, or you don't.' Vince didn't, okay?"

Amy's not sure why she's sitting there with Mrs. Mescolotto. She's not at all sure why she ran across to her like they were pals. Same reason, she guesses, that she went to Diane's. The story is closing in on itself. Her decision to follow Vincent has led to this. Alessandra, Fred, Vincent, Dom, Diane, Monsignor Ricciardi. Her life. Her *lives*. All so close. Tangled. The mess of it.

"What's your name?" Mrs. Mescolotto asks.

"Amy."

"Amy Winehouse. Amy Adams." Mrs. Mescolotto searches the sidewalk, her head a bit booze-wobbly now. "I'm trying to think of other famous Amys."

Amy smiles. "Amy Poehler."

"She's funny," Mrs. Mescolotto says, and she rises slowly, using the bottle for leverage. Her stockings have runs in them now.

Amy stands, too.

Mrs. Mescolotto slips her heels back on, clamping a hand on Amy's shoulder as she does it. "I like you, Amy the Angel," she says.

Amy wants to say, *I saw it happen.* She's not sure what that will lead to, though. Maybe Mrs. Mescolotto knows something but not everything. Maybe she doesn't know it was Dom. Maybe she thinks her husband had Vincent killed. Maybe it's better to leave it this way.

"You want this picture?" Amy asks, holding it up.

"You can just toss it. Makes me too sad." Mrs. Mescolotto stumbles back to Capelli's, slugging from the brown bag like a front-stoop drunk, her sunglasses still up on her head. It's beautiful, actually, watching her walk and drink, the little quake in her heels. She opens the door of the funeral home and lurches in.

Amy goes back to Chris's. Alessandra and Fred are still at the table, food spread out in front of them. Neither of them is eating yet.

"What was that all about?" Alessandra says.

"I felt like I had to talk to her," Amy replies.

"And?"

"Everything keeps getting stranger."

Alessandra stabs at a cheese blintz with a fork. "Why don't you just go into the wake and give everyone your regards?"

"Tell me what's really going on here," Fred cuts in.

"Your services are no longer required," Alessandra shoots back.

Fred looks crushed. "I'm nothing but a fuckup." He slouches over his plate. "I'm trying. I'm sorry."

"Fred, I got news for you," Alessandra says. "We're all a bunch of fuckups."

Amy's eyes have drifted back across the street. Andy Capelli comes out. Hearing aid. Turtleneck. Big wooden cross hanging over his chest. He's plucking at his right ear with his thumb and index finger.

"Is that Andy Capelli?" Alessandra says. "Christ, he looks like a pedophile. Who the fuck wears a turtleneck and one of those big crosses?"

Diane comes out next, accompanied by Monsignor Ricciardi. He's holding her by the arm, helping her watch her step, making sure she doesn't take a flop. Diane's wearing a black shawl with the price tag still on it and black slacks. Amy can't tell if she's leaving or if she's just getting some air. She stops walking and leans against the wall in almost the same spot where Mrs. Mescolotto had been.

Andy and Monsignor Ricciardi are yapping at Diane, probably saying comforting things about God's plan and how Vincent's in a better place and all the typical garbage that people say at a wake. Even on her most faithful days, Amy can't take that type of stuff. It's just talk. Monsignor Ricciardi's a pro at it. He isn't a bad guy, but he's most definitely a bullshit artist.

Then again, maybe they're not doing that at all. Maybe something happened inside.

Diane's looking up and down Eighty-Sixth Street. Amy wonders if Diane's looking for her, if she's counting on her showing up at the wake. She feels so sad for Diane. She can't help but think of the woman in ten or twenty years, battered by the world, dying alone in a slim, dirty bed with crinkled gray sheets, thin and raw-eyed. Amy obscures herself a bit behind a paper menu taped up in the window so that she can still see Diane but Diane can't see her, if her eyes wander over in this direction.

Fred and Alessandra are quiet now, resigned to a doomed situation, eating with their heads down.

Amy starts talking. "It was horrible when my mom died," she says. "I saw death everywhere. It was horrible having a father who'd left, who didn't give a shit. I've been searching for an identity my whole life, trying all these different lives. I've never felt comfortable anywhere." Her eyes stay on Diane, Monsignor Ricciardi, and Andy Capelli. They're huddled together. Monsignor Ricciardi has his hand on Diane's back.

Fred is listening closely. So is Alessandra. She seems shocked by how much Amy's opening up, by what she's saying. She knows how unlike her this is.

"I can't ever love you, Fred," Amy says.

Fred's crying.

Across the street, Dom throws open the door of Capelli's and struts outside. Mrs. Mescolotto is with him, wasted, staggering, and Tony trails behind her. They stand in a circle, Mrs. Mescolotto fumbling with a new cigarette, Tony struggling to light it for her, Dom looking at his phone.

You do things because you have to be near the beating heart of terror, Amy thinks. "What else is there in the end?" she says aloud, to no one in particular.

"What are you saying, Amy?" Alessandra says.

"I'm going back over there. I'm gonna tell Mrs. Mescolotto it was Dom. No way she knows. And I'm gonna show Diane who I really am. And Dom, well, I don't know." She's thinking, too, that maybe Vincent wasn't that bad. Maybe he just got chewed up and spit out by a world he couldn't figure out how to exist in. You can't pretend to know a stranger. All their secrets. Maybe he loved Mrs. Mescolotto with his whole heart. Maybe he was just another person out on the streets, hauling his pain around from decision to decision. Maybe the love was enough to give meaning to his life.

"Don't," Alessandra says. "Stay out of it."

"I can't," Amy says. "I'm already in it."

The door clangs behind Amy as she leaves Chris's again, Vincent's picture pinched between her fingers in her outstretched hand. This time, Fred and Alessandra follow, Fred scrambling to leave some money on the table, Alessandra slinging the backpack over her shoulder.

Diane notices Amy as she approaches Capelli's and looks relieved. Amy can tell that what remained of Diane's world hinged on whether this stranger who had been kind to her would show up at her son's wake. She has. And maybe that means there's something still worth living for. Diane smiles.

Amy greets her by touching her arm.

"I'm glad you came," Diane says, reaching for Amy's hair, her eyes revealing that she's relieved the wig's gone for good.

"I'm so sorry for your loss," Amy says.

Diane looks at the picture in Amy's shaking hand, but it's held in such a way that she probably can't see who's in it. Now she looks over Amy's shoulder at Fred and Alessandra, clearly seeking introductions.

Dom notices Amy then—it seems to take him a second to register it's actually her—and he keeps his head tucked into his chest. He pockets his phone.

All of these people standing outside the funeral home know a different Amy. She has been different things to them. Daughter, girlfriend, parishioner, stranger, friend, witness.

"What are we doing?" Alessandra says in a whisper, reaching out and squeezing Amy's elbow with urgency.

Amy doesn't respond. She's light-headed in a mystical way. Everything's slowed down. Alessandra's hand on her arm is spongy. Cars on Eighty-Sixth Street zoom by as if underwater.

"I'm not dressed for a wake," Fred says.

Amy's shaken back into full-speed reality. She walks into Capelli's, right past the Mescolottos. Dom doesn't say anything. Mrs. Mescolotto, puffing hungrily on her smoke, her bottle gone somewhere, doesn't even see her.

Inside: heavy flower smell, paintings of oceans and vineyards on the walls, swirling red carpets that seem flattened by grief. A sign that says Vincent's name points to the first room on the right. Amy thinks of her mother's wake, how she sat on a folding chair, people kissing her cheeks and her grandmother bringing her water constantly. Heavy flower smell then, too.

Her mother in the casket, with so much makeup on, wearing a black dress Amy had never seen her in. So skinny and severe against the white satin. The memory is as strong as the flower stench, crashing on her in waves.

Vincent is alone in the room, the only people left at his wake the ones now standing outside. High in his casket in the suit she retrieved. An eight-by-ten picture of him propped on a nearby table. The Popsicle-stick picture Diane showed her next to that. Amy moves close to pay her respects. Fred and Alessandra followed her in, and they sit in chairs off to the side, confused, swept up in whatever Amy has brought them into. Alessandra's got the backpack in her lap.

Vincent's collar covers where the knife went in. His suit has been ironed; it's stiff. He's stiff. There's a blue handkerchief in his pocket, and he's wearing a dark blue tie. His face is gaunt. She barely remembers talking to him. She doesn't remember what they said to each other at Mrs. Epifanio's. Clearer is what he looked like from behind as she followed him. Vaping. On his phone. Through the window at Homestretch. She tries to picture him kissing Mrs. Mescolotto's neck. She tries to picture them in bed together. Probably twenty-five years between them. She wonders when it started. When Vincent was in high school?

Amy holds the picture over Vincent, and then she reaches down and stuffs it inside his jacket, finding a slit for the interior pocket. She feels something hard lodged there as she pushes the picture in. She can tell it's the knife before she draws it out and turns it over on Vincent's chest. Dom must've put it there as a final *fuck you*. She jabs it back into the interior pocket. She kneels on the bench in front of the casket and studies Vincent's face. She tries to think of a prayer to say, but all her prayers are gone.

Noises behind her, everyone from outside tumbling back in. Amy's not prepared to make a scene, but she's not sure how to avoid it. She turns around slowly. Diane sits in the front row, Monsignor Ricciardi next to her. Andy Capelli is off in the back of the room, sweating under a painting of a Mediterranean beach. Sand, grapes on a plate, blue water. Tony is holding up

Mrs. Mescolotto, trying to talk her into leaving, but she's cursing under her breath, saying she wants to stay. What Diane thinks of this, Amy can't make out. She can't imagine she knew anything about Vincent and Mrs. Mescolotto. No one seems to have even acknowledged that she's bombed. Protocol. Dom is pacing in the hallway outside the room. Bernie from Homestretch is with him, and they're talking. Dom's heated. Bernie throws up his hands and then comes in to pay his respects. He stands next to Amy.

"Hey, it's you," Bernie says.

Amy half smiles at Bernie.

Diane stands and makes for the casket. It's as if she's seeing Vincent for the first time. She throws herself over his body and starts wailing. "'Que sera, sera,'" she sings through tears. "'Whatever will be, will be. The future's not ours to see. Que sera, sera. What will be, will be.'" She weeps harder, the song trailing off, her hands on his chest. Amy wonders if she'll feel the knife there.

As if on cue, there's music in the hallway, the rising thrum of "Eye of the Tiger." Dom's phone. He silences it fast, but not fast enough. Diane whirls around and looks to see whose phone the music came from. She knows right away it's Dom's. He's got his phone out in his hand. Diane looks at Amy, as if to say, *What's going on here?* The sadness in her eyes has transformed into fear. "Dom?" she says. And then she passes out cold, crumpling forward.

Monsignor Ricciardi leaps forward to try to catch her, but she goes down pretty hard. Andy Capelli jumps into action. He runs back to his office to get whatever he gets when people pass out. Probably a cup of water, a wet washcloth, maybe smelling salts.

Amy leans over Diane. Alessandra and Fred look on, dumbstruck.

"Diane?" Amy says, touching her cheek.

"That was some fall," Monsignor Ricciardi says. "Maybe we should call an ambulance."

Andy Capelli comes back with a bag of frozen peas.

"What's that for?" Monsignor Ricciardi says.

"What?" Andy says, not hearing Monsignor Ricciardi, falling to his knees next to Diane. "Hold it up against her head."

"Why do you have frozen peas in a funeral home?"

Andy drops the bag of peas to the carpet. "Is she okay?"

"We're not sure," Amy says.

Diane's eyes flutter open. Amy looks back to see if Dom's still there. He's gone.

Mrs. Mescolotto is now swatting at her husband's chest. "You did this, didn't you, Tone? You son of a bitch! You did this!"

Tony seems genuinely taken aback. "You're drunk, Karen."

"Vincent, my love!" Mrs. Mescolotto says, and Amy's glad that Diane's not fully conscious to hear it.

"This is wild," Bernie says.

Amy makes a move toward Mrs. Mescolotto, but she knows the woman's too drunk to have any sense talked into her. She wonders what Diane will think when she wakes up. Will she be able to piece together a narrative that makes Amy look like she did something wrong? *Did* Amy do something wrong? There's nothing wrong with staying quiet. It's a way of life.

The money. The money's wrong. She's put herself in a position where she'll have to tell everyone what she saw. Diane. The police. Head down, she sighs.

"Dude, let's go," Alessandra says, standing up. "This is fucking crazy."

Maybe escape's still an option. Seems like the only thing to do now. Walk away from these wrecked mothers. Amy can't let herself get sucked into a whirlpool like this.

Amy leaves Diane with Monsignor Ricciardi, saddened by the way Diane's hair looks spread out against the carpet, and she follows Alessandra to the door. The Mescolottos are a blur as she passes. Fred's staying close. She wants to shake him, but she's not sure how. She's already tried cruelty.

Back outside. Streetlights. A bus at the corner, wheezing low under the El.

Alessandra's frantic. "I shouldn't have come back here," she says.

Dom's sitting on a fire hydrant in front of the law office. Amy can't believe he's there. He claps his hands together. "I stuck the knife in his pocket," he says to her, laughing. "You catch that?"

She says to Dom, "I thought you were—"

"I had a drink at Homestretch to celebrate," Dom says. "You were right, Amy. What you said about me not coming to the wake. You were right. Bad idea to skip it. Plus, I wanted to give Vincent my little parting gift."

"Listen," Fred says, stepping in.

"Who are you?" Dom says.

"I'm Amy's father," Fred says. "I recognize you now, from the bar the other day. I'm a little in the dark here, but do we need to do something to make things right?"

"Amy's old man, huh?" Bad guy grin, all blind arrogance. "Your daughter's a little troublemaker. She likes to be in the middle of things. You teach her to be that way?"

"Watch that mouth there, bub," Fred says.

"I need to pick up my bag and then I'm going to get a hotel by the airport," Alessandra says to Amy. "I was fucking crazy, coming back here."

"I'll give you a ride wherever you want to go," Dom says, puffing out his chest. "Me and you, sweetie, I can see us going places together. Might be I'm headed to the airport anyway. Might be we're getting on the same plane."

Alessandra ignores him.

"I'm a ghost?" Dom says, standing and stepping toward Alessandra. "Let me give you a ride. Look at me in my suit. I'm a handsome motherfucker, no? You, you're model-pretty. I'd like to suck your toes. Stroke your little feet with a feather."

"You're a real pig," Fred says. "That's no way to talk."

"Think it's time to go back to the homeless shelter you came from, *bub*."

Fred, red in the face, stumbles into Dom. He raises his hand, looking like he might try to clock him on the side of the head, but instead his forearm thwacks against Dom's shoulder and it's Fred who seems hurt.

Dom laughs. "Watch the fucking suit," he says, and he pushes Fred off. Fred flops to the sidewalk, landing on his ass and letting out a wheezy groan.

Mrs. Mescolotto comes tumbling out of Capelli's, her husband nowhere to be seen.

"Ma," Dom says, and he goes over and puts his hand on her back. "You've had too much to drink."

Mrs. Mescolotto's blubbering. Amy's afraid of what she'll say.

"I know, Ma," Dom says, trying to calm her with soft circular pats on the back. "I know. Why don't you go on home? Have one of them peach yogurts you like. Put on *Law and Order.*"

"We had a future, me and Vince," Mrs. Mescolotto says. "We were gonna run away."

"He's dead, Ma," Dom says. "Don't make me mad by saying his name."

"Your father must've—"

"It wasn't Dad, okay? It was random, that's it. He walked down the wrong street at the wrong time."

"I'm sorry you found out about us the way you did," Mrs. Mescolotto says, dabbing at her eyes with her knuckles.

"Don't talk about it," Dom says, his voice hard.

"Dom, please."

"Shut up. Just shut up."

Tony comes out next, huffing. "Karen, let me take you home," he says. And then to Dom: "I'll talk to you later, Dommie. This five grand you got from Bernie—whatever you got up your sleeve, I'm gonna find out."

Amy's distracted enough by Dom and his folks that she doesn't notice Alessandra has started hustling away down Eighty-Sixth Street, her phone in her hand, still holding the backpack. Amy runs after her, calling out her name, sloshing through a puddle. When she catches up, Alessandra's crossing Nineteenth Avenue. "I'm sorry," she says.

"I just shouldn't have come here," Alessandra says. "It's not you. It's the neighborhood."

Amy keeps pace with Alessandra, looking back once and catching a glimpse of Fred, on his feet now, hitching up his pants and hopping along after them. Dom's still standing back by Capelli's with his parents. Two trains pass in opposite directions overhead. Everything's consumed by the noise. Alessandra's lips are making words, but Amy can't hear them.

After the trains are gone, Amy can hear that Alessandra's just saying, "I'm so fucking stupid," over and over.

"I'm the one who's stupid," Amy says. "Tempting fate."

"This is where I'm from. This is what fucking happens here. Are they following us?"

"Fred is."

"Get on the train, Amy. Now. If I didn't leave my bag behind, I wouldn't even go back to your place. So stupid. Get out of here. To Gwen's or wherever."

"You called a cab?"

"The Uber should be there by the time I get back. Give me your key. Split. This is dangerous."

"I'm coming with you. Just to the apartment, at least. I want to give you some of this money."

The whir of Eighty-Sixth Street around them: another rush of commuters coming down from the train; a Chinese restaurant with chickens hanging in the window next to a Chinese restaurant with a cramped fish tank in the window, gray sludgy forms puckered against the glass; faces in windows behind these displays, white hats, loud food orders from open doors.

They pass Lenny's. Amy's almost convinced for a moment that she could steer Alessandra in there for a slice and things would return to a time before any of this. They'd stare at the picture of Sylvester Stallone and John Travolta, taken during the making of *Staying Alive*, and nothing that happened would actually have happened. It'd be a portal into their first year together, how everything felt lit up with love, with raw kisses, with the possibility that things would work out, that the neighborhood would be good for them or they could at least reinvent it to suit their purposes. It wasn't the place Alessandra had grown up in anymore. It was changing. A new wave of immigrants. Chinese, Ukrainian, Russian, Albanian, Turkish, Georgian, Uzbek, Palestinian, Egyptian, Lebanese, Pakistani, Mexican. The old ghosts were finally going away, lingering only in the houses of those who hadn't died yet or hadn't been worn down or run off. There were still plenty of those folks left, but they were fading fast. If only that could happen for them now, a return to such a moment of promise. But it can't. This is ending, as all things end, badly.

Alessandra's jaw is clenched, making that little line on the side of her face she gets when she's angry or frustrated or fed up with failing.

"Talk to me," Amy says, sweating now, afraid of what's to come, what's not to come, what will never come.

"There's nothing to say," Alessandra says.

"I love you," Amy says.

"Haven't you learned that's not enough? Whoever you love, whatever you love, it's not enough. It'll never be."

"Jeez, Al."

They're between Twentieth Avenue and Bay Parkway on Eighty-Sixth Street now. Fred is still trudging along, about a hundred feet behind them. They pass a kid on a quarter ride, a little paint-stripped elephant bopping back and forth as if on a broken spring. The kid giggles, his mother and father rooting him on.

A food stand with a smoking grill. Smell of chicken kebobs.

An overturned garbage can on the corner.

They cross Bay Parkway. People waiting for the B1 on a small sidewalk island under the El. Markets still crowded. Old men and women with shopping carts, walking slow. Bruised fruits. Broccoli rabe. Junk stores overflowing and circus-like in the dark.

They're closing in on Twenty-Third Avenue, Fred getting farther away, losing steam. "I don't know what else to say," Amy says.

"There's nothing *to* say," Alessandra says.

Amy's phone buzzes in her pocket. A text from Gwen: *What's up?* She puts the phone away. She'll respond as soon as she can. Over the rooftops, she can see the cross on the St. Mary's steeple. That's something she'll remember wherever she goes, seeing the cross from everywhere. Over the El. Nudged between things. Just tall enough that it rises over the squatting two-story buildings that dot Eighty-Sixth Street. But she's got to be looking up to see it, as she is now. So often, she's looking down, focused on the sidewalk. Cracks, weeds, words, the sidewalks their own story.

"I'm not trying to convince you of anything," Amy says.

"Good," Alessandra says. "Listen, you can just get in the Uber with me. We'll drop you at Gwen's. Or wherever. Just get out of here."

"Can't I come to the hotel with you? Just for the night?"

"I don't think that's a good idea. You've got trouble all over you."

"So?"

"I don't know. I can't get mixed up in it."

"You thought I was being paranoid."

"I don't know what you did, and I don't know why you did it. I can't get mixed up in it."

"Trying to rob the rest of the jewelry out of the attic was your idea."

"It was stupid. You made me think there was a gold mine there, and I got greedy. Like the fucking end of *The Goonies*. I started thinking about how we could be rich."

"*The Goonies?*"

"Just let shit be. I'm worried for you, but I'll be fucking honest, Amy, I don't want to pay for these decisions you've made."

They hook a left onto Twenty-Third Avenue, close to the church now and the apartment Amy can't quite escape. There's always something drawing her back there. She puts her hand on Alessandra's shoulder, tries to stop her from crossing the avenue and walking up the block to the apartment, brushing past Mr. Pezzolanti and grabbing her bag from inside and hopping in the cab or the Uber or whatever it is and going somewhere that's not where Amy is. What does Amy want? What has she ever wanted?

"Get your fucking hand off me," Alessandra says, pulling away.

"Please."

"Please *what?*"

"I don't know."

"You don't know. I don't know. That's all there fucking is, Amy. *Not knowing.* Don't you see that?" A car passes. Alessandra pauses before crossing in the middle of Twenty-Third Avenue.

Amy's got tears in her eyes. She's trying to hold them back. Alessandra's not big on crying. "Why do we do anything we do?" Amy says. "What am I gonna do with my life?"

"How many ways can I say *I don't know?* People are just trying to find a way to live. You used to have records, at least. Find something to hang on to, something that's not God and not love."

Alessandra rushes across the avenue. Amy stays with her. They pass St. Mary's, dark as a dead place. Music plays somewhere up the street.

When they get to the apartment, Mr. Pezzolanti is out on the stoop, his front light on. He's wearing an oversized flannel and rumpled chinos. He's got a boombox between his legs, and he's playing "Big Girls Don't Cry" by Frankie Valli and the Four Seasons. That falsetto. Amy knows it from her grandparents. They loved Frankie Valli, always made her listen in the car.

Mr. Pezzolanti's moving his mouth to the music. It's not loud enough to bother anyone. He would never want to be perceived as someone who could bug his neighbors. "You girls like this music?" he asks.

"Give me the key," Alessandra says to Amy.

Amy fumbles for the key in her pocket and hands it to Alessandra, her hand shaking.

"Getting those extra batteries made me remember I had this radio upstairs," Mr. Pezzolanti says, "so I got my tapes. Sinatra, Frankie Valli, Johnny Mathis, Dion. The good stuff."

"That's nice, Mr. P.," Amy says.

"Sounds terrific, right? I'm happy it still works."

"Big Girls Don't Cry" fades out. "Working My Way Back to You" comes on. The car's not there yet, and Amy's grateful for that.

Inside, Alessandra throws Amy's backpack on the bed. She gets her suitcase and wheels it behind her back to the door.

"Just wait in here," Amy says.

"The car'll be here any second," Alessandra says.

Amy picks up the Joan of Arc medal from the table. "Take this, at least," she says, rushing over and thrusting it at Alessandra.

Alessandra nods. She unzips the outer pocket on her suitcase and drops the medal in, the chain dribbling after it.

"It'll fall out if you don't close the pocket," Amy says.

Alessandra goes outside, pushing through the front gate. She stands by the curb, waiting for her car to show up.

Amy lingers back by Mr. Pezzolanti, sensing that she's coming off too desperate. She's done that before; it's a sure bet to make Alessandra turn further away. If she can keep her cool, maybe they'll be able to talk in a few days and see where they are.

Los Angeles. A name that's still soft on her tongue. She sees them at a party in a backyard with a pool, lanterns all around, drinks on trays. She sees them at the movies. She sees them hiking. Matching boots. Klean Kanteens. The dream of it so pretty. The reality filled with hard distance and missing pages.

"Everything okay?" Mr. Pezzolanti says, lowering the music to a hush.

"Fine," Amy replies.

"She's waiting for car service?"

"An Uber, yeah."

"What's an Uber?"

"Just a cab."

Mr. Pezzolanti waves his hand through the air. "I don't know nothing."

Alessandra doesn't look over her shoulder at them. It feels late because of the dark, but it's not. Late afternoon, maybe early evening. Barely. Amy doesn't want to look at the time on her phone. She doesn't want to see numbers. Numbers tell only one story: time winding down.

"Alessandra," Amy says.

"What is it?" Alessandra says without turning around.

"Let me know you get home okay." Amy takes a breath. "Okay?"

Alessandra turns around now, a little quiver in her chin. "All that's going on, you be careful."

"What's going on?" Mr. Pezzolanti says.

Amy looks up and sees Fred turning onto the block, out of breath. As he crosses to their side of the street, a horn blares. A car blasts through the red light at Twenty-Third Avenue and comes screeching onto the block. Dom's Daytona. Fred looks up and sees the car. He tries to halt in his tracks. Dom slams on the brakes and swerves to the left, clipping Fred with his side-view mirror and knocking him off-balance. Fred staggers forward, collapsing to his knees first and then landing on his side with a thud on the glittery black pavement in the glow of Dom's headlights.

"Jesus Christ," Mr. Pezzolanti says, standing and then rushing over to help.

Amy is frozen in place. So is Alessandra. Dom slams the wheel with his fists.

Mr. Pezzolanti, kneeling at Fred's side, starts yelling: "Call someone!"

The same words Vincent said.

"Call nine-one-one," Mr. Pezzolanti says. "Someone call someone!" He's shocked to see that Dom's not getting out of the car, that Amy and Alessandra aren't dealing with this in any way whatsoever.

Amy finally takes out her phone and fumbles it to the sidewalk. It's not as bad as it could've been, she's telling herself. Dom's car barely touched Fred. He's just fragile. She picks up the phone and punches in 911 and says that a man's been hit by a car on Eighty-Fifth Street between Twenty-Third and Twenty-Fourth Avenue.

When Alessandra makes a move, it's away from the scene, past Fred and Mr. Pezzolanti and Dom in his Daytona, heading for the corner of Twenty-Third Avenue, hoping to cut off her Uber when it finally arrives.

Dom throws open the driver's-side door of his Daytona, tie undone, looking from Fred on the ground back to Alessandra. "Hey, sweetie," he says. "How about you stay right where you're at?" He leans into his car and gets the gun out of the glove compartment.

Alessandra ignores him.

Amy says Alessandra's name—quietly, and then much louder.

Dom swings around with the gun in his hand, aiming it in Alessandra's direction. He looks strained, confused. A battered minivan pulls up behind the Daytona, and the driver leans on her horn. The driver can't see the situation with Fred. And it takes a second before she notices the gun in Dom's hand and throws the minivan into reverse, screeching backward off the block, almost slamming into two cars in the intersection.

Amy rushes out onto the sidewalk.

"You see me here?" Dom says to Alessandra.

"Fuck off," Alessandra says, continuing on past the church, passing under a bright cone of light from a streetlamp.

"You think you're hot shit, huh? I'll show you hot shit." Dom fires above her, the bullet blasting high into the stained glass on the close side of St. Mary's, the glass sturdy enough that only a small hole webbed with cracks shows in a patch of blue robe.

"What the fuck?" Alessandra says, her hands over her head now, ducking, looking for cover behind her suitcase, behind a telephone pole, behind anything.

Mr. Pezzolanti is on his feet. "Guy," he says to Dom, "put the piece down, okay? What's this all about?"

Dom turns to Mr. Pezzolanti with the gun. "Mind your own business, old man," he says.

"Why are you doing this?" Amy says. "I'm not talking to anyone."

"You and your friend, get in the fucking car," Dom says, and now he's got the gun on Amy. "I should've killed you when I had the chance. This is what I get for being a nice guy."

Alessandra ditches her suitcase and takes off running, looping into the St. Mary's parking lot and then disappearing into the dark, unlit stretch behind the church.

Fred sits up, dazed. He looks shaken, but Mr. Pezzolanti helps him to his feet.

"Come on, put it down," Fred says. "Please."

Spooked, Dom swings to Fred with the gun.

Amy feels bad that she doesn't have too much concern for Fred. She should be thinking about him, worrying for him—not as a daughter, just as a human being. If what happened to him had happened to a stranger, she would've gone to help. She believes down in her bones that people in trouble need help. But she doesn't care about him, not really. And not caring seems to give her strength. She takes off after Alessandra, leaping over the suitcase, and cutting into the St. Mary's lot. She waits for a gunshot, and it's high and wide when it comes, hitting one of the glass front doors of the church, shattering it. She can hear Dom yelling for her to stop. She expects more gunshots, but there's nothing.

The lot narrows into an alley that passes between the school and the church. A Dumpster filled with garbage bags and a few broken office chairs is pushed up against one building. Amy scans everywhere for Alessandra and doesn't see her. The alley opens into another little lot on the Eighty-Fourth Street rectory side of the church, and she passes through the back gate and looks both ways. She sees Alessandra running toward Twenty-Fourth Avenue. She doesn't call out. Before the end of the block, Alessandra hops a low fence into someone's front yard and Amy loses sight of her.

The sound of an engine revving from around the corner. Tires peeling out on blacktop. Yelling. Another gunshot. No sirens yet.

Amy hustles past the rectory. When she gets to the yard where Alessandra disappeared, she turns in. A two-family brick house with an empty grotto in the front yard. Whatever religious statue once stood there is stolen or gone somewhere. Empty chip bags flutter in the weeds around it. The mailbox overflows with circulars, and the windows are darkened by heavy curtains. A note taped to the front door reads SMILE, YOU ARE ON CAMERA in bleeding-red Sharpie, the edges of the paper curled. A driveway on the right side of the house leads to a small backyard. A high chain-link fence separates it from the house next door. Amy runs down the driveway, passing a padlocked side door. She says Alessandra's name a couple of times.

The backyard is pretty typical of the neighborhood. Cracked cement, weeds, abandoned things—in this case, a high double stack of old tires filled with rainwater, an air conditioner half-covered with a blue tarp, a rickety manual lawnmower though there's no lawn in sight. A clothesline hangs across the yard from a hook above the back door to a telephone pole on the opposite side of the yard. Weather-blackened wooden clothespins dangle from the line. No clothes are hung, only a few sad dish towels, striped with stains. A length of broken gutter pokes down from the edge of the roof. The back of the house is dark, shades instead of curtains on those windows. No lights inside that Amy can see.

"What the fuck are you doing?" Alessandra whispers from somewhere.

Amy finds her crouched down behind the tires and joins her there. "What are *you* doing?" she says as quietly as she can.

"Running the fuck away, dude. Did he see you?"

"I don't think so."

"You don't think so, or you *know* he didn't?"

"I don't think he did."

"Jesus Christ. This place will fucking kill me yet."

They sit in silence for a little while, listening for shots, for feet pounding the pavement, for a car. With all the yards and alleys around, with all the different ways to run, all the different places to hide, there's no reason to think Dom will find them here.

"What're we gonna do?" Amy asks, knocking her leg into a length of metal pipe she doesn't notice leaning against one of the tire stacks. It clanks on the cement, the sound filling the night.

"Just shush," Alessandra says.

A light comes on in one of the back windows of the house. It casts a golden glow over the yard. Amy peeks between the tires to see which window. It's the one in the middle on the ground floor, light lining the edges of the shade.

"Fuck," Alessandra says.

The shade goes up quickly. An old woman, her face fully illuminated by the light behind her, presses her nose to the glass, cupping her hands over her eyes. She has dark eyes and glasses on her head. She's searching the yard for a sign of someone. She's agitated.

"Just don't move," Alessandra says.

The old woman pulls back from the window, leaving the shade up and the light on. A tabby cat jumps up onto the windowsill and dances against the glass.

A few seconds later, the back door is thrust open. It's an ancient door with tin panels and a sagging wooden frame, and it crunches on its hinges. The old woman comes out with a broom in her hand, swatting at the dish towels on the clothesline.

"Who's back here?" she says. "I'm calling the police, you don't get out of my yard."

Alessandra puts her hand on Amy's knee.

"You're in the wrong place," the old woman says. "There's nothing here for you. My yard is my yard." She's getting closer to the tires, leading with the broom, its bristles scratching against the cement.

Amy's sure now that the old woman can see them crouching there, that they're not as well hidden as they think.

"Get out of there now," the old woman says, hammering the broom against the top tire, as if trying to chase out a rat.

Alessandra and Amy stand up and face the woman over the tires. She's in her seventies, wearing a bulky sweater and jeans and cheap sneakers. She lowers her glasses onto her nose. She's surprised by the sight of them.

"What are you girls doing?" she asks.

"Please," Alessandra says.

"There's someone after us," Amy says.

"A rapist?" the old woman says.

Alessandra says, "He's got a gun."

"I knew I heard gunshots." The old woman's grip on the broom slackens. "I told Joe those were goddamn shots. Come inside."

They follow the old woman in through the back door. They're in a little room with a warped linoleum floor and a heavy wooden door latched from the inside. Canned food on sagging shelves. Rusty pans hanging from nails in the wall.

"I'm Ginny," the old woman says. Amy and Alessandra introduce themselves in return.

Ginny locks the back door four different ways: two slide locks, a hook, and a dead bolt. She leads them through the wooden door into a cramped kitchen. A table overflowing with newspapers, bills, church bulletins, receipts, empty Ensure cans. An old-fashioned yellow rotary phone on the wall next to a broken cuckoo clock. Some numbers penciled on a Post-it note stuck above the phone. The stove is dirty. A strong smell of stale coffee and rotten fruit hangs in the air. A pile of wet rags sits on the floor next to a plastic garbage pail lined with a brown paper bag. The fluorescent light overhead is flickering. "Sit," Ginny says.

Alessandra pulls out a chair at the table and sits down. Amy follows her lead, settling in the chair next to her. It's wobbly. Some kind of hair is clumped under the front legs.

"I'll call the cops," Ginny says.

"I already called nine-one-one," Amy says. "A man was hit by a car. And there were the shots."

"Who the hell was hit by a car?"

"Just some guy."

"I got a number here on the wall for a detective named Macrorie. Personal number. He told me to call if there's ever any trouble." Ginny shuffles over to the phone and scans the numbers on the Post-it. "That nine-one-one is a load of shit. You're lucky if they show. My neighbor Johnnie Annio called nine-one-one and they put him on hold. He had a guy out pissing in his front yard, swinging around a baseball bat. Drunk. The operator finally comes on and she's a no-good bitch. John went out and took care of it himself. Good thing he had that big can of bug spray."

"He sprayed the guy with bug spray?"

"Raid, right in the eyes. Guy went howling away up the block. Never pissed in anybody else's yard, I bet." She goes to the cabinet over the stove. "You girls want some coffee? I've got instant." Ginny takes a jar of Folgers from the cabinet and carries it with her to the phone. She runs her thumb along the Post-it until she finds the number she's looking for, then clutches the jar of coffee against her chest and dials the number. Every number is an effort. She curls her finger into the dial and draws it slowly to the right, waiting for it to clack back before repeating the process.

"What are we doing here?" Amy says to Alessandra.

Ginny finishes dialing and puts the phone against her shoulder, waiting for the ringing. Instead, there's an automated voice almost immediately. Amy can't quite make out what it's saying, but she can guess.

"No longer in service," Ginny says. "Nice guy. I wonder if he's dead."

"We don't need coffee," Alessandra says.

"I'm making some anyway," Ginny says. And then she turns to a hallway that opens up into a dark living room. "Joe, that cop's number is no good anymore!"

"You goddamn kidding me?" Joe, whoever Joe is, calls back. An old man's voice, wavering and frail.

"When was he here?"

Joe comes out of the living room. He's behind a walker, and he's wearing black-rimmed glasses and a track jacket with a big hole in the elbow and flannel pajama pants. "That was only about fifteen years ago. Number should still be good." To Amy and Alessandra: "Who the hell are you? Look like a couple of hot tamales."

"Joe, you keep it in your drawers, you hear me?" Ginny says, filling a kettle with water from the kitchen sink and putting it on the stove. "Nothing but a dirty old jadrool."

"Sue me!"

Sirens outside now.

"He's not my husband," Ginny says. "He's just my worthless brother."

"Hell's going on outside?" Joe says, lowering himself into a chair at the table, pushing the walker away as he lands with a sigh. He's sitting right across from Amy. He gives her slobbery eyes.

"Rapist with a gun," Ginny says.

"No shit?"

"We'll be out of your hair in a few minutes," Alessandra says.

"You stick around as long as you want," Joe says. "I'm just watching *The Intern* again. You see that one? With De Niro. He plays an old guy who's an intern. I love it so much. That actress, what's her name? She's great."

"Anne Hathaway," Alessandra says, picking up one of the empty cans of Ensure and tapping it against the tabletop.

"What? You don't like her? I think she's great. Just great."

Alessandra doesn't say anything.

Ginny fills four Styrofoam cups with crystals and boiling water, stirring them with a paring knife and then bringing them over to the table to Amy, Alessandra, and Joe one by one. "Black okay?" she says. "We don't have any sugar and milk. We're out of everything. Reggie comes tomorrow."

"Reggie's a family friend," Joe says. "He does our shopping for us."

"You don't leave the house?" Amy says, sipping the coffee. It's terrible, flat and watery and somehow sour.

"Not in a long time," Ginny says.

Which explains why Amy's never seen them at church or anywhere that she can remember. And she must've looked right past this dump of a house. It's like so many other places around, devastated by time. "There's an apartment upstairs?"

"Been empty twenty years. Since the Faluticos moved to Jersey."

Amy allows herself to fantasize for a moment about going up to the apartment with Alessandra and staying hidden for a few days. It'd be nice if it could be like it was at the hotel.

Alessandra is typing on her phone. "What's your address here?" she says to Ginny and Joe without looking up.

"Two-three-six-nine," Joe says.

"What are you doing?" Amy says.

"I'm trying to get the Uber driver to come here."

"He got in touch?"

"He got lost, thank God." Alessandra is typing again.

"That's a good idea?"

Alessandra shrugs. "I'm getting out, one way or another."

"You want a can of bug spray?" Ginny asks. "I've got some right under the sink."

"What about your suitcase?" Amy asks Alessandra, ignoring the old woman.

"What about it?" Alessandra says. "Forget it. I'm not going back over there. There's nothing I can't replace. I've got my wallet and the check from my Aunt Cecilia. I don't give a shit about that script. The pills I can get whenever."

"The medal?"

"Sorry, dude."

Amy sips the coffee. She's glad it's so bad. She deserves bad coffee.

More sirens from outside, though now it sounds like a fire truck. The firehouse is only a couple of blocks away, next to McDonald's on Eighty-Sixth

Street, just off the corner of Twenty-Fourth Avenue. Amy wonders if there's a fire. Dom's car, maybe. She pictures flames spouting from the hood of the Daytona, licking up the telephone poles, a crowd starting to gather. She hopes Mr. Pezzolanti hasn't been shot. And Fred, she's not sure what she hopes for him. Not death; she can't wish death on him. But she's not terribly bothered by the fact that he's allowed himself to be dragged into all this.

"This is some moron you got yourself messed up with," Alessandra says. "Why's he even after you again? He got what he wanted."

"You're so good at steering clear of trouble," Amy snaps back.

"Trouble has a way of finding me, but I get the fuck out of its way. You just had to go over to that funeral home."

"It was your idea to try to break into the attic. If we hadn't made that plan, we wouldn't have gone to find Fred and then I wouldn't have brought us to that Polish place."

"Whatever fucking crazy-ass decisions you made led to this. I just shouldn't have missed my flight."

"Ladies," Joe says, smiling, "if you're gonna fight here, the least you could do is take off your tops."

"Jesus Christ," Alessandra says, standing, knocking over her coffee with a wild backhand. It goes everywhere, pooling around all the papers, dripping off the edge of the table onto the floor.

Joe gets some in his lap. He tries to stand but falls back into his chair with an *oof.* "Look at this mess," he says.

Ginny swarms the table with a handful of rags. "I've got it," she says.

Alessandra storms out of the kitchen into the living room that Joe emerged from a few minutes before, going for the door. Amy's right behind her.

"Car's here?" Amy asks.

"Any second."

The living room is a garbage heap. Cardboard boxes stacked with magazines. Ratty recliners covered in even rattier plaid throw blankets. A TV sitting crookedly on a table not meant to hold its weight, playing with no volume. A painting of a sad clown on one wall. Browned pictures of a couple at Coney Island in what must be the forties or fifties, probably Ginny and Joe's folks. It's dark in the room, just a hurricane table lamp with roses painted on it giving off a dim light.

Alessandra pulls back the front curtain and looks out at the street. Amy half expects Dom to be out there with his gun, like it would happen in a horror movie. Him, waiting for them, grinning, knowing exactly where they are, even when they think they're in the clear.

"Let me come with you," Amy says. "To the hotel, at least."

Alessandra feigns exhaustion. "Just stop."

"You said you'd give me a ride to Gwen's."

"Forget it. Take the train."

Ginny and Joe are bickering back in the kitchen. Amy can't hear about what. This house should feel safer than being outside. It doesn't. It feels scary, confining, alight with the fear of a toxic future. Lives get smaller, ruled by paranoia and isolation, and there's nothing left to do but stay in retreat, stay hidden. Collect things, shield yourself, keep out of the sun.

A car pulls up out front, a white Chevy Malibu with tinted windows.

"That's your ride?"

"Good luck, Amy," Alessandra says, opening the front door and walking out into the yard.

Before Alessandra gets to the gate, Amy notices that her eyes have drifted to the left. Amy walks out behind her and looks at what Alessandra's looking at. Smoke churning up around the steeple. St. Mary's is burning.

17

Amy is stuck in place, nauseated, withering on the vine. What she doesn't feel about Fred, she feels about the church. It's been a refuge. No matter what she's going through now, what confusion she's experiencing, what loss, what dislocation, she understood—or thought she did—something in that sacred place. That will always have meaning for her. She thinks of the stained glass windows, of her St. Thérèse, the altar, the pews, the organ, the candles, the poor boxes, the smell of myrrh. She sees the faces of the people she knows intimately: Katrya, Connie Giacchino, Monsignor Ricciardi, so many others. Familiar hats, jackets, hands on missals, communion on tongues, voices singing together, the paten, the chalice, the poinsettias in winter.

She doesn't know exactly what's happened, but she knows this is no coincidence. The original church burned down fifty years ago and now this one is burning, too. Dom's done it somehow, which means it's her fault. It's her fault. It's her fault.

Amy Lynn Therese Falconetti, this is your legacy.

Alessandra walks to the car and goes around to the passenger side. She opens the door and looks at Amy with pity.

Amy locks eyes with her before turning back to the smoke. A fire truck has pulled onto the block from Twenty-Third Avenue, obstructing the way, its lights dancing everywhere.

Alessandra doesn't say anything. She gets in the car, pulling the door closed behind her. The car idles a moment longer, but then the driver throws it into reverse and backs out of the block, swerving onto Twenty-Fourth and headed in the direction of Cropsey Avenue, of the Belt Parkway, of escape.

Amy walks toward the church. Her heart's beating fast. She's not sure what she's headed for. But she can't walk away. She's afraid, but she's alive in her fear.

Firefighters drag hoses into the lot. They're saying things, but the sound of the world is dull to her. The fire must be making sound, too, but she can't hear it. There must be flames inside, but she doesn't see them. Only the smoke. The smell is strong. It smells like a church burning. A bank burning would be different. Or a bar. Or a house. A church burning smells like the end of everything.

The rectory is totally dark. Monsignor Ricciardi might still be with Diane. Maybe she needed to go to the hospital, and maybe he went with her. He would do that. He would sit with her for however long it took.

Since she can't cut through the lot, Amy rushes around the corner, past the school, and comes out on the Eighty-Fifth Street side of the church. A small crowd has gathered at the corner. Four cop cars and an ambulance, lights spinning. Another fire truck with pulsing hoses blocking off the lot.

Dom's Daytona is up on the sidewalk in front of the church, crashed against the iron gate just beyond the stoop, doors thrown open, trunk gaping, that bungee cord hanging loose from the lid. The headlights are still on, illuminating Alessandra's suitcase on the sidewalk. Meaning Dom backed up and sped forward onto the sidewalk, or maybe tried to turn around in the lot and things backfired. No sign of him. Or Fred.

The glass front door of the church that Dom shot out has been totally kicked clean. One of the glass doors beyond that in the lobby has also been broken, likely shot out and then pushed through. Amy can see fire in the church, on the altar, the canopy and coverings and altar protector screaming with flames.

Mr. Pezzolanti is standing by a group of cops, mopping his head with a white handkerchief. He sees her and comes over. "Amy?" he says, as if he can't believe any of this is really happening.

"I'm sorry," she says. "This is horrible."

He shakes his head. "That guy who hit your old man is off his goddamn rocker."

"What happened?"

"He got in his car and backed up and tried to mow down your old man again. Tried to get me this time, too. But he crashed and jumped out, then grabbed these bags he had in his car and headed for the church. Your old man went and confronted him, waving a finger in his face. I don't know where he got the energy after being clipped by the car. You should've heard him. 'You leave my daughter be!' He called him about fifty kinds of a son of a bitch. The guy was shaken up from hitting the gate. But then he got it together and started waving his piece around. That's when the first cops showed."

Mr. Pezzolanti is shaking with the improbability of the story. He seems less upset that the church he's gone to his whole life is on fire and more amped up by all the wild action. "Next thing, this guy kicks in through the doors of the church. Like Jimmy Cagney. 'You'll never get me!' That kind of thing. Real goddamn dummy, this guy. Your old man follows him in like he's on hero patrol, you believe that? The cops are yelling. They've got their pieces out, too. This fire starts somehow. I don't know what the guy did in there."

"They haven't come out?"

"Not that I've seen."

"I don't believe this."

Mr. Pezzolanti puts an arm around her. "You poor kid."

Amy can't believe that Mr. Pezzolanti's read of the situation with all that he's seen is that she's someone to feel sympathy for. The way she hardly did anything when Fred got hit. The way her decisions led to putting him and Alessandra and Diane and Fred and everyone in peril. The way there'd be no fire if she'd just had some common sense. She doesn't correct him. It's nice to feel like this poor kid he's seeing for a second.

"Your friend okay?" Mr. Pezzolanti says.

"She's gone."

"Her bag's still over there."

Amy shrugs.

"Why don't you come sit down?" Mr. Pezzolanti points to the low brick gate of the yard outside the apartment building on the corner.

"I'm okay," Amy says.

The cops have settled into doing not much of anything now. A little crowd control. They look like movie cops. Sleek uniforms, confused sneers. They're happy to stand back and let the firefighters try to save the church. The guy with the gun inside and the old man who raced in after him, she guesses they're chalking them up as dead meat.

To watch the fire is to look into an open wound.

She feels twitchy with the possibility that Monsignor Ricciardi will show up any minute and that he'll fall to his knees and break down crying.

"I'll be right back," Amy says to Mr. Pezzolanti, stepping out of his grasp, his arm falling awkwardly to his side. He seems to have no purpose if he can't comfort her.

The guilt is too much. She can't watch anymore.

What Amy's thinking is she'll go back to the apartment and grab her backpack and take off. She'll walk away from the fire, away from Mr. Pezzolanti, in the direction that Alessandra went in the Uber. She'll go to Twenty-Fifth

Avenue and catch the D train. She'll ride it all the way into the city and switch for the J or M there. She'll be with Gwen in a couple of hours.

As she moves away from Mr. Pezzolanti, she takes out her phone and texts Gwen: *Headed for train now.* Gwen instantly texts back an emoji, but because Amy's phone is old and not capable of handling the symbol, it shows up as a question mark in a box.

Her next thought is about Alessandra's suitcase, sitting out there on the sidewalk. Maybe Amy will take it with her. It's got wheels. That way, she'll have an in. She can call Alessandra at some point and offer to mail it. She's seen people just mail suitcases at the post office. Or she can have everything that's in it. Wear Alessandra's underwear and bras and T-shirts. Use that beach perfume. Take those pills. She'll be able to feel like Alessandra. And the medal that she'd stolen from Mrs. Epifanio, she'll keep it. She's strong. She'll wear it to remind herself that you can say *fuck you* in the face of fire. But that's ridiculous. She's no Joan of Arc. This fire is hers to carry.

She crosses the street in front of a police cruiser and stares at the suitcase in the headlights of Dom's car. Going for it wouldn't put her in the path of the firefighters. All she'd have to do is lean down, pick it up, and head for her apartment. She could be seen, sure. By Mr. Pezzolanti, or Monsignor Ricciardi if he shows. And Dom's unaccounted for, of course.

Still, she makes her move.

As she pulls out the handle of the suitcase and rights it, she thinks she sees something out of the corner of her eye. It's nothing. The suitcase is hers. She drags it behind her on the clunky sidewalk, headed for the apartment.

She thinks of Alessandra in that white Malibu with tinted windows, on her way to the airport hotel. She won't come back. There's no way. The neighborhood is a necklace of scars for her. Plus, that's just not Alessandra. She'll pick up someone at the hotel bar, try to find a new lie to help her forget what she wants to forget.

The front door to Amy's apartment is open. She knows she left it open. She props the suitcase out by the gate and runs in to grab her backpack.

She sees Fred first, and then she sees Dom. They're sitting at the table, soot on their faces, the purse and the yellow pillowcase—all that jewelry— lumped between them. Dom has the gun tilted on Fred. "I should've killed you when I had the chance," he says again to Amy.

Amy wonders if she could bolt out the door before Dom squeezes off a shot. If she could do that and make a break for the church, she'll have a halo of cops around her. She'll be safe, and she'll be able to point them to Dom. But he's turned the gun on her already, and she's not confident that she'd be able to pull it off.

"Put the gun back on me," Fred says.

"I like the gun where it is," Dom says.

"What do you want?" Amy says. "I didn't tell anybody. I won't tell any-body."

"You were talking to my mother," Dom says. "You were gonna tell her it was me who did Vincent. I couldn't have that. That's why I came back." He pauses. "She told you they were fucking, huh? They were. Vincent stole my shit with the intention of also stealing my mother. They were gonna run off together, you believe that? Old lady like her and a piece of shit like him."

Amy stares outside. She wishes someone would pass and look in. All she sees is the swirling blue police lights.

"I bet you got a lot of questions," Dom says.

"Why'd you have to set the church on fire?" Amy asks.

"He did it as a distraction," Fred says. "Used a candle to get it started. I tried to stop him."

"Shut up," Dom says.

"We got out through the back door of the sacristy," Fred says, his head down. "Cut through the yard of the rectory and a couple of other backyards to get over here. He had the gun on me. I'm sorry."

"I said, shut up," Dom says to Fred. And then to Amy: "Listen, what I need from you now is to get us out of here. You have a car?"

Amy shakes her head.

"Your landlord have a car?"

She doesn't shake her head. She doesn't nod.

"I'll take that as a yes."

"You're gonna kill me," Amy says. "Why would I help you?"

"You got no options, Amy. I need you to get the keys somehow. And then I need you to get me to this car. You play it right, maybe I won't have to kill you. I'll bring you with me where I'm going. You can be, like, my servant." That smile again. Pleased with himself. "We'll get out of here. Don't you worry. I'm not the smartest guy around, but I'm lucky as fuck."

Fred leans forward and smacks the gun out of Dom's hand. It goes skittering across the floor. "Run!" Fred shouts to Amy.

Instead of going straight out the door, Amy breaks for the bed and grabs her backpack just as Dom erupts from his chair and dives for the gun. Fred's after him, wrestling at his legs.

Amy slings the backpack over her shoulder and turns for the door.

Dom kicks loose of Fred and gets a hand on the gun. He's up on his knees and elbows.

Amy crosses the threshold, and she's back outside, her hand on the foil-covered railing, moving toward the gate. Dom fires, and the bullet sings past her, thumping into Alessandra's suitcase and knocking it over. She hopes the cops can hear it but doubts they can, with all that's going on. She's lucky, as was Alessandra, that he's such a bad shot.

He tells her to freeze.

She doesn't. She cuts left out of the gate and runs as hard as she can. She shouldn't look back, but she does. Dom's out the door. He's after her. Fred's after him, hobbling. The cops will have to see this. Dom's got the gun on her. That unsteady hand. Her luck, he'll take another shot and it'll kill a sleeping baby in one of these houses. Just slip through a wall or window and zip straight into a crib.

"Stop, Amy!" he calls out. "Or I'll kill your old man!"

Her head's twisted to keep an eye on him, but she doesn't stop.

He turns and fires into Fred. Two shots. Fred's so close even Dom can't miss. One in the chest and one in the stomach. Fred doesn't make any noise. He goes down, his arms at his side.

Amy stops, out of breath.

"I told you," Dom says, as if he's forgotten where he is and who's there and what's going on. He looks at Amy and then looks back beyond Fred. Three cops are charging him from the church, guns drawn, yelling for him to put down his gun.

Dom doesn't put down his gun.

Amy gets low and takes cover between two parked cars. She closes her eyes. She doesn't see what happens, but she can imagine it. A shot from Dom and then immediate return fire from the cops. When she peeks out from around the edge of the bumper, Dom's down, shot in the head. Two of the cops come to a stop when they get to his side, their guns still fixed on him. His gun has slipped away from his hand. He's nothing but dead. The other cop is with Fred, checking on him. Fred's still alive, she can tell.

She stands and walks past Dom and the cops. The cops turn on her with their guns. They're not a hundred percent sure of anything.

"That's my dad," she says, the word strange in her mouth.

They lower the guns and focus on their radios. More smoke rises from the church, ribboning over the block.

Amy arrives at Fred's side and kneels close to him. His eyes are open.

The cop who's there says, "The ambulance is at the end of the block. They'll be here in a sec." This cop has a baby face. He looks maybe twenty. A small mole over his lip. Thick eyebrows. Muscles everywhere. His neck, his chest, his legs. His body is flooded with awful muscles. He's kneeling, too, and his pants look like they might rip. She catches the glare of a streetlamp in his shiny boot.

Fred's trying to say something, his face smudged black, his color fading, his beard fluttering with every pained breath.

"Save your energy," Amy says.

"Hold me," he finally manages to say.

She nods. She gets closer and puts her arms under him and pulls him up into her lap. She looks down and sees where he's been shot. Both spots ugly, pulsing, wet.

The cop seems like he might protest the move, but then he thinks better of it. "You're his daughter?" the cop says.

"Yeah, I am," Amy says. Her father is in her arms. Now she feels the heaviness of blood, how they're linked, no matter what.

"I'm here," she says to him. She's not crying. She doesn't feel like she's capable of it. She can't help but think of all that jewelry back on the table in her apartment.

Fred's trying to make words again. "I'm . . . glad," he says. "Glad I'm . . . gonna die looking up at you." His lips twist into something close to a smile.

Smoke and silence. Her father. *He*. Amy feels like a glove being turned inside out. She will stay to witness this. It's the least she can do.

EPILOGUE

Amy is alone, down by Gravesend Bay. She's leaning against the hood of an '89 Chevy Caprice. Blue and clean. It was Mr. Pezzolanti's car. He said for her to just take it, but she wanted to pay him. She gave him a thousand dollars. The stolen jewelry is in the trunk. So is the backpack with the rest of the money, Alessandra's bullet-torn suitcase, and Amy's egg crate full of records and whatever else she'd initially thought she'd have to leave behind, back when it was too much to carry. She's even brought along her hot pot and electric kettle.

Her father's ashes are in a coffee can at her feet. Her plan is to empty his ashes into the water, and here's as good a place as any. The Verrazano in all its looming glory. The sun on the water. The rocks. The feeling that people biking and running and fishing on the promenade that goes from Ceasar's Bay Bazaar all the way to the Sixty-Ninth Street Pier in Bay Ridge are doing so with purpose.

The tin coffee can is striped with the colors of the Italian flag. Medaglia d'Oro. Mr. Pezzolanti gave it to her. At the funeral home, they wanted to sell her a container to store the ashes in. She had no need for that. She knew she'd just be scattering Fred somewhere. At first, she figured Queens. And then she thought on the road, in a quiet stream, or from some mountain cliff where neither of them had ever been, somewhere hidden and new. But here is fine. It's fine.

This past week has been a blur. She had to explain everything to the police and to Diane. What she saw. Dom killing Vincent. Dom threatening her. She's sure some of it didn't add up, especially to Diane, who would probably always believe that Amy played some bigger part in this, the wedge that divided Dom and Vincent. No one knows about the jewelry, not yet.

Amy avoided Monsignor Ricciardi until she couldn't anymore. He was broken up about the fire in the church. He didn't blame her for it. There was so much to untangle, and she couldn't do much to untangle it. Talking to Mrs. Epifanio was useless. Mrs. Mescolotto was in public mourning and washed down a bottle of sleeping pills with her expensive vodka and didn't die. Everyone knew what Dom had done to Vincent. They didn't quite know why. Everyone talked him up as a hothead, said he was bound for an end like this.

Amy's been staying with Gwen in Williamsburg. Her nights have been boozy and long. She's tired. Her eyes are heavy. She's back here to dump her old man in the water, and then she's taking off for good.

Alessandra texted her the day after Fred died to let her know she was home in Los Angeles, walking dogs and pretending to give a shit about yoga. She didn't ask what happened after she split, didn't show any concern or wonder how bad things had gotten. Amy didn't say much in response either, nothing at all about her plans. She wants Alessandra to be surprised if she just shows up one day out of the blue, with her suitcase and money to burn. *Look*, Amy would be able to say. *It came true, that long-shot dream. An opportunity presented itself, and I took it.*

But Alessandra's not what she needs; she knows that now. What she needs is to get lost on her own terms.

It hadn't been hard to keep all the jewelry to herself. No one knew it was sitting there in her apartment, and the cops didn't have a reason to go in there at any point. The only information she had was from Dom. Mr. Mescolotto didn't even know this stuff was missing, didn't even know what was at the center of this whole thing. Maybe he would in the weeks to come, but she'd be gone, trying to figure out how to sell it all. Now, his son shot dead by cops, his wife in the hospital, he had other things to deal with.

Amy's got a map on the passenger seat. She bought it at a shop in Williamsburg and circled all the cities she's been considering as possible stops:

Austin, Chicago, Minneapolis, Denver, Seattle, Portland, San Francisco, maybe even Los Angeles. She's memorized routes she'd like to explore, marked off tourist attractions and parks and lakes. She's going to pass through places she's never been, never thought she'd see. She's going to stay in cheap motels and watch cable TV and take sad showers with those sad little bars of soap and eat pancakes in truck stops. Eventually, she'll find an apartment with a big bright window where she can keep a cactus on the sill. Mr. Pezzolanti's car—*her* car now—has a tape deck, and she's going to listen to all her cassettes. She's going to play them loud. They're on the passenger seat next to the map, lined up in a shoe box. She likes to look at the names of the bands and the titles of the albums scrawled on their white spines.

She picks up the coffee can and walks out to the fence. The tide is low. The water is kicking up around the rocks. She sees a rat and slimy green moss spreading out, plus a few lost tennis balls and six-pack rings floating in the scum. The Belt Parkway thrums behind her. She'll be part of that sound soon. She pries the plastic lid off the can and dumps her father onto the rocks. "I guess everyone just needs a place to sleep," she says. "I guess you deserve that much, Fred." The ashes turn dark on the rocks and then the water sloshes over them and they're gone. Amy doesn't think to say a prayer. She throws the coffee can out in a black plastic garbage bag hanging from the fence.

Back in the car, she settles under the wheel and starts the engine and pops in a cassette. L7's *Bricks Are Heavy*. Her phone is dead. She doesn't want a phone anymore. She wants to be alone on the roads between here and wherever, just her and the music. She wants to arrive in the arms of a new city like someone would've arrived somewhere a long time ago: tired, out of touch, desperate for contact. Maybe she'll feel new for a while, this most recent wreck a movie she never wants to watch again.

ACKNOWLEDGMENTS

The author wishes to gratefully acknowledge the generosity, support, and encouragement of:

Nat Sobel; Judith Weber; Siobhan McBride; Sara Henry; Kristen Pini; Adia Wright; Katie McGuire; Claiborne Hancock; François Guérif; Simon Baril; Oliver Gallmeister; Marie Moscoso; Jeanne Guyon; Sebastien Bonifay; all the wonderful booksellers and readers in France; Alex Andriesse; Jimmy Cajoleas; Megan Abbott; Ace and Angela Atkins; Jack Pendarvis and Theresa Starkey; Tom Franklin and Beth Ann Fennelly; Chris Offutt and Melissa Ginsburg; Lee Durkee; Tyler Keith; Burke Nixon; Abby Greenbaum; Anya Groner; Kevin Fitchett and Rachel Smith; David Swider and the End of All Music; David Shirley; Gary Short; John and Heather Brandon; Willy Vlautin; J. David Osborne; Dave Newman and Lori Jakiela; Micah Adler; Richard and Lisa Howorth, Cody Morrison, Lyn Roberts, Bill Cusumano, Slade Lewis, Katelyn O'Brien, and everyone at Square Books; and, particularly, Katie Farrell Boyle, Eamon Boyle, Connolly Jean Boyle, Geraldine Giannini, and Rosemary Giannini.